STOP AT NOTHING

STOP AT NOTHING

MICHAEL LEDWIDGE

HEADLINE

First published in the USA in 2020 by
Hanover Square Press

First published in Great Britain in 2020 by
HEADLINE PUBLISHING GROUP

1

Cataloguing in Publication Data is available from the British Library

Hardback ISBN 978 1 4722 6576 0
Trade paperback ISBN 978 1 4722 6577 7

Offset in 12.36/15.92 pt Bembo Std by Jouve (UK), Milton Keynes

Printed and bound in Great Britain by Clays Ltd, Elcograf S.p.A.

Headline's policy is to use papers that are natural, renewable and recyclable
products and made from wood grown in well-managed forests and other
controlled sources. The logging and manufacturing processes are expected
to conform to the environmental regulations of the country of origin.

HEADLINE PUBLISHING GROUP
An Hachette UK Company
Carmelite House
50 Victoria Embankment
London EC4Y 0DZ

www.headline.co.uk
www.hachette.co.uk

STOP AT NOTHING

PART ONE

CATCH OF THE DAY

1

When the sun started to go down, Gannon was out alone on his boat in the Atlantic thirty miles northwest of Little Abaco.

His boat was called the *Donegal Rambler,* and it was a forty-foot Delta diving boat with covered seating at the back and tank racks that could hold twenty cylinders. But he'd removed most of the tanks when he'd headed out that morning, and in their place he had seven sea rods set up on outrigger mounts.

Up in the slowly chugging boat's open flying bridge, Gannon stood with his back to the wheel, carefully watching where the rods' green-tinged monofilament lines trailed back into the boat's bubbling wake like the strings of a submerged puppet.

The lines were baited with mackerel and squid and jig lures, and he was trolling them along at a steady nine knots to make them appear to be a swimming school of juicy fish.

Or at least that was the game plan, anyway.

Gannon folded his big forearms as the *Rambler*'s two inboards purred steadily under his Converse low tops.

He'd been out since early morning, stalking the deep Atlantic falloff, and so far hadn't gotten even a bounce on any of the rods.

A dwindling plastic sleeve of sunflower seeds sat in a drink holder at his left elbow, and he lifted it out and shook a few into his mouth. He was half-turned, spitting the shells into a waste bucket he kept beside the captain's seat, when he saw that the falling sun was about to depart behind a bank of dark clouds.

Gannon squinted down at the Simrad depth finder.

The best shot for a sword to hit was at the tide changes, especially high to low like it was now.

He looked back up at the sky and frowned.

Time and light were running out on him.

He was pondering this and just about to spit another shell into the bucket in frustration when the closest of the starboard rods whipped down and bounced back, and the air suddenly filled with the sweet zipping sound of eighty-pound test paying out.

Sunflower seeds went flying as Gannon slipped the boat into Neutral and flashed down the ladder without touching the rungs. As he grabbed the big, frantically unreeling rod up out of the mount, he smiled at the heavy tug on it. Swords usually liked to nibble first, but this one apparently had just gone for it.

He gripped hard on the rod and began reeling, rapidly taking up slack, racing the now-quickly-ascending fish to make sure it didn't get a chance to unhook.

The fish jumped for the first time thirty feet from the boat twenty minutes later. It was a gigantic white marlin, long and shining, with a dark blue bill and a beautiful Mohawk-like blue comb.

Even for an experienced fisherman, it was no small feat to hook a billfish during the day, and Gannon watched in boyish wide-eyed awe as it arced through the gold-tinged air, its body and tail trembling like a sprung diving board.

Then the hundred-pound-plus sport fish slapped back down into a swell with a loud explosion of water, and Gannon got giddily spinning again, sweat pouring off his face, the big rod bowing almost in half as he cranked and yanked.

He was tight on the fish and had it about twenty feet away and closing when it got stupid with panic and ran under the plunging bow. Gannon, pretty hyped up on adrenaline himself, immediately ran forward with the rod so the line wouldn't get tangled.

"Dammit!" he yelled as the bow of the boat bobbed up, and he felt the line immediately snag on something. A split second later, there was a loud crack, and all Gannon could do was watch as his snapped-free UHF radio antenna hit off the bow rail before it disappeared into the water.

Before he could even begin to deal with that, the fish spurted again and came back around to starboard and resurfaced ten feet from the boat. Gannon blinked sweat out of his stinging eyes and then whistled as he got a good look at it. He'd caught bigger sailfish before, but this was no contest the biggest white marlin he had ever hooked.

He was piecing together how to bring the monster around to the boat's port-side diving door when it suddenly twisted and went back under. That was when Gannon dropped the rod altogether. The reel clattered against the deck as he grabbed up the thick monofilament line with his gloved hands and began tugging the huge fish in hand over hand.

He had it just off the hull, holding the banjo-tight line firmly with his left hand, and was kneeling down on the deck lifting the gaff with his right when he felt it give one more mighty thrashing spasm.

"No!" Gannon screamed out as the frenzying line gave a funny jerk and the weight suddenly and completely disappeared on him.

He groaned as he stood and lunged over the gunwale with the gaff. But the huge fish was already gone. Gannon watched brokenhearted as its immense beautiful tail, already ten feet deep and counting, waved bye-bye down in the clear water as it dived.

Spit the hook a foot away! Gannon thought in agony as he slammed the gaff down loudly against the deck.

He glanced forward at the jagged, now-useless piece of metal clamped to the bow rail that used to be his radio antenna.

After busting up his boat!

He lifted the sea rod and reeled in nothing and shook his head in furious disgust as he stared at the empty hooks.

"Fish one. Gannon less than zippo," he said and after a moment began laughing as he looked for a towel.

He'd been a fisherman all his life, and it was either that or weep, he knew.

2

The sunset sky was glowing like a sheet of gold leaf by the time
Gannon reeled in everything and got all the gear and tackle
packed up and stowed tight.

After he washed up in the head, he went back up into the
flying bridge and set the GPS for Cooperstown on Little Abaco
to the south. Cooperstown was actually a little out of his way
as he lived farther south and east out on Eleuthera Island. But
with the radio antenna MIA, he wanted to be near shore by the
time it got too dark.

He slipped his face shield up and his Costa polarized shades
on and opened the boat wide to about thirty knots. Through
the breeze, the sky began to lose its glow, and the endless plain
of water took on the dark metallic tone of tarnished silver. Even
for a Monday, the fishing lanes northwest of the Bahamas were
deader than normal, the horizon empty in every direction. In
fact, the only other vessel he got a glimpse of all day was a faint

outline of a container heading west to Florida that morning when he started out.

His thoughts drifted to dinner. There was leftover lasagna in his fridge that he could nuke. Instead of fresh-grilled swordfish, he thought, shaking his defeated head in the rush of the wind. Oh, well. At least the beers would be cold.

It was about fifteen miles due east of Cooperstown when he saw something low in the sky off in front of the boat. He thought it was just a shine of light off a cloud. But then he saw that the light was moving, and he jacked up his shades onto his forehead, cupping his hands above his eyes.

Out from the postcard-Caribbean gold of the sky to the left came a plane, a small corporate jet plane, sleek and shiny and pale white. He watched it coming steadily due west at a right angle to the bow. He gauged it to be about four miles to the south. It seemed to be flying quite low. He waited for it to pull up, but it didn't. It kept zipping westward going fast, low and straight as a line drive.

He eased off on the throttle and grabbed his binoculars, putting his elbows up on the console to steady the view. Then he thumbed in the focus and something in the pit of his stomach went cold.

The plane *was* too low, flying maybe a hundred feet off the deck. It was also going way too fast like a stunt jet plane at an air show. It almost looked like a guided cruise missile rocketing just above the surface of the water.

Where had it come from? Gannon wondered, turning at the waist to keep it in the glass. There weren't any airports to the east. Hell, there wasn't *anything* east of the Bahamas. Maybe it had just left out of Marsh Harbour Airport?

It was directly off the front of his bow when he realized he couldn't hear its engines. Instead of a rumble, there was only a kind of whistling, a low whisper very faint in the distance of metal scratching air.

Gannon watched as the plane descended even lower. It had to be twenty feet off the water now. Maybe the pilot was being a hot dog, and in a moment, it would pull up, he thought hopefully.

Then the eerily whispering plane finally ran out of sky.

Its left wingtip touched down first, sending up a huge fountaining spray of water. In another moment, he watched as its belly struck down. Through the white water it threw up, you could see the fuselage vibrating violently. As it skidded along, a rough crunching, grinding sound started in the distance, like denim tearing. Fragments of metal began to shed off into the air behind it.

Even as Gannon watched this, he hoped dumbly that maybe it would be okay.

Like the Sully guy in NYC, he thought, as the back of the plane suddenly began to fishtail.

It swung all the way around backward and kept going. It was about to complete a full three-sixty when there was a rise in the tearing sound's pitch, and the plane went airborne again.

In the frozen silence, Gannon winced as he watched the spinning hundred-foot-long aircraft wobble up through the air sideways like a boomerang flung by a drunk.

Then there was a sound like a bomb going off, and all he could see in the binoculars was a hanging column of pure blinding white.

3

"Mayday! Mayday! Mayday!" Gannon called into his radio as he immediately throttled up, wheeling toward the crash site. "This is *Donegal Rambler, Donegal Rambler, Donegal Rambler*. VA number three eight seven five. I am at GPS heading twenty-seven point one-four-nine by seventy-seven point three-one-five. A plane is down! I repeat. A small commercial jet plane has crashed. How many people involved is unknown. Send help. *Donegal Rambler* is a forty-foot diving boat. Over."

He let off the handset's thumb key. There was nothing but choppy static. He checked to make sure that he was on the Channel 16 distress band then spun the volume dial as high up as it would go. The static only came in louder.

"Mayday! Mayday!" he was saying again when he remembered the snapped antenna.

He cursed as he roughly clipped the useless handset back into its holder. When he glanced forward over the dip and rise of the console, he made out the plane's tail fin on the horizon. Seeing that it was upright, a brief flutter of hope rose in his chest.

Then he looked with the binoculars.

No!

The plane had snapped in half. You could see its pale white tail section with its huge high fin and about twenty feet of it. Other than that, there was nothing. He panned over the water left and right. There was no nose, no wings. The whole front part of the aircraft was completely gone.

He was still trying to reckon this terrible fact when he began to encounter debris. A cluster of water bottles went by. A white garbage bag. A snapped piece of varnished wood paneling with drink holders in it. A man's black Nike sneaker.

On the other side of a swell to starboard appeared a huge white drumlike object. It was bouncing up and down in the water like a giant fishing bob. He couldn't think what the hell it was. Then he came close enough to smell the jet fuel and see the glistening steel turbofan blades still rotating inside of it.

A football field beyond the ripped-free jet engine lay the plane's dissected rear fuselage. Gannon eased the throttle back. He looked up at its aerodynamic rear stabilizers as he came alongside it. *G550* was written in high-sheen blue paint upon its pale side.

He slipped the boat into full idle as he came around to the front, where the cross-sectioned fuselage had breached asunder. From its top hung a spaghetti of aluminum framing and electrical wiring and tattered fiberglass. Yet through these ragged streamers, the rear interior of the aircraft was almost perfectly intact. There was cream-colored carpet on the floor, a window seat covered in bungee-corded luggage, a highly varnished wood sideboard.

Behind the sideboard was the open doorway of a restroom. Gannon stared into it, mesmerized. The white marble sink basin within it looked like something from a five-star hotel.

"Hello!" Gannon called into the fantastic floating ruin. "Hello! Is anyone in there?"

Gannon closed his eyes, listening intently. Thirty seconds passed. A minute. There was nothing. The only sound was the low chugging of his diesels.

He retrieved his binoculars and pointed them to the south. Far off beyond the wreck at ten miles or more, he could just make out the dark coast of one of Little Abaco's tiny uninhabited outer islands.

"What in the hell?" he said angrily as he scanned a three-sixty.

Why were there no boats in the water? he thought. Or choppers in the sky? Hadn't the pilot called in a mayday? Hadn't the airport in Little Abaco seen it disappear off the radar?

He went back up into the flying bridge and did another slower, tighter sweep with the binoculars. About another football field north of the tail section, he spotted a thick clump of objects floating in the water. It was quickly getting darker now, so it was hard to know what they were. Just five or ten black lumps bunched together, rising and falling in the calm swells.

"Please don't be what I think you are," he said to himself as he levered at the throttle and turned the wheel.

He'd chugged the *Rambler* in close enough to see that the items were only a cluster of floating pillows and seat cushions when he spotted something below in the clear water beneath them.

It was something large and pale.

4

Gannon came down the ladder and threw off his shirt and grabbed a diving mask from his equipment locker. The diving door was port side rear, and he swung it open and extended down the telescoping diving ladder with a loud clack and plunged feetfirst into the warm water.

In the darkening water below the hull of his boat there were some undersea limestone ridges at a depth of about fifty feet. In the murk, about fifty feet farther down their crusted slope, was the entire front of the jet with its huge wings and most of its forward cabin resting on a coral plateau.

He searched the plane and the coral all around it through the mask until he couldn't hold his breath anymore. Then he scrambled back up and stripped off the mask and kicked off his wet sneakers as he raced across the deck for his tanks.

It was three minutes later when Gannon plunged backward into the water. He clicked on all his lights and thumbed at the buoyancy compensator as he spun himself around and down into the dim water.

He was geared up with everything he could think of. His double 120 tanks, his flippers and wrist dive computer, his brand-new BCD vest. The light was almost gone now, so he'd also grabbed his powerful hand-strap Sola flashlight along with his GoPro camera diving mask because the camera had another light.

Descending along the crusted ridgeline toward the plane, he swung the powerful flashlight back and forth at the wreck, hoping to see air bubbles. But all he saw were bits of fiberglass and a couple of gray angelfish that came out of the coral, attracted to the light.

He finally came flat and level with the plane two long minutes later. The first object he made out inside the torn tube of its opening was the back of a large beige luxury leather seat. To the right of it across the narrow aisle was an empty leather couch of the same creamy beige color. A few feet in front of the couch beneath a porthole window was a low wood desk with a large black TV monitor on it that blocked his view farther in.

There was a brief moan in the plane's metal as Gannon floated there, considering his options. He checked his depth gauge with his flashlight. It said he and the plane were at one hundred fifteen feet.

He looked back at the plane through his mask. The ripped opening of the front half of the plane was strung with even more tatters of wire and shredded metal than the floating half above. But there was ample room for him to swim in as long as he stayed low.

He trimmed some more air out of his buoyancy compensator to get his horizontal balance even better, then went in slowly, careful of his hoses. He arrived at the beige chair and grabbed on to its armrest to pull himself forward.

He immediately face-planted down into the carpet as the

chair unexpectedly swiveled on him. He lost his balance, and his light and his mask went askew. He had just cleared the mask and was turning, pushing up off his knees, when he bumped into something with his chest, and he swung the light around.

And came nose to nose with the revolting open-eyed corpse sitting in the chair's seat.

Bubbles spewed, and he almost lost a flipper as he reared back in full-blown blind panic and terror. His mask went askew again and completely fogged into a gray mess as he clonked his head off the plane's low ceiling.

He turned and twisted and lunged away out of the plane as fast as his kicking flippers and fear-crazed windmilling arms could take him. He didn't stop swimming until his hand finally found his neon dive rope he'd dropped twenty feet to the wreck's south.

He cleared his mask again and floated there beside the faintly glowing rope. The hiss and gurgle of the regulator loud in his ears, his heart hammering.

Of course the people are dead, you idiot, Gannon thought angrily as he glanced back at the wrecked plane. *What the hell else would they be?*

He needed to stop this silliness, he thought as he looked past the plane into the immensity of the rapidly darkening ocean in front of him.

Diving alone in the open Atlantic was suicidal by itself without going into some coffin-sized wreck filled with who knew what. He was almost certain to get himself killed in another minute if he kept this nonsense up.

The rasp of his breath calmed a little as he fussed with his mask strap. He looked at the time on his dive computer. Then he glanced back at the wrecked plane again.

Oh, whatever. One more try, he thought, already swimming back toward it.

5

The dead man belted into the swivel chair back in the plane was a tall and lean distinguished-looking white-haired Caucasian male somewhere in his midsixties.

He looked polished, Gannon thought. Expensively groomed. With his white dress shirt with the sleeves rolled up and his gray suit slacks, he could have been a doctor from a daytime TV commercial.

When Gannon looked more closely in the flashlight beam, he could see there was actually something wrong with the man's photogenic face. There was a horribly pale bluish cast to his skin especially around his open eyes, and from his nose to his chin, there was a thin stripe of what looked like dried blood.

Behind his diving mask, Gannon squinted, perplexed.

How could his blood already be dry? he thought.

Gannon swam in a little to the right of the corpse. In two

more leather swivel chairs on the left-hand side of the aircraft's tight cabin sat two more dead men.

Like the first man, they were both white, both wearing business clothes. The one closest to him was about thirty-five or so. He had a closely cropped haircut and was stocky and rugged-faced. The other one seated farther toward the front of the plane was younger. He was bony, in his early twenties. He had long-ish hair and the wisp of a blond beard and was wearing white earmuff-style headphones.

Gannon passed the light from one to the other. Like the first body, they, too, had the same strangely pale bluish tone to their faces.

When Gannon finally turned to the right-hand side of the cabin beside them with the light, it took the entirety of his restraint to not rear back in another panicked bubble-spewing jolt.

In the forward galley before the cockpit was yet another dead man. He was floating upright as if standing. Unlike the others, this dead man was black and was dressed in jeans and a gray hoodie. Gannon watched as the corpse rotated around in a slow, horrid lifelike turn. There was the same blue sickly look to his features as well, and his nosebleed had been so bad, it had stained the top of his sweater black.

When Gannon pointed the light into the cockpit behind the body, he could see that there were two pilots in white-shirted airline-like uniforms still seated at the controls.

He tried to look to see their faces more closely, but the upright floating hoodie-wearing dead man in the galley was blocking the view.

And the chances of him moving the floating dead man out of the way or going any farther into the claustrophobic undersea mausoleum even another inch, Gannon thought, were exactly none at all.

Six dead. No survivors, Gannon thought with a nod. There was nothing to be done.

Time to go, he thought, flippering around in a hectic rush to finally get the hell out of there.

6

After what seemed some very long, slow minutes of following the coral ridge back up through the ten-story depth of the dark water, Gannon finally hauled himself back aboard his boat.

After he pulled himself up through the dive door, instead of sitting on one of the benches, he spit out the regulator and knelt and lay facedown on the deck in the sluice of the water.

He'd shrugged out of his clanging tanks and was still light-headed with the ebullient joy of breathing through his nose and being alive when he finally stood a long minute later.

And still, there is no rescue effort! he thought as he looked over the wreckage to the now-dark horizon.

Nothing. Not a boat. Not an aircraft. Not even a light anywhere in sight.

The boat pitched hard port to starboard in a swell as he peeled off his dripping gloves. As it baby cradled back and forth, he turned to the left and saw that the floating rear tail section of the shattered jet was lower than it had been. It had foundered to one side a tad, its pale cruciform tail fin slightly tilted.

In a moment, it would sink, too, Gannon thought, shaking his head at the absurdity of the whole crazy thing. In an hour, the dark Atlantic would swallow it like it had swallowed the first half of it. And but for Gannon's memory, it would be as if the plane had never existed at all.

Gannon had just pulled up the dive rope and was clacking up the dive ladder a minute later when the boat pitched again, and he heard the clatter to starboard.

He walked over and looked over the gunwale and saw some luggage there in the water, bumping up against the side of his boat.

The first piece Gannon brought aboard with the help of his gaff was a little dark green hard case that looked like something you'd put a camera in. He laid it on the deck and went and got a penlight. He clicked the light on, put it in his mouth, undid the case's clasps and flipped up the lid.

Inside of the case, sunk into the hard gray packing foam, was a gun. He could tell by its distinctive shape and black matte texture that it was a polymer Glock pistol. There were some large magazines and a suppressor half-buried in the packing material beside it. He peered at the length of the magazines then tilted the light at the pistol barrel. A thin number 18 was engraved along the side.

A Glock 18? Gannon thought with a whistle.

He'd heard of them. They looked like a regular pistol but they were actually small yet extremely powerful handheld machine guns with a rate of fire twice that of an Uzi.

A fully automatic machine gun pistol, he thought, looking at it curiously. But weren't only people in law enforcement or the military allowed to legally possess those?

He was still staring down at it with a hand to the back of his wet mind-boggled head a full minute later when he heard some more knocking and clacking against the boat.

The second hard case he pulled aboard was silver and far heavier than the first. He actually had to gaff it around to the diving door and almost threw out his back as he lugged it up over the lip. It had to be about seventy pounds or more, he thought as he brought it over and thumped it onto the deck next to the gun case.

He stood, chewing at his lower lip as he stared at it. Then he finally knelt down and opened it up.

And felt his breath exit his lungs in a mad-dash rush.

Gannon tracked the columns and rows. Right to left and up and down. And then he did it again.

The case was jammed tight with money. They were all hundreds. Packets and packets and packets of United States of America Benjamin Franklin one-hundred-dollar bills.

They were wrapped tight in red rubber bands. He edged one out. He thumbed at the cloth-like paper. He held it up to his face and smelled it and riffled its soft edge against his wrist.

"Seventy pounds," Gannon whispered as he stared.

But that's not all, came a TV game show host voice from somewhere in Gannon's mind as he noticed a huge lump in the cloth webbing on the underside of the case's lid.

Inside the flap, there was a big butter-soft black leather bag about the size of a laptop case. The word *Cross* was embossed along its bottom. He lifted it out and unzipped it and unfolded it on top of the pallet of money.

He was no jeweler, but inside of the leather bag was what appeared to be rough uncut diamonds. Some were grayish and some had a yellow tinge, but most of them were as colorless and clear as broken car glass.

They had been separated into clear plastic sleeves by size. A grouping of about ten of them in one sleeve section along the left side of the sheet particularly captured his attention.

He'd seen diamonds before. Just never ones the size of Jolly Rancher hard candies.

There were about enough diamonds to fill a cereal bowl, Gannon thought, shaking the bag. Hell, more. Several bowls. He bit at his lower lip some more as he began nodding idiotically. He was staring down at the damn entire box of cornflakes, wasn't he?

Seventy pounds of worn US hundred-dollar bills plus a fat satchel of uncut diamonds, he thought as he stood. Plus a fully automatic law enforcement–only machine gun pistol.

He glanced back at the sinking tail section.

Plus six dead men in a multimillion-dollar crashed luxury Gulfstream jet.

He knew what it was now. He had thought it already, but now he knew.

It was a drug deal. Some kind of crazy high-level drug deal. Down in South America. In Colombia or Bolivia or somewhere with the cartels. But it had gone super loco apparently.

Gannon blinked at the piled treasure.

He looked up at the dark vault of the sky, the first faint silver sprinkling of stars that could be seen there.

The opportunity he had here. All that money. Like a Powerball hit.

Only the kind you could never tell anyone about.

He slowly passed a hand over his scruffy jaw. He looked at the water, turned in every direction. All still dark. Still nobody coming. He looked at the cross of the listing tail section about to sink.

What would the Bahamian government do with it? Gannon thought. *Lower the tax rate? Give it to the poor?*

Sure they would, he thought as he took a deep breath.

Then he decided.

Was it even a decision at all? he thought as he went and found his gloves again and pulled them on.

Gannon hurried up to the bow and clicked on the electric anchor winch. As the chain began to chatter against the bow roll, he came back and dumped the money out onto the deck and tossed the bag of diamonds on top of it. He wiped down the empty suitcase with a wet towel before he brought it back to the diving platform and filled it with water and made it sink.

He thought about keeping the gun before he closed its lid and wiped its case down and heaved it into the sea from whence it came.

He tossed the diamonds and money into a dirty blanket he used as a pad when doing engine repairs and locked it in the head before he went forward and secured the anchor.

Gannon could feel butterflies in his stomach and his heart pounding crazily in his chest as he came back and climbed the ladder up into the dark flying bridge.

"Caught something after all," he said to himself with a crazy laugh as he turned off the running lights and slammed the twin diesels to full reverse, keeping his eyes on the dark horizon.

7

Coming on eleven at night, there was an accident on Miami's Palmetto Expressway that was backing up traffic just west of the I-95 on-ramp.

Pressed up against the left side window of the coast guard C-130 Hercules on approach to Miami Coast Guard Air Station, navy lieutenant Ruby Everett squinted down at the commotion.

In the police blue-and-red bubble light glare, she counted three vehicles involved, a pickup truck and two cars. She craned her neck back as the thunderous aircraft zoomed over the highway. She looked for debris, telltale skid marks. But it was fruitless. They were too far away.

Easy, tiger, she thought as she felt the aircraft's landing gear hum beneath her toes.

You'll have more work than you bargained for in about five seconds flat.

"Hey, can I ask you a question?" said the pilot in her earphones.

She turned away from the window and came forward in the jump seat. The pilot was leaning out of the cockpit, smiling back at her. There were two other crew members sitting behind her, but they both seemed to be sleeping.

Ruby listened to the roar of the engines behind her in the big cavernous cargo plane as she looked forward at the pilot and the smile on his face. There was something creepy about the guy that she couldn't quite put her finger on. He seemed normal enough. Plain looking. Midthirties. Very neat.

But maybe that was precisely it. He was too neat, too plain. He looked like one of those blend-into-the-woodwork, plain-looking neat guys from one of those Discovery Channel shows where women ended up floating in the Everglades after the first date.

"What was that?" she said as she pulled her blue camo utility cap down tighter over her dark brown pulled-back hair.

"What division are you in?" he said.

"Office of Naval Safety," she said, tugging at her matching blue camo blouse to make it as baggy as possible.

As usual, she'd changed immediately into her navy blue utility working uniform and boots when she'd gotten the call. She actually had to gun it back to her apartment up in Ensley to change and to grab her gear. She'd only just gotten back in time to hitch this cargo flight out of Pensacola Naval Air Station, where she was based.

"Naval Safety?" the pilot said, glancing at his instruments then back at her.

"I know. It makes us sound like hall monitors," she said. "We're basically the NTSB but for the military. We investigate aviation mishaps."

"Ah, a toe tagger," he said with a nod. "That's wild. You must have seen some real freaky stuff."

Ruby smiled back politely.

She'd been backup for plenty of accidents in the four years she'd worked at Safety but had only been on-site to two real ones. The biggest was an air force cargo plane that had gone down in upstate New York the year before.

It was a NATO base resupply plane coming back from an overseas deployment somewhere. It needed to refuel in Canada, and there had been some screwup with the liters-to-gallons ratio. They'd also eventually surmised that the gas tank low-level alarm never went off due to a burnt-out transducer.

She remembered finding the black box herself on the bank of a frozen creek in Chittenango State Park near Syracuse. She most definitely remembered the pilots' screams from it. Both pilots and the 140-million-dollar aircraft had been completely obliterated on impact.

"You like it?" the pilot said.

She glanced out at the lights of Miami-Opa Locka Executive Airport coming at them hard and fast in the aircraft's windshield.

"It's a job," she said.

That wasn't true. Ruby loved it. The engineering, the math, the detective work, the excitement. Not being chained to a desk.

Well, at least usually, she thought, squinting down at the floor.

For the first time in her professional life, she had been actually disappointed when her boss had called her in for a job.

It was because of her sister. Her little sister, Lori, was due any minute to give birth to her second child. When Ruby's phone rang two hours before, she'd actually been hanging out at Lori's place in Lake Charlene waiting for her water to break so she could drive her to the hospital.

It had been Ruby's hope to ride out her last night of being on call into her upcoming leave. She'd been pretty much banking on it actually. With Lori's husband, Mitch, in the marine corps on active deployment in the Middle East, there was no way Ruby wanted Lori, her only sibling, to have to give birth alone.

Ruby winced as she thought about her sister, big as a house, on the sofa with her little three-year-old son, Sean, running around like a monkey.

Hopefully, she could get the preliminaries started on whatever the hell this was and then pass it off to the other members of her team and skedaddle.

"What kind of plane crash you going to?" the pilot said, absently flicking off the autopilot on the console as he sat forward again. "A navy plane? Some arrogant navy Tomcat pilot seen too many Tom Cruise movies and became tarmac pizza?"

"I don't know yet. We do all branches. They didn't tell me much. They just said they needed me in Miami ASAP."

"One other question," the pilot said, looking back at her with his creepily plain grin.

Oh, boy, here we go, Ruby thought.

"Shoot," she said.

"You married?"

"Engaged," she lied.

She saw the spinning chopper right away as they landed. To the left of the big coast guard hangars was one of their famous rescue helicopters seen in the recruiting commercials, red with the white stripe. There was a crewman in a helmet and a dark blue flight suit sitting in its open side door.

What was it called again? she thought as she unbuckled her seat belt. A Dolphin, she remembered as she stood and shouldered her gear bag. An MH-65 Dolphin.

"Lieutenant, your chariot awaits," said a chief petty officer with a ruddy face and a beer gut on the other side of the Hercules's dropped ramp.

"What's going on, Chief?" she said.

"No rest for the weary, Lieutenant," he said over the wind rush and rotor whine as he led her through the humid night air toward the Dolphin.

"We have a cutter on scene, the *Surmount*, out of Miami Beach. The bird will take you straight out."

"Are there any other members of my team here?" she said.

"No. There's no one. Are you supposed to wait for them?"

"I'm not sure. I keep texting my boss, but he hasn't gotten back. Did you send anybody else out?"

"No, but my orders are to get you out there right away. I recommend you just head out now, and I'll send out your friends later if they show. This one's a four-alarmer, from the sound of my boss."

Ruby looked at the old salty coastie, at the bright blinking lights of the churning chopper waiting for her.

"Let's do this," she said, tucking down her cap as she plunged into the rotor wash.

8

A thousand miles due north of Miami, snowflakes fell steadily against the upstairs window of Robert Reyland's house in Falls Church, Virginia. There was a pretty good wind going as well. Downstairs in the brick chimneys of Reyland's big new house, the whistling gusts of it sounded almost musical.

But Reyland didn't see the flakes, didn't hear the wind.

He was too busy watching it become midnight on his encrypted secure cell phone.

He raised his large bald head and looked around the small silent room. There wasn't much in it. The eyebrow window above the gun safe, the cardboard boxes in the corner they still hadn't unpacked.

The Realtor had told them that the tiny space off the master bedroom suite originally was supposed to have been a nursery for the people who had built the place, but the wife had miscarried, so they'd just left it empty.

Unforeseen botched circumstances, Reyland thought, passing a hand back and forth soothingly over the shaved-smooth
skin of his head.

He placed his BlackBerry back down on the top of the gun
safe he'd just taken it out of.

My, oh, my, can I empathize.

He shifted his weight on his wife's tiny vanity chair he'd
brought in from the bathroom. He was still in the suit and overcoat he was wearing when he'd gotten out of the car from the
airport two hours before.

He'd been in London waiting to hear word from his boss
when he'd gotten the report about his plane falling completely
out of contact. The eight-and-a-half sleepless hours he'd just
spent on the British Airways flight back to DC had felt like the
most useless of his entire life.

He refused to even consider all the worst-case scenarios. At
least not yet. Even for him, some things were just too terrible
to contemplate.

He had gone immediately from Reagan International downtown to his office and called everyone he could. Twice. They
had done some projections, but there were too many factors.
The wind, the orientation of the instruments. It was a needle
in a haystack even with the satellites.

Reyland palmed at his head like LeBron on a mid-dunk basketball.

Now he was home to get some sleep.

Yeah, right, he thought as the phone suddenly rang.

He felt his heart thump like a kick drum as he looked at the
screen.

It was his right-hand man, Emerson.

Here we go, Reyland thought, closing his eyes as it rang again.
In his mind, he pictured a coin flipping.

Heads, you live. Tails, you die.

He forced himself to take a very deliberate breath before he thumbed down the accept button.

"Where?" Reyland said.

"The ocean. Atlantic Ocean, northwest of the Bahamas."

"The Bahamas! What?" Reyland said as he let out a breath. "How the hell did it get there?"

"It must have happened before the second turn in the flight plan," Emerson said. "They never made the turn, and it just kept going till the gas ran out."

"What a damn disaster! Is he alive?"

"No. It got ripped up on impact. Tore in two. Dunning is dead. All of them are dead. No survivors, just like they said."

Reyland pondered that for a long silent beat. His mentor, the great Dunning, was gone. Just like that. It was hard to wrap his mind around. He put it aside.

"How far out from land?" he said.

"Ten, fifteen miles offshore of... Let's see... Little Abaco. It landed underwater on a coral shelf."

"Who called it in? Civilian?"

"No. The coast guard found it. A drug-interdiction cutter out of Miami Beach. They spotted the wreckage with their radar. Thought it was a drug boat."

"Are we lucky it wasn't a civilian. But coast guard, huh? I don't like it. Did they see inside the cabin?"

"No, not really. The bodies are still in the part of the plane that's underwater. We lucked out there."

"Wait, wait, wait. What do you mean by 'not really'?" Reyland said, squinting.

"Well, the coast guard went through standard rescue procedures when they spotted it. One of the rescue divers went down to check for survivors. Don't worry. I'm already getting any and all tape and making plans to isolate the crew."

"We on the way?"

"Yes, Ruiz should be wheels up with our team by now. Luckily, there was a salvage vessel out of Norfolk out training. It's six hours away. Ruiz has some ex-SEALs with him. They'll go under and get everything that needs getting off. All in all, it's looking about as good as we could have hoped."

"I don't like it," Reyland said. "The coast guard is out of our purview. I don't have to tell you the lid we need on this."

"Don't worry. It won't be a problem," Emerson said. "I'll send word again that the coast guard is to completely stand down and babysit until Ruiz and the navy vessel show up, and we get it all the hell out of there.

"By the way, London called again. Twice. But I stalled them like you said. Also, have you figured out how you're going to tell Cathy?"

"Who?"

"Cathy. You know, Dunning's wife."

"Oh. No. I haven't. Not yet. Shit. She thinks he's at a conference in Italy. I mean, imagine? Add telling her the great Dunning is dead to the list of my magic tricks."

"I could do it, boss, if you want," Emerson said quickly.

Reyland's gray eyes squinted as he sat up, suddenly noticing the eager-beaver tone in Emerson's voice.

He was really all over everything, wasn't he? Reyland thought. London. Their military contacts. You bet he was. Trying to use the crisis to climb a rung or two.

What's the expression? Never let one go to waste?

There was a long beat of silence in the cold of the small room. Down in the living room, Reyland heard the wind in the chimney suddenly chime like a bell.

"You're right, boss," Emerson finally said. "I'll leave it to you."

9

After over an hour of monotonous black ocean, the sudden deck lights of the USCGC *Surmount* were as bright as a rock concert.

Ruby's stomach churned in time to the change in pitch of the chopper's turboshaft engines as they came to a hover. She loved flying in airplanes and was actually a licensed pilot herself, but like so many others in the military, helicopters always made her nervous.

As they swung in above the rear flight deck helipad, outside the window she could see several sailors in life jackets and hard hats along the 270-foot cutter's aft rail.

"Okay, Lieutenant, if you're ready, we're going to lower you down in the bucket," the Dolphin crew chief said with his Southern accent in her intercom headphones.

She turned and looked at him in horror as he showed her some kind of harness.

"What?" she shrieked.

"Gotcha," the helmeted crew chief said with a grin. "Don't worry, Lieutenant. Roy will land it. Maybe even on the boat, if we're lucky."

The officer who met her on the chopper pad's edge was fair-haired and clean-shaven and, like almost everyone else in the coast guard, looked young enough to still be in college.

"Welcome to the *Surmount*, Lieutenant Everett. I'm Lieuten-ant Martin," he said, shaking her hand as he led her up a short set of steps through a doorway.

Inside, there were three blue-uniformed seamen on the bridge. She dropped her bag in an unobtrusive corner, the air-conditioning delicious after the humid heat in the chopper.

"So you're the investigative team," Martin said as they watched out the pilothouse glass where a team of coasties with a hose was already refueling the Dolphin.

"The first," she said. "There are four of us altogether. The others are on the way. So what do you have? A downed aircraft?"

"It's a plane," Martin said, nodding. "One of our guys on watch spotted it on our radar about five hours ago. We do long-range drug-interdiction patrols out of Miami Beach, so we thought it was a boat in distress on the water at first.

"But as we approached, we saw its tail fin barely sticking up out of the water. That was only from its rear section. It's actually broken in two. The front part is under a hundred feet of water. I was about to call the local airport on Little Abaco for any miss-ing aircraft, but then I saw the bulletin. My father's buddy Al Litvak works at the naval safety office, so I called him first di-rectly. You know Al?"

"Yes," Ruby said. "He's one of my boss's bosses. You said there was a bulletin?"

"Yep. It was on our OPREP board. I saw it when I came on watch. It said something about a missing air force jet to be on the lookout for."

She thought about that. No one had told her about a missing jet.

"So it's a jet? What kind? Do you know?"

Martin took out an iPhone and brought up a picture.

"Not a military one, as far as I can tell. It's some kind of corporate jet. Our diver took a photograph of a dataplate on a piece of debris near the tail section. *Gulfstream*, it says. See?"

She looked at the image. *Gulfstream* was *all* it said. There was nothing stamped in the boxes for model and serial number and FAA certification.

Maybe it was an EC-37B, she thought. The EC-37B was the new military version of the Gulfstream 550 that had electronic warfare capability. It could jam radar and other electronic systems.

Perhaps it was on a test flight? Which was maybe why it hadn't been picked up by local airports' radar?

Ruby peered at the photograph again. She had never seen a blank dataplate before. It was like staring at a car license plate with no number on it.

"After we spotted it, we immediately did our rapid emergency rescue response to check for survivors. There was no one in the tail part. Then we saw that the sunken front portion was within diving range, so I had one of our rescue divers go down for a peek. Six aboard it, including the two pilots. All dead."

"That's terrible. Where are they now? Below deck?" she said.

"Who?" Martin said.

"The deceased," she said, blinking at him.

"No," Martin said, looking at her. "We didn't do the recovery yet. I got a call from my base commander to stand down and let you guys take care of it."

She gave him a funny look.

"Is that right?" she said.

"What's the problem? Is that not protocol? With the bodies, I mean?"

"No, it's not," she said. "I've never heard of the deceased being left in place before. We usually get brought in after all remains are recovered from the wreckage."

Martin squinted, puzzled.

"He was pretty insistent about us not going near the aircraft again until you guys showed," he said. "He said a navy salvage vessel is en route."

"My boss didn't tell me that. I thought he was waiting to hear from me first," she said.

"Well, looks like somebody's getting their wires crossed, I guess. What else is new," Martin said.

A burly older man in a bosun's mate uniform came out of a door on the other side of the ship's glowing control boards.

"Hey, Lieutenant, you got a call," he said.

Martin looked at him then back at Ruby.

"Give me a sec," he said.

10

Ruby went to the window. As the Dolphin lifted off, she looked down and saw a diver in a wet suit talking to a seaman along the main-deck starboard rail.

"Hey, guys. I'm Lieutenant Everett from Naval Safety investigating the crash," she said as she arrived in front of them. "Did you go down and see the wreckage?"

The diver nodded. He was a cute kid, lean and blond and green-eyed with a fresh green tattoo of a shamrock on the webbing of his right hand. He was short, about five foot five or six. Sitting gracefully in his Body Glove suit, he could have been a teen surfer resting between waves.

"How far down was it?" Ruby said.

"About a hundred and twenty feet," the blond diver said.

"Can you go deeper?"

"You'd be amazed," said the older deckhand with a wink as the kid blushed.

Ruby glared at the joker, a thick-featured, dark-haired thirty-something with a goatee. She looked at his deckhand's green hard hat. What was the navy term for green hats? Oh, yeah. Deck apes.

"We're trained to go up to two hundred or so or even more, but you need special tanks with added helium," the young diver said.

"Were the deceased in uniform? Air force personnel or navy? Could you tell?" she said.

"Lieutenant?" called a voice from above.

Ruby turned around to see Lieutenant Martin at the pilot-house rail above, waving.

"Excuse me," she said to the diver. "We'll talk later, okay?"

"I'll be here," the diver said.

"Me, too," said the deck ape with a wink.

She went back up the stairs and followed Lieutenant Martin inside. He led her across the bridge through a short corridor into his wood-paneled office.

"Coffee?" he said, closing the door.

"Please. Black."

She stood silently waiting as he poured. The mug he handed her had a picture of a cute little blond boy in a funny puffy Hulk costume on it.

"Please, sit back and get comfy, Lieutenant," Martin said, gesturing at a bench-like padded couch bolted to the wall. "There's been a change in plans apparently."

"What do you mean?" she said.

"We've been advised to completely stay away from the wreckage. We're actually leaving now. We're supposed to babysit at a distance of a quarter mile. We're not supposed to touch any debris. Just keep people away. Starting now. No personnel are to go near the wreckage until the navy salvage ship arrives. Including you."

Ruby's brow wrinkled.

"What? Why?"

"I don't know."

"But how does that make sense?"

Lieutenant Martin leaned forward in his bolted-down office chair and thumbed back his hat as he thought about that. He took it off and began spinning it off a finger.

"I have absolutely no clue," he finally said. "But as it turns out, I shouldn't even have called you. My boss is pissed that I jumped the chain. I should have called him first, he said, even though he's on leave with his family on vacation out in California. You ever see something like this with a crash before?"

Ruby looked down into her coffee and then back at him before she slowly shook her head.

"Not even close," she said.

11

The clock in the dashboard was at 2:53 when the dirt road Gannon was looking for suddenly leaped out of the darkness into his headlights on his right.

His GMC Sierra skidded slightly as he brought it to an abrupt stop on the right shoulder and flicked on the cab light. There was a map of Eleuthera Island's southern end on the passenger seat, and he reached over and lifted it up. He looked at the map then looked back at the dashboard, where he'd been clocking the distance on the odometer. Then he flicked off the dome light and shifted the truck into Reverse.

He'd finally arrived home around ten and put up the boat at his berth in Davis Head Harbor and went back to his house in Tarpum Head.

Weeds leaped and danced in the bobbing headlights as he turned off the asphalt down onto the slightly sloping bumpy dirt drive.

Now it was four hours later, and he was twenty miles south of his house in a mostly unpopulated part of Eleuthera known as Bannerman Town.

After a few hundred yards, he stopped again, shut off the engine, got out and stood looking.

There wasn't much to see. The old road led into fifty or so acres of deserted pineland that had belonged to a run-down resort that had been abandoned years before after hurricane damage had finished it off.

He crossed the rocky, sandy dirt to the rear of the truck and dropped the tailgate. In the bed was another vehicle, a golf cart–like utility quad ATV 4x4 known as a Gator. It, too, had a kind of truck bed that was filled now with diving tanks and coils of lights and ropes.

Gannon dropped the ramp and backed the Gator down. He winced at the tremendous roar of its four-stroke engine as he fired it on.

Not exactly stealth mode, was it? he thought. But there was no helping it.

He went to the back of it. Down between the tanks was a bulging faded-green canvas sea bag and he zipped it open.

Sealed up watertight in thick plastic vacuum-sealed garment bags were the money and the diamonds and his GoPro camera.

He hadn't planned on adding the GoPro to the rest of his salvaged contraband until he'd wisely decided to take a look at it back at the house and realized he'd actually filmed the whole dive into the plane.

It was some pretty creepy footage. Not to mention incriminating.

He certainly hadn't meant to memorialize the event, but he must have accidentally hit the camera's record button when he turned on its light while he was in the water.

He zipped the canvas bag back up again. As he stood there in the dark it occurred to him that he could still cease and desist from what he was doing here. That even now there was still time.

Then the moment passed, and he found himself hopping in behind the Gator's wheel and flicking the lights on.

12

The narrow foot lane he was looking for was another two hundred feet down the pitch-black drive.

It was off to the left atop a thickly overgrown slope, and thistles and sharp pine brush and branches scraped like claws through the Gator's open door as he throttled up to it.

About a football field from the tree line where he'd come in, the path began to slope steeply downward as the pine forest trees began to thin. The trees gave way to a shrubby glade, and he hit the brakes a moment later as the path suddenly ended.

Beyond in the headlights of the ATV was a large depression in the earth about the size and shape of an ice hockey rink. It was rimmed with steep, almost sheer ten-foot-high pale rock walls, and at the bottom of it was a large pond-like body of water.

The large quarry-like opening in the ground was known as a blue hole. All over the Bahamas, blue holes were cave-like water-filled sinkholes that had been formed by eons of rain eroding through the soft Bahamian limestone.

There were several that were famous diving tourist spots but not this one. The only reason Gannon knew about this one out here in the boonies was because he had dived it three years before with a geology professor from Australia who had hired him to watch his back while he did research.

Gannon had thought the old Aussie was a little off his rocker until he dived down with him and saw the amazing subway-like network of corridors and caves with his own eyes. Several channels were almost a mile in length and went down hundreds of feet in depth. Every day for two weeks they had explored and mapped the cave network with guide ropes and radiolocation transmitters.

From behind his seat, Gannon produced a cardboard tube and tipped out the rolled-up laminated map that he and the professor had made of the cave system.

Then he clicked on a flashlight and uncapped a Sharpie marker.

It was almost 3:30 on his wrist dive computer when he finally managed to get his game plan sussed out and all his equipment and the money bag lowered on ropes down to the water.

He had just climbed down himself and was about to get into his tanks when he realized he had forgotten something after all.

"If it's not one thing, it's another," he mumbled to the darkness as he scurried back up the rope and rock in his bare feet.

He went to the Gator and lifted up the green cloth fishing rod bag he'd left in the foot well. He couldn't strap the small cloth bag to his back because of the tanks, so he decided to tape it to his lower right leg with a few wraps of black vinyl electrical tape he'd brought along.

Two minutes later, Gannon was finally back down in the warm water of the blue hole completely geared up.

Here goes nothing, he thought, as he finally untied the heavy money-filled bag and let its weight take him down.

Most of the top part of the hole was like the bowl of a giant wineglass. But at seventy feet, its bottom tapered, and three corridor-like passageways opened up, two to the west and one to the east.

Gannon took the eastern passageway that went another thirty feet down in an angled sort of corridor that was like a steep stairwell with no stairs. At the bottom of the stairwell was a short corridor-like passage that went in two directions, east and west.

Remembering the directions he'd memorized, Gannon went to the left, east, and passed two more branches: one to the left and one to the right, and then a third on the left that he took. A hundred feet in on a level plane, the walls and ceiling of the hotel corridor–like passage began to close narrower and narrower to that of a barely diver-wide pipe.

Just when it looked like it was going to dead-end, the pipe suddenly opened up into a huge rectilinear chamber that rose up thirty or so feet.

Gannon pulled himself in through the manhole-sized opening and swung his light up at the stalactites. The professor had dubbed the chamber "the cathedral" because of its height.

Along the high wall to his right, about twenty feet up, he stopped the light where a horizontal lip of rock jutted out.

Gannon shone the light down onto the sea bag and opened it and took out the twenty-pound weight. Then he adjusted his buoyancy and floated and swam up to the ridge with the bag.

Arriving at the ridge, he peeked over at the shelf of rock he had noticed when he had explored the chamber with the professor. When he placed the heavy sea bag down onto the shelf, it fit almost perfectly, but it kept floating up a little. After a few more failed tries of stuffing it down, he swam down to the cathedral's floor, retrieved the weight, swam up and put it into the bag.

Gannon paddled back a little bit and looked with the light at the almost-invisible ridge of rock. He smiled around the regulator in his mouth.

The money bag was settled now. Invisible.

Better than a Swiss vault, he thought.

Gannon was squeezing into the pipe-sized tunnel out of the cathedral when he realized the green cloth fishing rod bag was still taped to his leg. He backed into the cathedral chamber and cut the tape with a knife from his ankle and held the bag in his hand as he looked around.

Just above the tunnel exit he found a rock ledge, and he took the narrow tube-shaped cloth bag and dug it down into the silt and rocks there.

Now we're done, he thought.

13

"Okay, here we go. Which famous English writer was called 'the prophet of British Imperialism'?" a tall, skinny coast guard sailor at the next table read off a Trivial Pursuit card.

"Harry Potter," somebody called out in the bright sunny bacon-scented room. Then somebody called out "Joe Mama" in a funny voice, and they all cracked up.

Ruby put down the beat-up Nicholas Sparks paperback she'd found in the lounge next to the mess and looked out at the bright light coming through the big window at the other end of the cafeteria.

They were shore bound now, still in the Bahamas on Andros Island on a US naval base called the Atlantic Undersea Test and Evaluation Center.

She had actually heard of it. It had some deep ocean trench close by off its coast where they supposedly tested submarine stuff, sonar and torpedoes and missiles and depth charges and who knew what else.

As if she could care what they did here, she thought, checking her watch and seeing that it was coming on two in the afternoon.

Why the hell was she here?

It wasn't clear. Three hours after Lieutenant Martin had received his babysitting orders, a navy salvage ship called the USS *Recover* had arrived.

When the navy ship had relieved them, she had thought they would head back to base in Miami. Silly her. Lieutenant Martin had been ordered south directly to Andros Island to dock here at the obscure base until further notice and that was all.

Or at least, Ruby thought, that was all she was being told.

She lifted up the paperback again but then put it down, stood, went to the window and looked across the base yard at the USS *Recover.*

It had arrived at one of the deep-sea docks a half hour before. They had some kind of big dividers or something set up on its deck. As if they were actually hiding the damn wreckage or something.

She stared at the boat, trying to decide which pissed her off more: that they'd stuck her here without explanation or that someone else was doing her job.

What was also great was she'd tried to call her boss to get her the hell out of here, but there was no service. There was Wi-Fi, but it was password-only, and what do you know? No one at the base would give any of them the password.

Ruby wanted to find Lieutenant Martin to complain, but he was conspicuously absent.

Out of bitching range, she thought. *He'd move up quickly.*

Just called out here to stand down, she thought as she looked at the stupid navy ship. Which really, really wasn't working for her since she was supposed to be on leave by now helping her sister, Lori, due in less than twenty-four hours.

Ruby shook her head as she pictured Lori by herself out in Lake Charlene, waiting for her water to break. If it hadn't already.

"Screw this," Ruby mumbled as she crossed for the door.

It was incredibly humid outside, the hot air still, the sun beating. She walked down the mess hall's rust-tinged steps and across the bleached concrete base yard. There were some more rust-flaked steps onto the deep-water dock on the other side, and she was already sweating like it was going out of style as she came up them.

As she walked along the three thousand–ton navy ship's looming football field–length of gray steel for the boarding ramp, she could hear some clanking coming from it, faint voices, the hum of equipment.

It sounded like a crane up there or a Bobcat or something moving things around. People working up there, arranging the wreckage.

But not Naval Safety people? she thought, looking up at the ship, huge and gray and still. She swiped sweat off her forehead with her blue camo blouse sleeve. Some other mysterious people up there, the Keebler elves of the navy or the Smurfs maybe, up there stealing her job.

"I'm sorry. You can't be here," called down a sailor way up on the ship in a booming voice as she arrived at the other end of the gangway ramp.

He was a tall blond guy with a goatee and a bullet-shaped head. A petty officer first class, by the three red stripes on his shoulder.

Unbelievable. Why would they put such a heavy hitter at the ramp? she wondered.

"I'm Lieutenant Everett from Naval Safety. Is the plane up there? The jet they found? I'm supposed to be working on it," she called back.

"Sorry," he said. "No one can come aboard, Lieutenant. Captain's orders. Call your CO."

"I can't. I don't have the damn password for the Wi-Fi."

The sailor at the other end of the gangway shrugged his large shoulders.

"No one can come aboard, Lieutenant. Sorry," he said, not sounding very sorry, his face like a slab of stone.

14

Ruby walked across the yard, cursing to herself, sweat dripping down her back. She was slow to anger normally, a get-alonger by nature. But she'd about had it.

Most of the *Surmount*'s sailors were outside now at the bottom of the mess steps. They were smoking and kicking a hacky sack around. One of them had a football, and they were laughing and carrying on like middle schoolers with the teacher gone as they tossed it back and forth.

Beyond them in the shadow of the mess hall was a bleached-white wooden picnic table next to an old grill that was Cheeto-orange with rust. Ruby sat down at it, looking out at the endless turquoise Caribbean behind the building.

How far to Florida, she thought, if she started swimming now?

"Hey," said a voice behind her.

The short blond surfer kid diver looked even younger in his

ironed uniform. And cuter in a cute little brother sort of way. He looked like a Catholic grammar school eighth-grader on picture day.

"Hey," Ruby said as he sat down across from her.

"This sucks, huh?" he said. "I saw you head over to the ship. What's the story?"

"They won't tell me."

"I'm Steve, by the way. Steve Vance," the diver said, offering his hand with the green shamrock tattoo on it.

She shook, smiling at him.

"I'm Ruby," she said, dispensing with all the navy protocol rank bullshit that she actually despised.

"Hey, Ruby, you want to see something?" he said, waving his phone at her.

"Tell me you got the Wi-Fi password," she said, tenting her fingers in prayer.

"No. Better," he said, handing over his phone.

There was some kind of video queued up on the screen. When she pressed the play triangle, it showed a bright beam of light in dark water. After a moment, coral passed at the edge of the light and then a pale aircraft fuselage appeared along with a porthole plane window.

Ruby hit the screen, pausing it.

"No way!" she said. "But I asked Martin for the dive footage, and he said it was unavailable."

The diver gave her a wink.

"Yeah, well, can't hurt to take a copy for myself, can it?" he said, looking around. "Believe it or not, Lieutenant Martin can be a prick. He got a shippie shit-canned for getting loaded on board last trip out, a good buddy of mine, who was the best sailor in the entire seventh. I tried to tell Martin that he had just found out his girl was leaving him, but he couldn't care less.

"I yelled at him pretty good in front of everyone at dinner about a week later, and since then, he's been busting my chops pretty good. Any screwup, he could just blame me, right? So that's what the folks at GoPro are for. I'm documenting everything I do. I have to cover my ass."

Ruby pressed Play again. She sat up when she saw the first older dead man in the captain's chair.

What in the hell? she thought, looking at the white-haired guy. He didn't look military. He looked like a lawyer or a businessman or something.

The moment she saw the blue patches on his face and the dried blood, she knew what had probably happened to make the plane crash.

There had been a sudden loss of cabin pressure, Ruby realized.

The bluish face on the screen was almost identical to a picture of a plane fatality victim she had seen in one of their training manuals about cabin pressurization system failure.

At high altitude, pressure system failure was extremely deadly. First, the rapid change in pressure often induced nosebleeds. Then because of the low percentage of oxygen at 40,000 feet, a rapid loss of consciousness would almost immediately occur. Even after only thirty seconds of losing oxygen at a high enough altitude, pilots could become completely incapacitated.

A sudden loss of cabin pressure knocking out everyone on board also explained the challenging search for the plane, Ruby realized. If the autopilot was on at the time, the only limit to how far the plane could have traveled was based on how much fuel was in the tank. If the Gulfstream's tanks were even relatively full, it could have come from virtually anywhere, Ruby realized. South America. Heck, maybe even Europe, she thought.

Ruby shook her head when she realized that the plane might have even had military-grade radar-jamming capability.

No wonder they had been so frantically looking for it.

It had been a true ghost plane.

She watched as the camera lit over the rest of them. Still no uniforms. They all looked like civilians, four civilians. Even the pilots' uniforms looked like commercial ones.

She remembered the dataplate again. The blank dataplate.

What in the hell *was* going on? she thought.

She watched it a second time. She had the odd urge to wipe her hand on her uniform shirt after she finally handed back the phone.

"You tell anybody you have this?" she said.

"Just my buddy Matt. The guy I was talking to when you spoke to us last night."

"The deck ape?" Ruby said.

Steve laughed.

"That's Matt," he said.

"Okay, Steve. Listen to me. Don't tell anybody else about this video, okay? And tell your buddy Matt to shut the hell up about it, too. Keep it to yourself."

"Why?" he said.

Ruby turned back to the gray boat looming there. The dividers up there on the deck. The big stone-faced petty officer guarding the rail.

"Silence is golden," she finally said.

15

An hour and a half later, a Chevy Cobalt drove out of the base without incident. Then a Nissan Altima came in. Then a Kia Soul headed out, and the guards by the fence came out of their shack and stopped it.

On the side of the guardhouse were two signs: POSITIVE ID REQUIRED and RESTRICTED AREA AUTHORIZED PERSONNEL ONLY—KEEP OUT.

Keep out? Ruby thought. "With pleasure," she mumbled from where she stood beside a brick barracks two hundred feet to the gate's south. *Hell, I didn't even want to come in here in the first place.*

Her decision to leave after seeing the video had been a no-brainer. It was obvious they were all being detained because of the mystery plane. Some upper-echelon ass-coverer had probably gotten word that the plane had something to do with some classified horseshit and had frozen everyone in place until he figured out which was the best ass to kiss next.

Under normal circumstances, she could put up with the government and the navy's top-down bureaucratic bullshit about things. But these weren't exactly normal circumstances, were they?

Plane or no plane, she was technically on leave now, and if she didn't get back to Florida this afternoon, her little sister, Lori, would have to give birth by herself.

What she needed to do now was get on a plane. She'd learned there was a commercial airport that was actually within walking distance of the base, but the question was, would they let her off?

She didn't know. She certainly wasn't going to ask anyone. She'd been in the navy long enough to know that if you wanted to get something done, you just went for it. It was far easier to ask for forgiveness than permission.

Ruby was still squinting at the gate that she needed to get past a minute later when a white Ford Focus drove onto the base. Its driver showed something to the guard. As it came up the road, Ruby smiled and shook her head when she saw the familiar smiling Asian face behind the wheel.

"Hey, sailor. What's a nice girl like you doing in a place like this?" said her Naval Safety coworker Mark Thanh with a wink as he rolled down his window.

Ruby grabbed her bag and ran over, beaming.

"Mark! Am I glad to see you," Ruby said, chucking her bag into the back of his rental. "I thought everybody died. What the heck took you so long?"

"I just got back from leave and wasn't a minute into the office when El Jefe turned me right around to come down and relieve you. Your sister still hasn't had that baby yet, right?"

"That's what I want to know," Ruby said, glancing at the guard shack. "You need to get me to the civilian airport double time."

They made the U-turn. As they approached the checkpoint,

she stifled a groan as the big sergeant-at-arms at the gate held up a hand for a second.

He peered at Ruby's face, confused. But then he saw Mark's face again and realized he'd just seen him, and then he tentatively waved them on.

As they came out onto the base road, Ruby turned around and looked back. The guard hadn't moved from the spot. He was looking at her again with the same confused look.

Ruby felt weird then, sort of guilty and suddenly and oddly quite afraid.

"Rube, you all right?" Mark said.

"I'm fine. Just worried about my sister," she lied as the gate and the white buildings of the base behind them got smaller and smaller under the hot blue sky.

16

The steel diamond-plate steps rang loudly against Reyland's shoe heels as he came down the steep flight from the top deck of the USS *Recover*.

He was going to need to get some polo shirts or something, Reyland thought, unbuttoning his suit jacket in the Caribbean heat as he reached the bottom of the steel steps. It had actually been snowing at Bolling Air Force Base in DC when he took off two and a half hours before.

He glanced at his encrypted phone as it buzzed in his pocket. London again. Screw them. They'd have to wait. Everybody would have to just back the hell up for five seconds.

"Watch the chrome dome, boss," his tactical team head, Thomas Ruiz, called out as he led Reyland to the right down the hot dim corridor.

Reyland smiled at Ruiz as he ducked under a sharply jutting electrical box.

The short and stocky former Delta Force sergeant didn't walk so much as barrel through the world with a rooster-like strut.

The below-deck corridor was lined tight on both sides with cables and massive pipes and water hoses. They stopped at the end of it, and Ruiz knocked twice on a closed bulkhead door. The metal door squeaked and then opened inward like a bank vault. Just inside stood a very muscular black man wearing sunglasses in the same buff-colored tactical uniform as Ruiz.

The formidable man snapped his heels together as he gave them an ironically formal salute.

"Knock it off, Shepard," Ruiz said, elbowing the man out of the way as they walked past.

The low warehouse-like hold they entered was roofed with steel beams. The bodies were laid out in the middle of it on a blue tarp, two by two. They were in dark green plastic body bags, and as Reyland came closer, over the boiler room smell of the ship's machine oil, he caught the first fecal whiff of their rot.

Ruiz stopped before them and nodded at Shepard, who knelt at the first body bag. The rest of Ruiz's men, a half-dozen veteran professional operators, sat a ways off in a dim corner of the hold. Aloof. Yawning. Not even looking at them. Some standing, some squatting, all in complete monk-like silence. They weren't even talking to each other.

As the bags were zipped open, Reyland watched Ruiz take a cigar from his pocket. The Zippo he lit it up with had an ace of spades engraved in the side.

"Here," Ruiz said as he offered the stogie to Reyland, soggy end first. "You're going to need this."

They went over to the first one.

Reyland let out a breath as he looked down.

His boss, Arthur Dunning himself. *Holy Toledo.*

Even in death, his boss had an austere bearing. Even now his standing expression was that of a crafty old coach about to throw a chair across a basketball court.

A memory came suddenly. Dunning, competitive in all things, was a scratch golfer, and they would play twice a month. He remembered the time he had almost beaten him a few years before on the course out on Griffin Island. He'd been up one on the last tee. Then right in the middle of his back swing, the sly old bastard had actually coughed. Reyland remembered slicing it, burying it in the woods good and deep.

"Shit happens," Dunning had said, giving him a smug little smile.

Reyland fought off the strange desire to smile a little smugly himself as he looked down at his dead mentor laid out on the beat-up below-deck windowless room like a bunch of garbage in a split-open Hefty.

Sure does, boss, he thought, nodding. *It surely does.*

Reyland looked at the other dead men.

"How'd the plane go wonky? The cabin pressure like they said?"

"No clue," Ruiz said, blinking at him. "I'd expect it's something like that because of the blue patches on their faces there. Looks like they suffocated. But there's no way to tell unless we bring in the mechanics and experts. I'm no structural engineer, boss."

"Now tell me, Tommy," Reyland said, looking the hardcase commando in the eye, "we're the only ones to see this abortion, correct? Our team and the coast guard diver and a few coast guard people?"

"Well, actually," Ruiz said, raising a brow.

"Actually what?"

Ruiz folded his stocky forearms.

"They sent an investigator from Naval Safety before we got the call. The cutter captain has an uncle in the navy and went VFR direct to him, jumped the chain."

"No!" Reyland cried.

Ruiz nodded.

"They even flew her out to the cutter. But as far as I know, she didn't see this or anything else. The cutter was ordered away before she could see any of the wreckage. She actually left the base. There's another investigator now. Some navy fool who keeps asking to get on the ship."

"Why bring her up?"

"No reason. I know how thorough you like to be. Especially in a situation of this, um, magnitude. I thought you might want to make a note of who's coming and going."

Reyland nodded at his tough little security man. Ruiz was as sharp as he was ruthless. He never missed a trick.

"Okay, good, Tommy. Noted. Now, where are the packages?"

"Ah, the packages," Ruiz said, gesturing with his chin.

Reyland followed him into the corner of the hold opposite his resting men.

As they arrived, Ruiz kicked at a silver hard-pack suitcase with his tactical boot, sending it spinning. Reyland looked at it. It was open and empty.

"What's this?"

"We found this at the site in some coral thirty feet from the plane," Ruiz said. "Empty just like this."

"No!" Reyland said, staring at the empty case. "You have got to be putting me on. Someone is playing games, huh? Did a little five-finger salvage job? One of the coasties? Or maybe the navy inspector who left?"

Ruiz shrugged.

"Not her. We watched video of her leaving the base. She only took her kit bag."

Reyland pulled his phone out and called Emerson topside on the *Recover*'s deck.

"Yes, boss?"

"Plan B. Call HQ. I want full intelligence jackets on everybody on that coast guard tub from the captain to the guy who scrubs the urinals. Also, tell that peckerhead base commander who drove us in here we need some rooms to conduct interviews."

"On it," Emerson said.

Reyland looked at Ruiz in the dimness of the hold, looked at the empty suitcase. A bead of sweat rolled down his hairless head and neck into the back of his starched shirt collar as he tucked his phone away.

"Looks like we're doing this the hard way, Tommy," he said.

17

Late Tuesday afternoon just before sunset, Gannon was at his bungalow in Tarpum Head.

In his favorite pair of camo cargo cutoff shorts and the last of his clean button-down shirts, he was out on his covered back porch, lying back on a plastic chaise.

There was a warm bottle of beer in his hand, and he took a sip of it, looking out on things. On his backyard. On the thorny brush that edged it. On the blue glitter of the Caribbean to the south.

He'd come home around dawn and wolfed down the entire half tray of lasagna he had made two days before and proceeded to sleep like the dead. He'd woken up around three in the afternoon and had to call a resort he had just started working for to apologize for the diving appointment that he had missed.

"If this happens one more time, you're fired," the manager had screamed at him.

"You got it," Gannon had said pleasantly before he hung up. "Goodbye now."

He was freed up now, wasn't he? he thought, smiling, as he put his hands behind his head in the warm breeze.

Freed up in a whole entirely new way.

He yawned and listened to the birds chirp in the warmth of the evening. He had just taken a shower, and his hair was still wet. He thought about bringing out the little Bluetooth speaker to get some tunes going, but he was too comfortable.

He looked out across the crabgrass. Alongside the edge of his yard were three chewed-up tennis balls he had forgotten to throw away. They had belonged to his late-departed boxer, Buster, who had died of old age two months before.

For the twentieth time, he told himself that he needed to find a new dog. Fishing, especially, had always been so much finer with Buster beside him. But something always seemed to come up.

He lifted his beer again.

It was probably because his good old Buster was so awesome, Gannon thought. He didn't want to replace him yet. That was it.

He sipped his beer and nodded.

It was out of respect.

He closed his eyes and thought about all the problems he could erase now. The loan on the boat, the one on the house, the costly leak in the line between the *Rambler*'s tank and the fuel pump he was ignoring. Wipe those pesky critters away with one swipe.

Not right away, of course, he thought with a smile. *No, no, no.* He would wait and wait and wait. All he had to do was wait now. He sighed. He had no problem with that. When he put his mind to it, he could be quite a patient man.

He smiled. What was especially delicious was the secret of the whole thing. He had nothing to do with the local area of Little Abaco. He knew no one up there. There was no way to know that he had been there.

Besides, even if they surmised that the money had been picked up by someone, there were what? Five thousand fishing and pleasure boats in the Bahamas? Ten?

It made him giddy how free and clear he was.

18

He was finishing his beer and thinking about walking on down the beach road to his local watering hole to procure an actually cold one when his phone rang.

He smiled as he looked at the caller ID. His son usually took a minimum of twenty-four hours to text him back.

But in this case apparently, he was making an exception.

"Dad? What's going on?" Declan said, sounding stunned. "I just read your text. What are you talking about? You're joking, right?"

Gannon smiled as he sat up under the rusty awning.

"Hi, son. It's no joke. Pack your stuff. When opportunity knocks, you have to answer the door."

"But, Dad, I told you Larry won't give me the time off. He can't. We're already down a guy. He'll go ballistic. I'll lose my job."

"Don't worry about that, son," Gannon said. "You're going,

and that's final. Actually, scratch that. *We're* going. I'm heading over to go with you."

Declan had been an outstanding pitcher ever since Little League, but he'd broken his arm skateboarding in his junior year, and they thought that was that.

But about six months ago, he'd started rehabbing as a goof after work with one of his buddies who'd played a little minor-league ball, and now like some returned gift from on high, he was apparently hitting the midnineties with ease. His friend had arranged a meet with a scout and just like that Declan had actually been invited to a tryout for the Brewers.

The rub was the tryout had to be in the middle of the week, and Declan's boss was a jerk and wouldn't give him any time off. The kid was already living lean with three roommates in a town house in St. Pete and couldn't risk losing his job, so he was up a creek.

When Gannon found out about all of this, he had felt bad for not having even a couple of grand for his son to pursue his dream. With the boat maintenance and his bills, he'd pretty much blown through his entire savings over the last year or so.

That was why he had gone out fishing with close to the last couple of hundred bucks to his name. He thought if he caught something big, he could sell it at the dock market and help out his son like a real father instead of a broke beach bum.

But all that was water under the bridge now, wasn't it? Gannon thought.

He smiled.

He had him covered now.

And then some.

"This is...incredible!" Declan said. "But I thought you said you were broke. That the boat's pump or whatever is on its last legs and that guy screwed you on the money he owes you for that three-day thing you did?"

"He paid me," Gannon lied.

"No! Really? *Really?*"

"Yes. Really. You're going. I got us covered. And if that ass, Larry, cans you, I'll help you find another job. Call me crazy, but I think Tampa probably has more than one air-conditioning and re-frigeration tech apprentice position somewhere. I just can't believe your arm is back. That's what's really unbelievable," Gannon said.

"You're telling me," Declan said. "I don't even like talking about it, I'm so afraid it'll crap out again. When will you get in?"

"Earliest flight I can get is Wednesday. I'll meet you at the airport there in Tampa around five or so and then we'll both get a flight to Phoenix."

"But won't that all cost a fortune? Especially last minute?"

"Don't worry about it. It's how these things happen, son. We're just going to go for it."

Gannon smiled again as Declan laughed like an excited little kid.

He was still smiling, enjoying the moment, when he heard the sound from the front of the bungalow. It was the crackle of tires, the sound of a car slowly coming down his little remote cul-de-sac.

Gannon sat up, squinting. He wasn't waiting on any visitors.

When he heard brakes, he stood and peeked all the way around the side of his concrete blockhouse. In the gap between his pickup and the house, he could see the front of a vehicle. It was a Jeep. A white-and-blue Jeep.

A familiar white-and-blue Jeep.

Gannon bit his lip, thinking quickly.

No, he thought.

No way. Calm yourself. It can't be. No way. Not this quick.

"Dad, I'm going to pay you back. I promise. Every penny. Hey, you there?" his son said as Gannon glanced at the back of his pickup in the carport.

The Gator and the tanks were still up there in the bed. Dammit. Why the hell hadn't he put them away?

"Dad? You there?" his son was saying when the doorbell rang.

"Um, bad connection, son. I'll call you back," Gannon said quickly as he hopped off the back porch.

19

"I'm right here, Sergeant Jeremy," Gannon said to the uniformed cop as he was about to get back into his white-and-blue Bahama PD police Jeep. "Right here. No need to call up the SWAT team."

Gannon smiled as he came out into his front yard through the carport, walking unhurriedly. He had undone another button on his shirt and had a fresh beer with him.

"Ah, so you are, Michael," the cop said with a smile back as they shook.

As always, the muscular, handsome black man in his early sixties looked impeccable. His big general's hat was squared neatly on his head and his white-and-blue police uniform shirt was crisp and highly starched.

Gannon had met Sergeant Jeremy three years before working for a small resort on Windermere Island. A tourist kid out sea kayaking had gone missing in the Atlantic, and he and Sergeant Jeremy had gone out in the *Rambler* looking for him.

For hours, they had scoured the entire treacherous rocky east shore. The kid had turned out not to have gone kayaking at all, thank goodness, but during the search, he and the good sergeant had commiserated on everything from fatherhood to eighties music to the current insane state of the world.

Sergeant Jeremy, who was a deacon at St. Anne's up in Rock Sound, often roped Gannon into usher duty during his sporadic church attendance, and they sometimes played poker.

Gannon turned back, checking to see if the sergeant could notice the Gator and tanks back there in the bed of his pickup under the carport.

Maybe, maybe not, he thought.

"You're here early for the poker game. Isn't it at Teddy's next week?" he said.

"No, no. It's not a social visit, Michael. I was wondering if you might be able to help me. Did you hear about the accident?"

Gannon looked at him.

"Accident?"

"You didn't hear?"

"I didn't turn on the radio today. What's up?"

"There was a plane crash in the water on the north side of Little Abaco last night. My son's friend Alan in the coast guard got called in."

"That's terrible. Bad? Was it an airliner or something?"

"I don't know. Probably not or it would be an even bigger deal. Lot of activity, though. I know you fish up around there sometimes. I thought maybe you might have seen or heard something."

Gee, thanks for remembering, Gannon thought.

"That's crazy. No. I didn't see anything," Gannon said.

"You did go fishing, though, yesterday, right? Like you usually do Mondays?"

Gannon looked at him. Sergeant Jeremy seemed cheery and laid-back as they came, but he was nobody's fool. There wasn't much in the island's resorts—and even more so with the island's residents—that happened without his knowledge. Especially on his beat in the lower southern part.

"Yep. I went out in the morning as usual. But I actually didn't go out that far. I tried my spot off Governor's Harbour first and got a hit. It was a white marlin, but it went under the bow and the damn line broke my radio antenna. So I stayed in close to shore here at home."

Sergeant Jeremy tapped a finger against his lip. Then he smiled.

"Any extra fresh swordfish you'd like to share with your good friend?"

Gannon took a hit of his beer and wiped at his mouth with his fingers.

"No. Sorry, friend," he said, swiping his hand on his shorts. "None for me either. After all that, the big nasty son of a gun spit the hook five feet from the boat. You should have seen this thing."

"Ah, yes. The one that got away. Big as my Jeep, was it?"

"No way," Gannon said with another smile. "Way bigger."

Jeremy looked at him. Then looked down his little street.

Gannon looked with him at the palm fronds waving there in the breeze.

"Was that Little Jorge with you?" Sergeant Jeremy said with an eye roll.

As he usually did, Gannon grinned as he thought about his young, somewhat sketchy first mate.

"No," Gannon said, squinting. "First mate Little Jorge is still...on vacation."

"Vacation? A young man of leisure. Very interesting."

"Anything else I can do for you?" Gannon said. "I'd offer you a beer, but with you being on duty and all, I wouldn't want to insult you."

"Always thinking of others, Michael, aren't you? That's probably why I like you so much," Sergeant Jeremy said after he closed his door. "Shall I expect to see you Sunday? It's my turn for the sermon. It's called 'God Has a Mission for You.' I'll even keep it under half an hour this time, I promise."

"Deacon," Gannon said, blessing himself as he backed for his house, "to be present on such an auspicious occasion, I will do my level best."

20

The too-bright cement windowless room Emerson led coast guard rescue diver Stephen Vance into was in the basement of the base's power plant building.

Used as an emergency brig, the walk-in closet-sized room had raw cement block walls and a threadbare linoleum floor that was a pale institutional green. The curtain blocking off the cell's back corner toilet was opaque and yellowing at the plastic edges and seemed in several spots to be coated in black mold.

Beside it in the room were only four other items: a folding table, two folding chairs and a little mirror on the wall opposite the door.

Perfect, Reyland thought, watching through the peep show one-way glass. The toilet curtain especially. Just atrocious.

Reyland smiled at the haughty expression on Emerson's face as the two of them sat. He always loved watching the way suspects became instantly intimidated by Emerson's six-foot-tall

height and dark-haired preppy good looks. He had played var-
sity lacrosse at Boston College, and his resting countenance was
still one of pure big-man-on-campus arrogance. The men in the
unit actually called him Prep School behind his back.

Emerson had confided to Reyland at the last Christmas party
that he could have joined a Wall Street bank like his brother but
had chosen the Bureau instead on purpose. In his junior year, he
had read a book about the way homicide cops did interrogations,
how they were legally allowed to screw with and to bully people, and he finally realized what he wanted to do with his life.

He had drunkenly told Reyland that what he loved most about
his job was the back-and-forth of grinding down a subject until
he made him, as Emerson put it, "his soft sweet little bitch."

Reyland smiled as he watched Emerson take out a laptop
and clack it down and fold it open with slow ceremony onto
the table.

Though he was smart enough never to admit it out loud, that
was Reyland's favorite part of the job, too.

"Hi, Stephen," Emerson said as he pulled in his chair. "My
name is Agent Emerson. Can I call you Steve?"

"No," the little diver said, getting huffy straight off. "You
can address me as Petty Officer Third Class Stephen Vance."

Emerson sighed.

"That's not the way you want to play this. This is no big deal.
Just some questions for my report, and we're done."

"No big deal?" the diver said. "Why have I been separated
from my crew? What the hell do you want from me? I wrote
out an incident report of my dive in detail for my commanding
officer. Read it. I got nothing more for you or anyone. Bringing me into this disgusting pit. Is this Nazi crap supposed to
scare me or something?"

Emerson sighed again.

"All right. Fine," Emerson said as he stood and gracefully
crossed the room.

He even moved like he had money, Reyland thought. Tan in his crisp khakis and polo shirt, he could have been a country-club golf pro.

"Have it your way," Emerson said as he casually knocked on the cell door.

"What do you mean? You're acting like I'm not cooperating?" the diver said, getting a little nervous now. "I cooperated. Just read my report."

"Oh, I've read it. Don't you worry about that," Emerson said, smiling, as there was a sound of approaching steps out in the hallway.

"Take off your shirt, please," Emerson said, as there was a loud knock on the door.

"What?" Steve the diver said, screeching back the chair as he stood.

"You heard me. Take off your shirt," Emerson said, unlocking the door. "For your polygraph."

Reyland stifled a laugh at the lie. You didn't have to take off the subject's shirt. Emerson was just brilliant. He really did love this. It was personal with him. You could tell. You couldn't fake being this sadistic.

What an asset.

He was a master.

"Sorry, buddy. That's not happening. I want my CO in here right now," Vance said.

But he was already sweating. You could see it on his brow. See it shining on his upper lip.

Vance jumped, knocking over the folding chair as the door burst open and Ruiz and Shepard came in with the equipment. Huge Shepard with his ever-present aviator sunglasses was especially intimidating in the tight confines of the concrete room.

"Take off your shirt, please," Emerson said again. "Or we will do it for you."

A minute later, the young diver sat shirtless and small on the folding chair. Ruiz put on the blood pressure cuff while Shepard put the two bands called pneumographs around his narrow chest.

Emerson himself attached the galvanometer's two finger straps to the pointer finger of the diver's left hand. He stood looming over him, almost on top of him. Like a daddy putting a bandage on his kid's boo-boo.

"What's this? Some kind of LGBT thing?" he said to the diver, pointing at a thin band of gold on his pinkie as Ruiz and Shepard left.

"It was my mother's wedding band," the diver said. "She died when I was small."

"Take it off," Emerson said. "No jewelry for the test."

"Thank you very much," Emerson said brightly when the diver finally dropped it in his outstretched waiting palm.

Bravo, Emerson, Reyland thought proudly. Skin-on-skin contact, violation of the subject's personal space, forced removal of precious items.

Textbook.

Emerson slowly and meticulously attached all the leads to a little black box that was then connected with a USB cord to his laptop. He turned the laptop's screen around so Vance could see it.

"Pay attention. This is important," Emerson said. "See these? These four moving lines? The upper two are respiratory rate and electrodermal, and these bottom ones are for your blood pressure. These instruments monitor your vitals. Your breathing, your pulse, your blood pressure, your perspiration, and any slight movements of an arm or a leg.

"Now, before we get started, I want you to read something," Emerson said, taking a laminated card out of his pants pocket.

"Do you understand what this document says?" Emerson said after a minute as the diver stared down at the card. "It basically says that if you lie to me during this polygraph examination—if any of your vitals indicate falsehood—you will not just be subject to court-martial, you will be guilty of obstruction of justice, a federal felony punishable by up to five years in prison."

"What?"

"Every time you lie, it will be a felony, *Steve*. Do you understand, *Steve*? Every falsehood you tell is a year in Leavenworth."

"But you can't do this! You can't do this! It's illegal. Please!" the diver said.

"Not only can I do this," Emerson said, turning the laptop back around, "I have to, *Steve*. It's my job."

21

Reyland left after the first hour when the diver began to stutter uncontrollably.

It was a humid night outside in the open shipyard, but there was a nice breeze off the darkly gleaming Caribbean. It was steak night in the officers' mess hall, and there was a pleasant, happy, summer vacation kind of smell of charcoal from the grills.

From the mess, he grabbed a tray and a plate of sirloin and mashed potatoes and took it upstairs to the office space above the mess that they were using as a staging area.

Reyland was sitting at a conference table, sipping a cup of lukewarm coffee with Ruiz, when Emerson came in two hours later. They waited for the interrogator to hit the head and come out and crack a Diet Coke from the fridge.

"So what's the story?" Reyland said.

Emerson put down the soda.

"My first read is that he didn't take it. He doesn't know about the missing money."

"But?" Reyland said, looking at Emerson's clouded face.

"He has a secret," Emerson said. "It's something about the video."

"The video? We got that off Martin first thing," Ruiz said.

"Yes. But there's something there about him handing it over. Every time the video comes up, there's a hiccup. Tiny but there."

Reyland sat up.

"That's the most important thing of all," he said. "Containing and burying the inside of that plane. A video getting out is beyond comprehension."

"I know," said Emerson.

"So bear down," Reyland said.

"What do you think I've been doing, boss? He's digging in. The little prick is actually tougher than I first thought."

"Short and spunky. Terrific," Ruiz said, taking a quarter out of his pocket.

"So you're thinking he might have made a personal copy of the video or something?" Reyland said.

"Maybe," Emerson said with a nod.

"Do you have his phone?" Ruiz said.

"Yes. It's an iPhone, but he won't give me the passcode," Emerson said. "Little Porky Pig was adamant about that. Told me to go f-f-f-screw myself."

Reyland blew out a breath. Here he was thinking they'd have some smooth sailing and now this. He looked over at Ruiz, who nodded. They'd already been going over worst-case scenario contingents concerning the diver.

The B plan was drastic and had its own downsides and risks. But this whole situation was about as desperate as it got.

"Okay, Emerson. Good job," Reyland said. "Why don't you get some sleep?"

"What? You don't want me to try some more?"

"No. Don't worry about it. You've done your part. We'll leave him to Ruiz and his men."

Emerson had a disappointed look on his face as he picked up his soda and left.

"So if the diver doesn't know where the money is, where is it?" Reyland said.

Ruiz brought his right fist up onto the table, walking the quarter back and forth over his knuckles. He spun the quarter on the tabletop and then slapped it flat and peeked at it.

"A local must have taken it," he said. "Saw the wreckage, grabbed a bobbing suitcase before the coast guard found it. A fisherman or a sailboater."

"A local civvie," Reyland ruminated, taking out his phone as he watched Ruiz spin the coin again.

They really would have to do it the hard way, he thought.

22

Sergeant Jeremy made a funny humming sound as he bumped along the uneven field with his grandkids at his farm in Greencastle.

There were six of them altogether stuffed into the tiny cab of the old blue Ford tractor. The two older boys were hanging out the open left side and the two girls out the right. The littlest one, three-year-old George Junior, sat in his lap laughing as Sergeant Jeremy hummed and let him steer.

As usual on his day off, Sergeant Jeremy was "tilling the earth," as his wife sarcastically called his on-again, off-again interest in working their ramshackle farm. He had exchanged his uniform for a T-shirt and jeans and a Miami Marlins baseball cap, and he and the grandkids were coming back from spreading compost at the top field. Now after helping Pawpy, they were taking the long way back before Granmama's Bible class.

He saw the man as they arrived at the end of the field. He

was standing in a patch of sunlight a hundred feet down the old cow path. The man was white and tall and was wearing a dark polo shirt and business khakis.

"Run along now, children," Sergeant Jeremy said as he stopped the tractor and ratcheted on the hand brake.

"Hi, there. Are you Officer Jeremy Austin?" the visitor said as the children jumped down and started running past him for the house.

"I'm Sergeant Austin," Sergeant Jeremy said as he cut the engine altogether and came halfway out of the cab without stepping all the way down. The man was bald and so tall they were still almost eye level. He looked into the man's pale gray eyes.

Like a wolf's, he thought.

"I hear you're the man to talk to in these here parts," the white man said.

"And you are?"

"Me? Oh, I'm from the FBI."

"Ah, an American," Sergeant Jeremy said as if this delighted him.

"Yep. All the way from the US of A," the large bald man said, grinning. "We're looking into that plane crash that happened north of Little Abaco a few days back."

"Oh, I see. We haven't heard much about it after the initial report. Your navy is handling it, I believe."

"Yes, my navy is taking care of it, but you see, we're looking for information, Sergeant. Information about anyone you know who might have been out on the water that evening."

"Is that right?"

"Yes. I know there are a lot of boats on the island, but everybody down here is pretty cozy, aren't they? Especially the fishermen and workers on the boats. Everybody has his personal little fishing spots here and there. At least that's what I hear."

Sergeant Jeremy kicked free a clod of mud that had gotten caught up in the huge tread of the tractor's tire.

"What is it you're trying to find out?"

"You don't have to worry about that. We're just looking for the names of anyone you can think of who might have been out on the water when the crash occurred."

Sergeant Jeremy toed loose some more soil with his boot.

"Which night was this, now? Monday?"

"Yes. Two days ago. Monday night."

Sergeant Jeremy looked as the bald man pulled free a strand of tall dried grass and spun it in his fingers. He was comfortable, serene. Not a care in the world. Like he was on his own land, Jeremy thought. Like everywhere belonged to him.

"What time did the crash occur?" Jeremy asked.

"This would have been probably, oh, around seven or so," he said.

Sergeant Jeremy pursed his lips as if deep in thought.

"No one comes to mind right off. Folks around here rarely go up that far. Even charters. Most of the locals around here are pretty stingy with the gas."

As if I would tell you anything, you arrogant American prick, Sergeant Jeremy thought.

"Well, if you can think of anyone, give me a ring, would you?" the bald man said, smiling as he offered a business card. "I don't know if you've heard, but we're giving out grants now. Expanding our network here in the Caribbean. I would love to get some of those Washington grants out here to you to help you and your station. You could always use new equipment, yes? New vehicles? Perhaps even a boat. We can always use good partners."

Sergeant Jeremy took the card and beamed down at it exaggeratedly. The fake smile on his face like he'd just won the lottery.

Reyland, the card said under the FBI logo. Deputy Assistant Director Robert Reyland.

"If I hear of anything, Mr. Reyland," he said, giving the arrogant American official his best vacant *welcome to the Bahamas, mon* grin, "you'll be the first to know."

Reyland stood there for a moment staring at him, staring at the empty field around.

"Can I give you a lift back to the road?" Sergeant Jeremy said, stepping up into the tractor cab.

"No, thanks," Reyland finally said with a dismissive wave of his hand. "You can go ahead now, Sergeant. I'll find my own way out."

23

There were about a dozen fat gulls atop Mama Lizbeth's grocery store's dried wood awning, and they all seemed to give Gannon the stink eye as he jogged in off the beach the next morning at a little after 8:00 a.m.

As he caught his breath, he spotted an old red Toyota sedan with missing hubcaps and tinted windows at the other end of its sandy asphalt lot.

Gannon smiled as the island beater gave off a brief honk.

As he stepped over, its driver's door swung wide. A thin, smiling, mischievous-looking young black man with long dreads stepped out and gave him a funny little bow. His white wifebeater and khaki shorts were immaculate, pristine.

"Oh, so you really are still alive," Gannon said as he came over and gave his on-again, off-again first mate, Little Jorge, a hand slap and hearty man hug.

Little Jorge laughed.

"Alive and kicking, Captain Mike, always," he said in his musical island drawl.

Gannon shook his head at him.

When he first came down to the islands, Gannon took an instant liking to the cute, funny, hustling kid who hung around the docks with his older brothers. He'd actually been pretty good buds with Little Jorge's whole large family ever since he had taught the motley lot of them how to dive free of charge in an effort to keep them out of trouble.

The sun caught the glint of gold in Little Jorge's pirate's smile.

Gannon definitely had his work cut out for him there.

Little Jorge wasn't exactly what one would call a reliable employee, but when the wiry twenty-two-year-old showed up for work, he was actually top-notch. He knew the waters around the Bahamas better than anyone and was one of the most skilled, natural fishermen Gannon had ever seen.

"How'd your, um, vacation go?" Gannon said.

"Just got back this very minute when I saw your text," Little Jorge said.

"Three weeks this time?" Gannon said.

Little Jorge shrugged and laughed again.

His family was originally from San Andrés Island in Colombia, and sometimes, he and his brothers—like other reckless young island men—would try to make a quick and extremely dangerous buck by acting as pilots on the Picuda go-fast drug boats that played cat-and-mouse in the Caribbean with the coast guard from South America to Miami Beach.

Gannon had tried to talk to him about it, about what a .50-caliber bullet could do to a young man's future, but every time he would explain how unwise it was, the amiable young man would just giggle until he stopped.

Little Jorge was giggling now.

"I was actually starting to get a little worried this time," Gannon said.

"Worry? No, no, Captain Mike. About me? Never. Like the man says, 'Don't worry. Be happy.'"

Gannon rolled his eyes then laughed himself at the goofy, crazy kid as he shook his head.

"So tell me, did you replace Buster yet?" Little Jorge said.

"No," Gannon said. "I keep forgetting."

"I miss watching the lines with old Buster," Little Jorge said. "So what is it, Captain Mike? Where are we heading out this morning? The resorts? Is it diving or fishing or both?"

"No, I'm heading to the States for a bit, but I have some fishing appointments coming up, and I was hoping you could cover for me."

"You mean you want me to go out on the *Rambler* on my own?" Little Jorge said, blinking at him in shock.

Gannon blinked back. He was a little wary about it himself, but he wanted things to seem as normal as possible while he was gone.

And who knew? Maybe the responsibility would do him some good, Gannon thought.

"First time for everything, Little Jorge. I thought you could take Peter with you."

"No, my brother Peter is away, but Andre is here."

"Go with Andre, then," Gannon said. "The boat's at Davis Head. We need everything. Water and gas and bait. Oh, and a new radio antenna. I left some money under the seat with the schedule."

A touched expression crossed the young man's face when Gannon handed him the boat keys.

"I'll take good, good care of her, Captain Mike," Little Jorge said, looking down at his hand.

"You damn well better," Gannon said, giving the kid another clap on his back before he went up the steps for the store.

24

Inside the store, Mama Lizbeth's grown daughter, Joni, was manning the cash register. Gannon waved, but as usual, she ignored him as she turned to the little TV that perpetually played from the edge of the beat-up Plexiglas counter.

Joni was usually all smiles with everyone, the locals and the day-tripping boaters who came in on their grocery store's dock, but for some reason, she seemed to hate Gannon's guts with a fierce-burning passion.

Why? he thought for the millionth time as he passed down into the aisle.

What had he done? Run over her dog and not noticed? Looked like someone who'd robbed the store?

He could never figure it out.

He walked to the back. On the shelves, products were laid out in no particular order. Soup cans next to paper plates next to shaving cream.

He saw there were some packages of Oreos on a shelf.

When was the last time he had eaten one? he thought as he picked them up. But then he checked the date on them and put them back.

On the shelf below, there was a box of some desperate onions and a dwindling tray of sorry yams. Getting produce out here in the island sticks was the absolute worst.

He found what he was looking for in the center aisle. A jug of Tide and some Clorox bleach and a package of sponges. He wanted to get his laundry done and tidy up before he left on his afternoon flight.

When he came back up the aisle, Joni was turned almost fully around now, seemingly absorbed in some news on her little TV. He tapped his foot to get her attention, but that did no good, so he watched with her for a minute.

She was watching the BBC broadcast. There was something about a British singer who had OD'd and then something about protests in London over the latest computer hacker, and then there was a lager commercial that made her finally turn around.

He was coming out of the island bodega, blinking at the sunlight, when he saw Sergeant Jeremy. It would have been hard to miss him. His Jeep was parked almost butt up against the bottom of the grocery store's sandy steps and he was sitting on its hood.

"Hello, Michael, my friend," he said.

"Hey, buddy. How's the crime rate?" Gannon said, smiling broadly as he came down the steps.

"Everyone's still looking into that plane crash. I actually got a visit from a US official about it. He came by the farm."

Holy shit, Gannon thought.

"Yeah?" Gannon said, shifting his bag to his other arm. "Somebody from the coast guard?"

"No," Sergeant Jeremy said, folding his arms as he looked him in the eye. "It was a man from the American FBI."

"No way. An actual G-man, huh?" Gannon said, nodding like a fool as he tried to hide his awe and shock.

"Yes. They're asking around about anybody who might have come across anything. They wanted a list of anybody out on the water Monday night."

"Is that right?" Gannon said.

Sergeant Jeremy took off his hat and wiped his brow with a neatly folded white handkerchief he took from his pocket, then meticulously squared his hat back on his head again.

"Yes," he finally said. "I thought about you and your fishing trip, but you already told me you were far away from the crash site that night, so I said I couldn't help him. He said he wished to speak to anybody at all out that evening. But he was a very pushy, very arrogant man. I didn't think you wished to speak to him, so I left you out of it."

Gannon let out his breath as he began to nod.

"Well, thank you for that. I'm glad they got to the man who knows how to, um…properly handle things around here."

Sergeant Jeremy looked at him very closely.

"Tell me, what are your plans this week, Michael?"

"Plans? Oh, I was thinking of giving my boy a visit. I'm flying to the States this very afternoon, in fact."

"Oh, yes, your son. What's his name? David? No, Dean, is it?"

"Declan. Yeah. Haven't seen him in a while, so I'm going to hang out with him for a few weeks."

"That's sort of sudden," Sergeant Jeremy said.

"Yeah, well, I didn't get a chance to see him over Christmas."

"But the tourist season is just picking up for you, yes?" Sergeant Jeremy said, peering at him.

"I'm going to have Little Jorge take out the boat."

Sergeant Jeremy gaped at him for a beat. Like everybody else on the island, he knew all about Little Jorge and his family's sketchy reputation for going on sudden "vacations."

"Time to give that boy some experience out on his own," Gannon added. "Do him some good."

Sergeant Jeremy hopped down from the Jeep's hood.

"That's a good plan, Michael. At least the part about you going away for a bit. That's probably best."

"Best? What do you mean? Why's that?" Gannon said to the sly old codger.

Sergeant Jeremy winked as they shook hands.

"We can never spend enough time with the ones we love," he said.

PART TWO

GIVE MY REGARDS TO BROADWAY

25

Up on the wall behind the counter was the lineup of all the usual suspects. There was Elmo, of course, and Dora and several of the Power Rangers. There were also a few newcomers since last time, a Wonder Woman and PAW Patrol dog and one of those yellow one-eyed Cheez Doodles Minion things.

Then Ruby saw it and smiled because there was obviously no contest at all.

"I'll take that one," she said, pointing at the giant inflated pink baby bootie balloon that said *IT'S A GIRL!* across the incredible length of it.

"Oh, and one of these as well," she said with a yawn as she picked up a bottle of 5-hour ENERGY from the display beside the register.

"Actually, make that two," she said, cracking open the one in her hand and grabbing another.

What a day! she thought.

She'd gotten back to Pensacola at eleven at night, and at a little after three, her sister Lori's water broke. With the jet lag and panic, she'd driven like a nut to Sacred Heart Hospital, almost breaking the mechanical stick that blocked the parking lot entrance.

But it had all worked out. Seven hours later, at 5:11 p.m. Eastern Standard Time, her first and only niece, Alice Wells, a brand-new, healthy tiny human, had arrived on earth only slightly before her scheduled due date.

Lori and Ally were doing great, thank God, and her husband, Mitch, had been able to watch it on Skype from Afghanistan on her phone. If Ruby hadn't already been crying in the delivery room, the enormous roar of Mitch's fellow marines when he screamed "It's a girl!" at them would have done the trick.

Now, exhaustion or no exhaustion, it was crack-of-dawn victory lap time. In addition to the balloon, Ruby was going to grab a bottle of champagne and Lori's favorite roast beef hero from Firehouse Subs and then swing by Lori's neighbor's house to grab her nephew, Sean, so he could meet his little sister.

No rest for the weary, she thought, yawning as she came out into the early morning Party City parking lot.

Or for sisters slash aunts of the year.

She'd just managed to get the hatchback of her Kia Rio down over the pink blimp when her phone rang. She fished the phone out of her purse and checked the caller ID as she pulled the driver's door open.

Wally Derwent? she thought, dropping behind the wheel. He was her cubicle buddy from the naval safety office.

"Hey, Wally," she said.

"Hey, Rube. Sorry to bug you on leave, but I picked up your phone here a minute ago. Some guy is real frantic to get into contact with you. He called yesterday, too."

"That right?" Ruby said, bleary-eyed, as she slammed her door. "Did he leave a name?"

"No, he wouldn't say. All he said was he knew you from the *Surmount*, and he left his number and said he really, really, really needed to get into contact with you."

The *Surmount?* she thought.

Then the 5-hour ENERGY started to work.

She remembered.

The *Surmount*. The coast guard. The crazy plane everyone was being weird about.

Her sneaking off the naval base.

Oh, shit, she thought.

"Guy sounded young," Wally said. "Don't tell me you're robbing the cradle."

She remembered the cute young diver. What was his name again? Steve. Steve Vance. Fan of deep dives and green shamrock tattoos.

And unauthorized GoPro videos.

Oh, shit, she thought again.

"What's the number?" Ruby said.

26

"Hello," said a hushed voice, picking up on the first ring.

"Hi, this is Lieutenant Everett from Naval Safety. My office just called. You wanted to speak to me?"

"Hold up," the voice said.

Ruby ripped open the second 5-hour ENERGY. It was empty when she placed it down into the Kia's drink holder.

"Hello?" the voice said.

"Yes? This is Ruby Everett. Is this you, Steve?"

"No, this isn't Steve. My name is... Screw it, I won't even say in case they're listening."

Listening? Ruby thought.

"Listening? Who's listening?" she said.

"It doesn't matter," the voice said. "We met on the deck of the *Surmount*. You said to Steve, 'Can you go deeper?' and I said like a jackass, 'You'd be amazed.'"

Ah, yes, the deck ape, Ruby remembered.

"Now listen to me very carefully," he said. "They took Steve."

Ruby stared at the steering wheel as she tried to absorb the statement. She glanced at the empty parking lot asphalt, at the traffic going by on Interstate 10.

"Took him?"

"Yes. The government took him. He's been medically quarantined, they said. Whatever the hell that is. But no one knows where he is. It's like he's been swallowed into a black hole."

Ruby held the phone, silently trying to understand. She was having trouble. She tried to think despite her exhaustion.

"Wait. Slow down. Where are you now?" she finally said. "Still at the base?"

"Yes. They have us in a dormitory now. Tuesday, around five, they started interrogating all of us about the crash. Lie detector tests. They were complete pricks. They threatened us with jail time if we failed the test."

"Who were they? Military investigators?"

"No. Some Washington stuffed shirts. FBI agents or something. They wouldn't say. You should have seen how badly they treated us. They took us all into this disgusting prison cell. Asked us if we took anything from the crash site. If we knew anyone who was hiding anything they might have found. I feel like suing them.

"Now they're saying we're all quarantined due to some virus going around. But that's bullshit. None of us are sick. But that doesn't matter. We have to find Steve. Everybody came back except for him. They claim he's really sick and is being treated at a hospital nearby. It's complete shit. It's all lies. He's been secretly arrested or something."

"C'mon," Ruby said. "For real? Is this a joke?"

"I wish. Shit, wait! Someone's coming," the deck ape said quickly. "I have to go. Listen, there's a guy in New York you need to contact for us. An independent investigative reporter.

We told him what's going on, but he needs corroboration, more info from a credible source. Here, take down this number. You got a pen?"

"Wait. No. Listen. You don't want me. I'm actually off this," Ruby said. "I'm on leave now. You need to contact my coworker down there. His name is Mark Thanh. He's in charge now. He relieved me yesterday. Are you in contact with him?"

"What are you talking about? There's nobody here except us. It's just our crew."

Ruby took a deep breath, trying not to lose her patience.

"You need to talk to Mark Thanh. I know he's there. I saw him myself. He drove me to the airport. He's a wiseass Asian guy from New York?"

"I don't have a damn clue who you're talking about," the deck ape said in a kind of plea, emotional now. "Please. We haven't seen him. We haven't seen anyone. There's nobody else down here. Please take down this number quick. I don't know if they're listening."

Ruby rifled through her glove box.

"Okay. Shoot."

"The reporter's name is Eric Wheldon," he said after she had taken the number down. "You can see him on YouTube. He has a channel."

"An internet reporter? You mean like some conspiracy guy or something?"

"He's the real deal, Lieutenant. He works with a lot of whistle-blowers, especially military. One of the guys here had a brother in the merchant marines, and he was screwed until he told Wheldon, who got the story in the *Washington Post*."

"I don't know if I can do that," Ruby said.

"You *need* to talk to him and verify everything you know about the crash and how they got us stuck here on the base and especially that Steve is missing, okay? Contact him, please. I have to go."

"I really don't think I can help you," Ruby said.

"You have to. You're the only one who can," the deck ape said.

Then the line went dead.

27

"Hey, Wally," Ruby said into her phone as she pulled from the parking lot out onto the Dixie Highway.

"What's up, Rube?"

"Have you heard from Mark since he relieved me?" she said.

"Mark? No, not since he got sick down at that base you guys were at."

She stopped abruptly as she almost went through the red light.

"Hey, wait. You feeling okay? You're not sick, too, are you?" Wally said.

What the hell was going on? she thought.

"Ruby?" Wally said.

"No, I'm fine," Ruby said. "What's the matter with Mark?"

"Apparently, he's got a really bad flu or something, they said. He can't even come home because of a quarantine now. Something like that. That's what the boss told me. I thought you knew."

"Did we send another team?" she said.

"No. Jackie and Irrizarri just got back. They wouldn't even let them on the base. They're postponing the entire investigation until after the doctors clear the base."

Ruby remembered the diver's video. The old polished businessman. The tougher-looking middle-aged guy. The younger scruffy kid with the headphones. The black guy with the hoodie.

What in hell was on that plane? she thought as her phone started pulsing with a new incoming call.

"Thanks, Wally. I'll call you back," Ruby said abruptly.

"Hello, is this Lieutenant Everett?" said a new voice.

It was a man's voice. An older man now. Not the deck ape.

A horn suddenly honked from behind her because the light had turned green.

Ruby screeched off the strip road into an empty Chick-fil-A parking lot and stopped.

"Who the hell is this?" Ruby said.

"My name is Eric Wheldon. I'm a reporter. I got your number from the *Surmount* crew. You're in Naval Safety, right? You went to investigate the crash in the Bahamas?"

She suddenly felt dizzy. How could this be happening? What was she supposed to say?

"I don't know how you got my number," Ruby said, "but I can't help you, sir. Please don't call me again."

"Lieutenant," Wheldon said calmly. "Please don't hang up. I know. A reporter calls out of the blue. Panic time. But it's not like that. Let me explain."

Ruby sighed.

"I used to work for the State Department," Wheldon said. "I quit when I witnessed some very corrupt behavior by the federal government. Then I worked as a reporter for a major paper and saw a lot of covering up of that same exact corruption, so I quit that, too. Since then, I've been reporting on my own and helping whistle-blowers to get their stories out to the public."

"I'm sorry," Ruby said. "This is too much. I didn't get any sleep last night. I'm about to drop. I—"

"I understand," Wheldon said. "All right if I call you back this afternoon? It'll give you time to see my work on my YouTube channel. Bottom line, I think something serious is going on with that ship and crew. Especially with the rescue diver who saw the plane. They seem to have renditioned him."

"They what?" Ruby said.

"Taken him off base to a secret black site. A different country, most likely, for forced interrogation."

What in the hell? Ruby thought, struggling to keep up.

"What was up with that crashed plane, Lieutenant?" Wheldon said. "Steve dived down and saw it. Now Steve is gone. I'm thinking there's a connection there."

"Listen, Mr. Wheldon," Ruby said, rubbing at her forehead. "Let's get something straight. I'm no longer assigned to this investigation. I can't be of any help to you."

"Too much too soon," Wheldon said. "Okay, I understand, Lieutenant. If you would just check out my videos and see what I do. Then you can call me back."

"I have to go," Ruby said.

"Just one thing, though. If you talk to anyone, talk to me. Whatever you say to the so-called 'real press' will go straight to the people doing this. It happens every single time. They don't protect sources anymore. Industry wide, they're under pressure from the government. They'll roll on you so quick it'll make your head spin."

"I have to go now," Ruby said again, suddenly desperate to get off the phone.

"Lieutenant, one more thing. If you don't want them to track you, take your battery out of your phone. They can still follow you by the cell towers if the battery is still in it."

"Track me? Me? What did I do? Who would track me?" Ruby said, incredulous.

"They, Lieutenant. There really is a They. You're about to find that out, I think. When you do, call me first thing, okay? I can help you," Wheldon said.

28

Gannon's noon flight out of North Eleuthera was only an hour to Miami. But he had to wait two more hours for the connecting flight, so he didn't get into Tampa until almost five.

At six, he was sitting at a bar in Tampa's Airside C terminal when he saw his son coming through the crowd in front of the food court.

Gannon stood, smiling. Declan was fair-haired like he was but stood several inches taller at an impressive six foot three. He had actually filled out a little, too, Gannon noticed proudly as he came over. He was thicker at the shoulders, at the neck.

Gannon wasn't a hugger, yet he found himself hugging his strapping son right there in the middle of the bright bustling concourse.

He held him for a second after, looking at him. His mother's straight nose, her hazel eyes. Gannon smiled as he remembered him as a hyperactive kid, holding him on his knee for hours at family events so he wouldn't take down the Christmas tree. It had been six months since he'd last seen him.

Then he thought about his wife, Annette, who had died when Declan was just a freshman in high school.

How proud would she be of this solid young man here? he thought. Just beside herself, he knew. Over the moon.

Especially about the tryout. How many times had he come home from work to see them in the backyard hitting Wiffle balls to each other. She had actually been the biggest baseball fan in their family.

"Look at you, huh?" Gannon said, finally letting him go. "You weren't kidding about working out, were you? You're a monster. You're like hugging a soda machine."

"Dad, I can't begin to thank you for all of this," his son said, looking out at the concourse. "I mean, look at us. We're actually doing this!"

"No worries. You just rest that sweet arm," Gannon said, patting it gently.

"Just you wait, Dad. You won't believe your eyes. When do we leave here, by the way? At seven?"

"Yeah, a quarter after. It's a Delta flight. Gate whatever it is over there," Gannon said, pointing at a cluster of seats to the right. "We go to Atlanta first and should get in to Phoenix around midnight. I couldn't get a direct flight."

"No problem, Dad. Are you kidding me? Direct flight. I'd take a Megabus. I'd just about given up and then here we are right out of the blue."

"Yep, it's right out of the blue all right," Gannon said, hiding a smile as he took another pull of his beer.

When Declan left to hit the head, Gannon saw that the gate was filling up with people, so he strolled over to check that their flight was still on time. Declan was already sitting at the bar with two more fresh beers by the time he arrived back.

"Hey, Dad, look," he said, pointing at the TV above the bar. "They're talking about your neck of the woods."

Gannon looked up. A cable news channel was playing. On the screen was a petite blonde female reporter with the sparkling blue Caribbean behind her. Gannon's eyes went wide as he read the caption beneath her.

Plane Crash in the Bahamas, it said along the bottom of the screen.

Gannon waved over the bartender.

"Could you turn that up, please?"

"What's up? Did you hear about this?" Declan asked him.

"A little," Gannon said, straining to listen.

"...fifteen nautical miles off the coast of the Bahamian island known as Little Abaco when the US Coast Guard out on long-range patrol out of Miami Beach came upon it."

Golly tamale, here we go, Gannon thought, holding his breath as they showed footage of a coast guard cutter.

"The plane, a Cessna Denali seen here," the reporter continued as they showed a stock photo of a prop plane, "is a seven-passenger single-engine turboprop with an impeccable service record and a range of eighteen hundred miles."

Gannon's mouth dropped open.

A Cessna what? A little turboprop? he thought. What the hell were they talking about? It was no prop plane. It was a jet. It was a huge corporate Gulfstream 550 jet.

Were they talking about another crash? he thought, completely confused.

"The plane belonged to this couple," the reporter said as the screen changed to show a skinny curly-haired white guy and a pretty East Indian woman.

"Ben and Chandra Tholberg of Miami, Florida."

Who the hell were they? Gannon thought, even more stunned.

There was no woman on the jet. It had been men. All men.

"The Tholbergs, who lived in Coral Gables, had a vacation

house in Puerto Rico that they were returning from. Officials said Mr. Tholberg, an account executive at Century Bank and Trust in Coral Gables, had been an experienced pilot, so it will take some time before the mysterious cause of this tragic crash is known. Back to you, Brian."

Gannon kept blinking up at the screen even after it cut back to the studio.

"What's up, Dad? Did you know them or something?" Declan said.

Something, Gannon thought, his mind reeling.

"You okay, Dad?"

Gannon finally pulled his eyes off the screen and looked around at the airport bar. It had a tiki theme. There was straw on the wall behind the bottles and surfboards everywhere.

"No," Gannon finally said, mustering a smile. "I mean, yes. I'm fine. It's the, um, woman. She looked just like this girl I knew in high school. This aggravating Indian girl who used to sit behind me in math class."

He quickly gulped at his beer. He thought about Sergeant Jeremy. What he had said to him about the FBI poking around, asking questions.

He had one himself.

Why would the US government completely lie about a plane crash? he thought, glancing back up at the TV.

29

There was heavy evening traffic on the Beltway, so even with the lead car blooping the siren, it took them almost an hour from Dunning's house to get to the base. The driver had radioed ahead, so the uniformed guards at the gate were at crisp attention as they came right through.

It turned out to be some pretty perfect timing. Through the tinted window, Reyland could see the lights of the AC-130 turning in the dark sky as they came alongside the hangar. As they slowed just beside the tarmac, Emerson, riding shotgun with the driver, turned to see if he should open the door, but Reyland shook his head.

"I've been meaning to ask you something, Mr. Reyland," Dunning's very attractive black-haired daughter, Belinda, said as they stopped.

She was sitting opposite from him across the rear of the limo beside her devastated mother, Catherine.

Reyland folded his hands in the blue serge lap of his Brooks Brothers suit.

"Please, like I said, anything," Reyland said.

"I know you've told Mother here, but I'd like to hear it from you. How was it that my father died exactly?"

Reyland blinked at the thirtysomething. She was tall and chic and stunning in her all-black and sunglasses. Like other rich women, she had been a ballerina once and still retained that thin, gracious, model-like comportment.

A flash of memory came to him. Stopping by Dunning's villa once with some paperwork, he'd come upon Belinda soaking wet in a white one-piece with her other smoking-hot private high school BFFs by the pool.

Reyland swallowed.

"The doctors at the hospital in Rome said it was a massive stroke, Belinda," he said quietly. "They assured me that he wouldn't have felt anything. He just went to sleep and that was it."

Reyland watched Belinda slowly absorb this.

"Will we get a chance to see him?" Belinda finally said.

He glanced at the curve of her *Swan Lake* throat, perfect and smooth and pale between the stark black collar of her coat and the salon-perfect line of her dark hair. She was wearing a most-enchanting scent. A hint of peach over something mysterious and sumptuous that Reyland couldn't quite name.

"At the base here? No. I'm so sorry," Reyland finally said. "The civilian funeral home representatives need to take him straight from the plane in order to make the final preparations."

Reyland glanced over to where the hearse waited. A marine honor guard was standing at attention in the doorway of the hangar beside it, starched white gloves and the black patent leather shining.

He certainly couldn't complain about the optics, he thought.

Even Dunning, who was a hard-ass stickler in just about everything, would have approved.

"C'mon, Mother," Belinda said. "I can see the plane. Father's coming in."

"It's perfectly fine if you need more time. We still have a few minutes," Reyland said, bringing his hands together as if in prayer.

"Okay," Catherine Dunning finally said. "Okay."

The vice president's retinue showed up as the plane made its taxiing turn. The president, still on his Asian trip, couldn't make it, but he would be back just in time for the funeral. The VP came over and gave Belinda a hug and patted Catherine's hand, whispering to her. He smiled at Reyland as they nodded at each other.

"Nice to see you again, Ron," the VP said to him.

"You, too, sir," Reyland said, not correcting him that they had never met before and that his name was actually Robert.

It didn't matter. DC was a kinetic place. Factions were already making movements, readjustments.

He wouldn't make that mistake twice, Reyland thought in the roar of the approaching plane.

The turboprops roared even louder in the cold as the big plane crawled over to where they stood. Its back ramp was already down as it finally stopped before them. The marines, on the march, entered and went up with robotic precision.

The casket they came out with was straight lined and much smaller than Reyland expected. Under the flag, it looked like the kind of cardboard box that ready-to-assemble Walmart furniture came in.

The pallbearers stopped before the widow, and two of the marines from the honor guard marched over, giving the flag the required thirteen folds. As they did this, Reyland looked at himself in the limo's tinted glass and smoothed his black tie. When he glanced over at the photographers in the media pen set up beside the hangar, he could see that they were going stone-cold bat shit.

Roll 'em, boys, and don't forget my good side, Reyland thought, raising his chin high.

And why not? It was a moving performance. Solemn, austere. All of it. A splendorous display of reticence. Emerson had suggested taps, but Reyland had nixed it. Better to save it for the burial.

As the soldiers finally slid the boss into the dead-mobile, Reyland nodded to himself, pleased. There were still some long hard miles to go before he slept, but at least the press was already swallowing the Rome thing like a widemouthed bass. By tomorrow, the arrow of the bullshit wheel would be firmly landed upon one of the grandstanding press's all-time favorite chestnuts, A Nation in Mourning.

As the marines headed back to the hangar, Reyland glanced over at the tears flowing freely past the soft bud of Belinda's brilliant diamond-pierced earlobe a foot in front of him.

As she began to tremble, Reyland leaned ever so slightly forward and placed his hand on her perfect shoulder, careful to keep his chin up for the photographers as he mournfully closed his eyes.

30

It was coming on 3:00 a.m. when the vrooming Honda Ruckus moped slowed and came to a puttering halt on a dirt road on the southeast outskirts of Culiacán, Mexico.

There was a fork in the high-desert country road, and the handsome middle-aged man astride the rumbling bike sat for a moment before it with a ruminative look on his face.

He sat studying the two roads, the moonlit plains of chaparral they carved through, the mountains in the far distance. After a moment, he removed a pair of reading glasses from his crisp shirt's breast pocket and carefully consulted the GPS on the phone in a holder between the moped's handlebars. Then he put the glasses back and kicked up some dust as he rolled up the right-hand branch.

The small up-country compound he stopped before ten minutes later had a solid steel plate gate in the center of its nine-foot-high cement block outer wall. He unlocked the gate with the key from his pocket and squealed it open. Then he rolled in the moped and squealed the gate back and firmly relocked it.

The small building inside had once been a gas station. Before one of its old rusted pumps was a portable gasoline generator with a cord that went in under the station's closed door. He ripcorded the generator on and unlocked the old station's front door and came through its unlit empty front room into the back.

Beneath the tarp he pulled back was a steel cellar door built into the concrete slab floor. It was secured with a thick Master key padlock that he unlocked with his key ring. The well-oiled hinges made no sound at all as he opened the door up and out.

He squatted, looking down into it. Seven feet below was a dirt-walled cell that looked like a large grave dug into the earth. Light from the standing floodlight below fell across just the legs of the prisoner in the corner.

One couldn't tell if it was a man or a woman. It was just a figure, a small pale bare-legged figure with the knees drawn up and the arms hugging the shins. The feet were black with filth.

Good, the torturer thought as he saw how the prisoner was shivering.

He adjusted the floodlight as he got to the bottom of the ladder. As he did this, the figure raised a thin arm up as if to ward off a blow. The torturer looked at the bright green of the shamrock tattoo on the American's hand. He had spent some time in America and knew the symbol was supposed to stand for good luck.

The torturer had to catch himself from tsking at the irony of it, at the cruel difference that often arose between one's hopeful expectations and the actual brutalities of blind uncaring fate and chance.

The torturer stepped over slowly and looked down at the naked man. He had fought them from the very beginning, raged. You wouldn't think a man his size could reach such volume.

Now, after leaving him without food or water here in the dark for twenty-four hours, it was time for a new tack.

"My name is Dr. Segurro. I am here to tend to you. Are you awake? Hello?" the torturer said in his excellent English as he knelt beside the American.

The torturer was wearing a nice dress shirt and slacks and had a stethoscope. He warmed it in his palms before he put it to the man's chest.

"Put out your tongue," he said.

The prisoner did so, snorting and gasping.

"Yes, very good. Very good," the torturer said, shining a penlight into the man's eyes.

"Listen to me very carefully," the torturer said. "Something in you has ruptured. It's your spleen. Do you understand? You're broken inside, and if we don't get you to a hospital, you're going to die. These men obviously want something from you. If you tell them, I can get you out of here. But if you do not, you will die. This is your final chance."

"Okay, okay," the American said immediately. "I'll tell you."

The torturer smiled at the man's instant reversal. He had seen this happen more than once. Twenty-four hours in the dark with the rats was incredibly effective. One of his very favorite techniques. It was heartening to build up a store of knowledge of his craft.

"I copied the videotape of the dive," he said. "It's on my phone. The passcode is 6543. I showed the video to the lieutenant from the navy. She watched it twice. Now, please, some water. Please."

"I have water outside. I will get it in a moment. Just please speak louder. You're running out of time," the torturer said, putting his recording phone to the American's bruised face.

"The girl fr-fr-from Naval, Naval Safety. The pretty brown-haired girl. I showed her the video," he said again.

"Lieutenant Everett, yes," the torturer said, remembering his memorized notes. "You showed it to Ruby. Yes."

"Yes. Ruby. I showed her. Now help me, please. Please. I don't want to die. Save me. I need water."

"Yes, of course, of course. You have done well. What's your passcode again?"

"6543."

"I will tell them. I will be right back."

The torturer went up the ladder, relocked the cellar door, placed the tarp back over it, went outside and killed the generator.

He had a little kit bag beneath the motorbike's seat, and from it, he removed a sanitary baby wipe that he used meticulously on his hands and face before he took out his phone.

"Mr. Ruiz?" the torturer said, lighting a cigarette as he sat on the moped out in the silent country under the glittering starlight.

"Yes. Good news," the torturer said. "There's been a breakthrough."

31

Out in the cool of the morning off Interstate 10, Gannon watched his son raise his left arm, turning the baseball in his long, graceful fingers.

They were in Arizona now, somewhere west of downtown Phoenix. It was just after sunrise, and they were standing in the open desert a couple of miles from their hotel beside an empty truck stop pull-off.

The early morning workout had been Gannon's idea. In full coach mode now, he had gotten Declan up and moving the second he woke up.

Nothing like getting the blood pumping, to smooth out any pretryout jitters he might be having, Gannon thought.

"Ready, Dad?" Declan said.

Gannon was about to say yes when a car came off the two-lane highway into the strip of truck stop beside them. Gannon watched it. It was a silver sedan.

He kept watching as it pulled to a stop in front of their rented Silverado truck. There was only one person in it. He couldn't tell if it was a man or a woman.

Shit, was it a Ford? he wondered suddenly. Didn't the feds drive Fords?

No, he saw. It was too small. It was some kind of Honda. He stood silently watching it anyway. After a moment, it pulled away again and was gone back onto the road.

"Dad?" Declan said again.

Maybe his son wasn't the only one who needed to work out a jitter or two this morning, Gannon thought as he punched his catcher's mitt.

"Okay, let's go. Batter up! Play ball!" he yelled as he finally crouched down.

They went for almost an hour, then piled back into the rented Silverado. They were heading off the exit ramp back for the hotel when they saw the Starbucks sign.

He'd left Declan in the truck and was inside waiting his turn in the crowded morning rush line when his eyes glanced off the newspaper in the rack by the door.

Gannon stared. When he suddenly realized what he was looking at, he couldn't decide which was making his suddenly kick-started heart beat faster.

The above-the-fold page-wide photograph.

Or the huge three-word headline above it.

He zombie-shuffled numbly back through the people behind him to the rack and lifted up the paper.

He stared at the photograph some more. The thick white hair. The somber and austere expression.

No. There was no mistaking it.

FBI DIRECTOR DEAD, Gannon read again and then stared back at the face of the old white-haired man he'd seen dead under the water on the crashed jet.

FBI Director Dunning Dies of Stroke in Rome.

32

Fenwick's on 13th Street across from Franklin Square had a gleaming mahogany bar and tufted leather banquettes and waiters who wore white tuxedo jackets even at breakfast service.

It was always ranked in the top five of DC's oldest and most highly regarded establishment institutions. The joke was that the old Fenwick waiters had served not just Washington's senators but also the *actual* Washington Senators, the black-and-white-TV-era American League baseball team that had been disbanded in 1971.

At a quarter after nine in the morning, Reyland sat center court, smoothing down his silk Hermès tie between the bespoke lapels of his best Hackett of London navy suit. He glanced to his left, where Emerson sat looking the way he had ordered him to, neat and lean and preppy and highly polished.

Prep School, he thought, glancing at him, pleased. He hired

only people who could pull off that throwback J. Edgar Hoover FBI look.

He looked around the room ever so casually. He usually did his power noshing at the Hayes across from the J. Edgar Building on E Street, but he needed to be seen in the legend seats now that he was a shoo-in for deputy director.

And so far, his PR appearance seemed to be coming off pretty well. He'd been there only ten minutes before the UN ambassador to the Conference on Disarmament had come by to kiss his ring as well as the senior adviser to policy planning at State. Richie Dempsey, the famous four-hundred-pound owner of the legendary eatery, had waddled out of the kitchen to say hello and even his hardcase elderly mother had texted as he was leaving the house to give him a rare upvote for his debut appearance on the front page of the *New York Times*.

That wasn't even the best news, he thought, as he dabbed some country ham into the yolk of his perfectly runny poached egg.

Last night, Ruiz's Mexican contractor had finally broken the diver.

As they had already been theorizing, the diver, Stephen Vance, had in fact copied a backup video of the dive onto his phone. Not only that, as they had also been theorizing, Vance had indeed shown the video to the female naval inspector, Ruby Everett, who had left the base.

That the diver had done this was quite troubling now that the cat had been let out of the bag about Dunning.

But the good news was that Vance hadn't *given* her the video. They had done a full forensic on his mobile phone, and the video of the dive had not been uploaded to anyone.

So in essence, there was no proof. The leak was still very much sealable.

It was now just a matter of picking up the naval inspector, some surprisingly attractive hick nobody out of Ohio coal country named Ruby Everett.

Ruby, the rube, was out on leave to points unknown, but that wasn't going to be a problem since his team had been on it since three this morning.

Speaking of which, Reyland thought, stifling a smile as he saw one of Emerson's zonked-looking computer guys come in and stand at the end of Fenwick's storied mahogany bar.

Reyland touched Emerson's elbow as he stood to leave the banquette.

"Tell that stooge he can't come into a place like this looking like that. He wants to work for me, he better buy a tie, shave, and maybe start eating some salads."

"C'mon, boss, cut him some slack just this once. That's Billy Rayne, my MIT ace in the hole. He's a genius."

"Rayne," Reyland mumbled. "Rain Man is more like it."

Emerson came back to the table three minutes later, all smiles, with a folder in his hand.

"Good stuff, boss. We've found our errant little naval safety inspector."

"Finally! Where?"

"She has a sister that just squatted out a new hillbilly," he said, smiling as he placed the printed Google map onto the table. "The sister's house is here just north of Pensacola Air Station."

"And, oh, look. She even bought some goodies from Party City. Isn't that special?" Reyland said, flicking the report page to her USAA credit card statements.

"The arrest team will be out of where? Jacksonville?" Reyland said.

"No, Mobile," Emerson said, taking out his phone as the old tuxedoed grandfatherly waiter refilled their water glasses.

"Shouldn't take them more than an hour to get there," he said.

33

Sweating under the overcast morning sky, Ruby chugged along doing a long, lazy loop, jogging the Pensacola neighborhoods north of the naval base.

She'd let out an hour before from Lori's house, where she was still staying over. She'd lived in the modest neighborhood when she first joined the navy and could have practically done the familiar five miles past the sunburned bungalows blindfolded. Lake Charlene north to Glendale, Glendale to Fairfax Terrace, then out to the strip of New Warrington Road that they just called Navy Road because it led into the base.

She jogged steadily at an easy pace past the curving blocks, not pushing it. She always loved running in the morning, that pleasant, still half-asleep hopeful feeling of being outside in the freshness of the new day. She'd run cross-country track in high school well enough to get a partial scholarship to the University of Miami and tried to keep it up. She'd sprained an ankle the year before and then work got busy, and she just kind of let it go for a bit. But now she was gradually coming back after the layoff in fits and starts.

As she ran, her mind wandered to all the crazy phone calls she had gotten.

She still hadn't done anything about any of them. What could she do? Were Mark and the diver actually sick? Which seemed fishy. Or had the government gone nuts? Which seemed even fishier. Or was it something else?

She thought about the reporter. His YouTube videos. His advice on taking the battery out of her phone.

No, she thought as she ran. No way.

From personal experience, she knew the government was often careless, often even stupid. But it wasn't crazy. It wasn't actually malevolent. There had to be some rational explanation.

But she had to do *something*, didn't she?

She suddenly stopped and began jogging in place to let a minivan back out of a driveway.

Once she got back, she thought, as she began running again, she'd bite the bullet and call up Wally and ask again about Mark.

Her thighs were starting to burn on an upslope of her return loop five minutes later when her phone vibrated. She took it out of her waist pack and blew her sweaty bangs out of her eyes to look at the screen.

"Hey," she said, relieved to see it was only Lori.

"You okay?" Lori said, sounding sleepy.

"Of course. What's up? Is Ally okay?" Ruby said as she slowed and stopped.

"Yes, yes. Fine. Did you forget your key or something?" her sister said.

"What? No. I'm not home yet. What is it, Lori?"

As she stood listening, she heard baby Alice start crying.

"Somebody is knocking on the door," Lori said. "That's not you?"

Ruby sprinted across Penton and up to Lori's corner on Norton Street.

And saw them—all of them—there in front of the house.

34

Midway down the street in front of Lori's little house were a half-dozen vehicles. They were gray unmarked cop cars, and they were parked sideways out in the street, completely blocking it.

Alongside them stood half a dozen figures in blue raid jackets.

Ruby gasped when one of them turned and she spotted the three impossible-to-miss frightening Day-Glo yellow letters scrawled across the back.

FBI? Ruby thought.

There was a roar of a diesel engine and then from the other end of the street came some kind of armored van. It was a giant gunmetal gray SWAT truck and from its running board hung a team of tactical officers. They had shaved military jarheads and khaki-colored ballistic armor and military rifles that looked like something out of a middle schooler's video game.

Then it happened. As the heavy armored FBI SWAT van

mounted the sidewalk in front of Lori's house, the reality of what she was in the middle of finally slammed into Ruby like a wrecking ball to the chest.

She suddenly remembered the reporter's words.

They are real, Ruby. There really is a They.

"Ruby, what should I do? Someone's knocking hard now. What the hell is this?" Lori said in her ear.

Ruby stood there speechless. She stared mutely at the agents, at the houses around her. There was no one around. No one to notice the world going nuts.

Move, dammit! she thought. *Snap out of it! Do something!*

Ruby ripped her eyes from the cars and mayhem down the block and took a deep breath and quietly crossed the intersection. When she made the other side, she looked at her phone and saw that Lori's call had dropped off.

She ran at top speed into the dead end at the end of the side street. She hopped over someone's short back fence, darted across the yard, came around the house back into another cul-de-sac and made a right down McNeil, the street that ran parallel to Norton.

When she was about halfway down across from Lori's house, she quietly hopped another fence and went into someone else's side yard and crouched by some ornamental grass.

Over the house's backyard fence, she could see onto Norton. There was one of the double-parked FBI cars there with two male agents and a female one.

She looked at the hard expressions on their faces. Their drawn guns down by their legs. Like they were coming after a hijacker. A terrorist holed up with a weapon of mass destruction.

Her fear suddenly flipped to pure anger. What bastards, she thought, looking beyond them at Sean's Playskool scooter and kick balls under Lori's modest brick bungalow's carport.

They couldn't see that there were kids in the house? People's children. They didn't care about that?

She was watching the agents consult solemnly with one another when somewhere off to the left someone yelled out in a football coach roar.

"Open up! FBI! We have a warrant!"

And then there was a crunching boom and a shatter of glass as the sons of bitches actually broke down Lori's door.

Even from a block over, she heard Lori scream as a file of FBI agents ran in over her front lawn.

Ruby stood up breathing hard, a hand to her mouth. She was feeling nauseated now, helpless and numb, like she was coming out of herself.

The sound of little Sean's screaming cries snapped her out of it and she lifted her phone.

"911. What's your emergency?"

She was going to say "There are FBI agents entering my sister's house," then stopped herself.

"Help me! Someone just kicked in my door! A break-in, a break-in! Someone's in my house! 334 Norton. 334 Norton. Help me, please. Send someone, please. They have guns. Help!"

She hung up and stood in the side yard of the house stock-still with her hands clasped in prayer as she waited. When she heard the sirens another long two minutes later, she hopped back out of the person's side yard and headed back into the street.

As she ran out toward the corner, she saw them coming at her up 70th. Two radio cars, Pensacola's finest, roaring up, lights flashing, as they made the left onto Norton.

She speed-walked down to the corner and saw the cops getting out, some of the agents rushing over showing credentials. Lori's neighbors were now out on their porches and scrub grass front yards wondering what the hell was going on.

Then Ruby started running, booking for all she was worth, past Norton and down 70th before they figured out she wasn't there.

35

Ruby ran all the way, a full three miles more, up to the Mobile Highway. The first car rental place she found was on the strip between a mattress store and a Church's Fried Chicken. The bell on its door jangled loudly as she nearly took it off the hinges coming through at an almost dead run.

"Hello and what have we here?" said a guy sitting at a desk behind the counter. He was young and had one of those silly mountain man hipster beards that went to the chest of his corporate polo.

"I need to rent a car," Ruby gasped, red-faced, sweat dripping onto the carpet tile.

"Let me guess. Got tired of running? Figured, let me try this car thing," said the rental clerk snarkily as he laid down the cell phone he was playing with and stood.

"I just got into a damn car accident!" Ruby said loudly, acting only a little more in shock than she actually was. "My Mazda got completely totaled! The fire department had to cut the door off! I almost died."

"No way," the clerk said, wide-eyed, no more snark or irony in sight.

"Yes. Two miles down the road there. Some dumb little twit was texting on her phone and T-boned me. If her front end came in another inch closer, I'd be dead right now."

"I'm so sorry," the guy said. "Are you okay? Can I get you something?"

"No. I'm sorry for yelling. I'm still shook up a little, I guess. I just need a car real quick. My mama just had back surgery over at Sacred Heart. I need to pick her up. She has a bad heart, too, and she worries."

"You poor thing," the clerk said. "We'll get you fixed up. We just got a minivan in, a Honda Odyssey, a nice new one. Would that help you? I'll even charge you for a compact."

"Perfect," Ruby said. "Thank you."

"We'll get you right out of here," he said as he handed her a pen and a clipboard.

She sat in a chair, dripping sweat onto the paperwork, as he left to get the van. The clipboard shook in her hand as the enormity of everything came crashing down around her ears.

She thought about her sister and the children. She thought about Mark Thanh, her coworker, quarantined somewhere. And Steve, the diver, gone missing. He was just a kid.

She looked out at the traffic. On her run, she had been thinking that she would head to someplace safe in order to figure out what to do next. Call some friends. Maybe call a lawyer.

But she knew what she had to do now.

Ruby took out her phone and opened the back and pried out the battery as the guy with the beard arrived outside with the van.

36

Maryvale Baseball Park, Cactus League home of the Milwau-
kee Brewers, was a sprawling, newly revamped spring training facility in West Phoenix.

Gannon, standing by the third baseline seats, glanced out onto
the sunny infield where Declan was demonstrating his bunting
skills to some scouts and coaches. He fouled off the first, but then
dropped down a beaut up the third baseline as he began to book.

Gannon placed his phone down in his lap and clapped.

"Way to go, son. That's the way," he yelled and immediately
lifted his phone back up and went back to reading yet another
completely fake news story about Director Dunning's tragic
death by stroke in Rome.

"Hey, is that your kid out there?" said a guy from behind him.

"Yep," Gannon said without turning around.

"Wow. That's some slider he has. Just nasty. You have to be
pretty proud."

"Yep," Gannon said as he flicked at the screen.

The gaggle of baseball people broke up after a minute, and Declan jogged over to where Gannon was sitting.

"What's up, son?" Gannon said, his eyes still glued to his phone.

"We're still waiting on the assistant GM himself," Declan said. "Then we're going to start the simulated game."

"Is that right?"

"Did you hear me, Dad?"

Gannon looked up.

"I'll be right back," Gannon said, standing.

"Right back? Where the hell are you going?"

Gannon headed back outside the stadium altogether into the truck. He turned it over and cranked up the A/C as he pressed on the video he had just found on YouTube.

He turned up the volume on his phone as a lean middle-aged man appeared on the screen, walking along what appeared to be a New York City street.

The man had neatly cut light brown hair streaked with gray, and he was wearing a nice overcoat over a business suit with no tie. It almost looked like a camera crew was following along with the guy, taping him as he walked, but he was probably holding one of those selfie stick things, taping himself.

The man's name was Eric Wheldon, and Gannon had already quickly learned that he was some kind of alternative news reporter with a YouTube channel.

His channel had hundreds of videos with thousands of hits on each. The videos had all-caps titles like: BREAKING: STATE DEPARTMENT DENIES AMBASSADOR JOYCE'S TIES TO MUNICH HOOKERGATE! And, LATEST NSA HACKER UPDATE: IS MESSERLY STILL IN LONDON? And, CHINESE DELEGATION MEMBER LU DIES IN SUSPICIOUS HEART ATTACK!

What was of special interest to Gannon in his current state of panic was the title of the video he was now watching.

MYSTERIOUS PLANE CRASH IN BAHAMAS. IS IT REALLY WHAT THEY'RE SAYING?

"Hey, everyone, greetings from freezing-cold NYC and welcome to episode 349," Wheldon said.

"What shall we talk of today, my friends?" he said. "How about plane crashes? Yesterday, a little birdie told me about a very curious one down off the coast of sunny Florida. This little birdie works in one of our vaunted armed forces divisions, and said he was recently sent out to a site near the Bahamas."

Wheldon paused, smiling into the camera. Gannon looked at the building he was passing. It had brass doors, and in the granite beside the door, a shining brass plaque said 485 Park.

"Is that right? I said to my friend," Wheldon continued. "I believe I heard about that Bahamas crash on the news. You're talking about that Cessna Denali turboprop that went down, right? About that poor married couple who tragically lost their lives? Well, my friend said. The crash was in the Bahamas, that's true. But it was no prop plane. No? I said. How do you know that?"

Wheldon stopped walking and stared into the camera.

"Because how could it be a prop plane, my little birdie told me, when we fished two Rolls-Royce jet engines out of the water?"

Gannon felt the hair on the back of his neck stand up. He couldn't believe this. The FBI director. Now the crash.

Everything was starting to snowball. It was all blowing up now.

And he was smack-dab dead center in the middle of it.

"That's a pretty darn good question, isn't it?" Wheldon said.

"I'll say," said Gannon, dry-mouthed.

"Anybody out there know the answer?" Wheldon said.

37

Atop the concrete subway steps, Ruby stopped and stood still in the massive flow of hurrying people.

She gaped up at the giant TV screen billboards. The cartoons and lingerie ads. The streaming ABC News electronic billboard beside her that said it was twenty-nine degrees.

She checked her watch. It was almost midnight. Her train had arrived in New York City at eleven fifteen, but it took a little while in the chaotic disorienting swirl at Penn Station to figure out which subway she needed to take to get to Times Square.

Disorienting, Ruby thought, looking around.

Yep. Disorienting was the theme of her week all right.

Even after a full minute, she kept standing there, staring. She knew she looked like a tourist, but she didn't care.

She had one or two other things on her mind right now, she thought.

She found a Starbucks half a block west of the subway and

went in and got a tall black. Looking out through the foggy, greasy glass to get her bearings, she could see there was some kind of frantic commotion going on at the corner. People were stopped and staring and some of them were pointing phones at some other people there on the ground.

She thought maybe it was a fight. But then the crowd parted, and she saw it was a smiling Buzz Lightyear and green-painted Lady Liberty break-dancing together on a flattened cardboard box.

"My, my, my," she said.

On the morning of the day before, she'd left the rental van in the parking lot of a mall near Savannah/Hilton Head International Airport and taken a series of cabs to Yemassee, South Carolina, where she got on the Amtrak to New York.

It was Eric Wheldon's idea that she ditch the van for the Amtrak. She'd called him the moment after she bought a new prepaid burner phone. The first thing he told her was to take out as much cash as she could from an ATM and not to use her credit card.

She had wanted to call her sister, Lori, to make sure she and the kids were okay, but he said no way. That they would definitely be tapping her line. Which thoroughly sucked, but at least her brother-in-law, Mitch, would be home by now.

She slammed back the last of her coffee and dropped the cup into the trash hole and pulled the door back out to the grim, frigid sidewalk. She was supposed to meet Wheldon on the corner of 44th and Broadway, and when she arrived, there was a crowd on the corner. It was some kind of nightclub opening, and there were photographers standing by a red carpet and a velvet rope.

She looked at people, searching for Wheldon as she passed. In his YouTube videos, he was a neatly dressed reporterish-looking middle-aged white guy.

There was no one who looked like that in front of the red

ropes, so she went to the corner and waited on the light. On the opposite side of it, she saw a couple of dog walkers standing there, allowing their dogs to greet each other.

Of course, she thought.

Why not take the dog out for a stroll at midnight in Times Square in the freezing cold? To meet Buzz Lightyear for a break-dancing lesson maybe? Makes sense.

As she arrived at the opposite curb, she realized one of the dog walkers was staring at her. He was a pale, fiftyish man in a long dark overcoat.

Was it Wheldon? Ruby thought. The neat hair and reporterish look were the same, and he seemed to be about the same age. Though he hadn't mentioned any dog.

Or had the FBI found her? Ruby thought, gnawing on her lip. They looked reporterish, too.

They didn't break eye contact as she went past him north up Broadway. She was coming to the corner of 45th when she noticed that he was coming up behind her. She stopped short, freaking out a little. He handed her something before he kept going like a shot with the dog around the corner of 45th.

She kept going straight up Broadway and waited until she got across the next side street before she looked at it.

It was a flyer for an Irish pub on 50th Street.

12:30 was written in Sharpie along its bottom.

38

The hearty, happy smell of steak and Guinness made Ruby smile when she came in out of the cold through the door of O'Lunney's Times Square Pub.

After all the traveling and cold and walking and worrying, she suddenly felt ravenously hungry and very tired.

She looked at the people at the half-filled bar, the jewel-colored rows of shining bottles behind it.

"Hey, there you are. This way, miss," said a pleasant-looking goateed man in a dapper gray suit as he came out from behind the bar.

He led her down some steps to a downstairs bar and past it to a dark booth where the neat man from the corner stood as she approached.

"Welcome to the jungle, Ruby," Wheldon said as she stepped over.

"Where's your dog?" Ruby said.

Wheldon laughed as she sat.

"What dog?" he said with a wink.

"You are Eric Wheldon?"

"At your service," he said.

"An Irish coffee, please," she said to the waitress when she came over.

"I'd also like a menu, too, if we're staying. I'm starving," Ruby said, unbuttoning her coat as the waitress left.

"No, we should actually be leaving in a minute," Wheldon said, glancing at the stairs. "We should keep moving."

"Are you kidding? I haven't slept an hour straight since I called you. I'm about to drop. Is it really necessary?"

Wheldon took out a folded sheet of paper from inside his long coat and put it on the tabletop. He flashed the light from his phone on it to show her.

Ruby swallowed as she looked at her photo from her military ID.

"You tell me," he said.

"What the hell is that?"

"It's the FBI wire on you. You're a hot commodity."

"Oh, no, no, no… Am I like on the news now?"

"No, not yet. That's an interoffice sheet. They want to bag you discreetly, if they can."

"AWOL?" she said as she read the charges. "Bullshit! I'm on leave! And 'Suspicion of Terrorist Activities'! Are they crazy?"

"Yep, that's how they do it. If it's a national security top secret matter, they just go to their rigged secret court and get one of their cronies to rubber-stamp it. They don't need probable cause or to show any evidence. They just say it's a sensitive security issue and, boom, they get the warrant."

"I can't believe this. Are you being watched, too?"

"Off and on," Wheldon said. "They don't seem to like me or my YouTube channel very much. Weird."

The waitress brought her coffee.

"How the hell do you know all this stuff?"

"I told you I used to work in the State Department. I still know a few people, good people, who have had it up to here with what's happening."

"What *is* happening?"

"We'll get to all that. We need to get out of here first. I have a friend. You can crash on her couch. You'll like her. Everybody likes Rebecca."

"Then what?"

"Then tomorrow, we talk. Trade notes. Figure out your situation. How does that sound?"

"Honestly, sort of crazy," Ruby said as she stared at her very first personal WANTED poster there on the paper. "Five seconds ago, I was at my sister's house feeding my new niece. Now the FBI is after me, and I'm here in New York with a conspiracy theorist."

"Not theorist," Wheldon said, smiling as he dropped a couple of bills on the table. "Analyst, Ruby. The conspiracy is real. As you know yourself now."

Ruby took a sip of her coffee as Wheldon stood and yanked open a door beside their booth.

"Are you ready?" Wheldon said.

Ruby looked out the door. Beyond it there was a bunch of garbage bags and beer case boxes and a set of metal fire escape–style stairs heading up. A frigid ear-nipping wind rushed in.

"No, but let's do it anyway, I guess," Ruby said as she finally stood.

39

When Reyland woke it was around midnight and there was a sound of violins.

When he opened an eye, up on the big wall-sized screen, he could see men in Civil War uniforms being carried on stretchers. Scarlett O'Hara appeared, looking to and fro, and then the camera panned back to dramatically reveal a sepia-colored train yard filled with the dead and dying as the music turned to a sad strain of Dixieland.

Reyland yawned. Movie night had been his nine-year-old son Jason's idea. The kids were all off from school the next day because of some teachers' conference, so they'd all come down with popcorn and Mike and Ikes and blankets. They'd decided after several votes on the vintage Disney classic *Freaky Friday*, and then after the kids fell asleep, his wife had put on *Gone with the Wind*.

That had done it for him. He hadn't lasted through the opening credits.

"Okay, you lazybones," Reyland called out, clicking off the projector with the remote.

No one moved. His littlest, Sadie, was closest, and she squealed as he tickled her awake at her bare foot with his toenail.

"Mom, make him stop," she said as everyone finally got up.

At first, he had thought that the theater room the previous owners had done up with red curtains and even a little ticket stand in the hall was the corniest crap he had ever laid eyes on. But even he couldn't deny how much he actually loved it. The sound system especially. He'd never go to a real movie theater again.

As Jason, Tyler and Sadie zombie-stumbled off to bed, he helped his wife, Danielle, collect the popcorn bowls. He smiled, checking out his wife from behind as they came up the stairs. She'd just turned forty, but she worked out like crazy, and she still had a great rack and an ass you could bounce a quarter off.

She was still the hot LSU cheerleader he'd picked up at the Orlando Hard Rock Cafe after the Citrus Bowl back in the roaring nineties. Or at least mostly. He remembered Christmas in St. Barts two years before when they had left the kids in the hotel and gone sailing. How would he ever forget? Shirtless and tipsy, she had climbed to the bow and done a mermaid impression for him in just her Santa-red thong.

He frowned as he thought about work, Dunning, the missing navy girl.

Why? Reyland thought. Couldn't life just always be champagne and sailboats and Santa-red thongs?

"Bring up some bottled water, okay?" his wife called by the back stairs as he clicked off the basement lights.

"Yes, dear," he mumbled into the dark.

He was closing the Sub-Zero when he saw Emerson's three

missed calls on his phone on the charging pad on the other side of the kitchen island.

"Tell me the good news," Reyland said as he stood at his back door, looking out into the dark yard.

"Everett's in New York."

Reyland's face instantly brightened.

"New York? In custody?"

"No. You're not going to believe this, boss. It's not good. She's met up with that internet jackass Wheldon."

"Who?"

"You know. Eric Wheldon. He leaked the Oliveras thing about four months ago. He was the reason the *Post* finally picked it up."

"Oh, no, no, no," Reyland said, knocking at the French door glass with his Notre Dame school ring. "Tell me we have eyes on them right this second."

"No, but we're on this. New York already has a great jacket on Wheldon. We have his apartment and his office. You want me to get a forward team together?"

"Yes. Wake up Ruiz and call aviation. We need a plane three hours ago," Reyland said.

40

The late morning traffic on the BQE outside of LaGuardia Airport was catastrophic. But as the cab glacially got off the BQE onto the LIE, it did the impossible.

It actually got worse.

From the dead-stopped interchange five miles south of the airport, Gannon looked out, amazed at the evacuation-level volume of work vans and big rig trucks and taxis and cars. Then he looked forward at Manhattan, where the machine belts of vehicles were being fed.

The great gray barbed skyline on the western horizon looked like some giant instrument of torture set and ready for fresh victims.

Gannon zipped up the Carhartt coat he had bought from a sporting goods store in Arizona on the way to the airport.

And look who's headed straight into the jaws of it, he thought.

Gannon closed his eyes. Damn did this suck, he thought. Especially leaving Declan flat all by himself back at the stadium in Arizona. He hadn't even had time to stay for the simulated game in order to catch the next direct flight.

But what choice did he have?

What was going on, he didn't know, except that this wasn't a damn game. This wasn't some lucky fantasy scheme where he walked off into the sunset with a secret bag of doper money anymore. He could kiss all that good-night and goodbye.

He needed to get out in front of this and damn quick, he thought as he passed a hand nervously through his hair.

Before he found his sorry ass sitting in a prison cell.

They stopped and sat motionless for so long the cabbie actually put the car in Park.

"It's worse," Gannon finally said. "How could it have gotten worse?"

"What's that?" said the driver, pulling one of the hissing earbuds out of his head.

He was a skinny young Asian dude with a Mets flat-brim cap and a white North Face vest. He looked like a college kid.

"Nothing. I just hate this," Gannon said.

"Hate what?" he said.

"This. This city. It's a crumbling black sinkhole filled with hate and dirt and pizza rats."

"What? Come on, man. How does anyone hate the Big Apple? That's ridiculous. It's the biggest, greatest, most happening city in the world. Like where are you from, bro?"

"Here," Gannon said, staring out. "I'm from right here."

They drove for a bit then stopped again. The kid put his earbud back in, but then after a second, pulled it out again.

"If you hate it so much, why come back?"

"This is a onetime shot, believe me," Gannon said. "I had to come back. I have something to do."

"Must be something pretty important, huh?"

"Yep."

"What?"

Gannon took out his phone and looked at it stupidly for a moment then put it back into his pocket.

"I'm not really at liberty to divulge that information," he said.

"You're a real man of mystery, aren't you?"

"Buddy," Gannon said, looking out at the shark-toothed skyline. "You don't even want to know."

41

Just north of Little Italy, the icy breeze was so strong Gannon had to fight the cab door to get it open.

He'd just made the unmarked Chevy on the northeast corner of Orchard Street when its driver's door opened. The big man who got out of it smiling had shoulder-length dirty blond hair and a black leather jacket.

With his Fu Manchu and big Red Wing boots, he didn't look like a cop. He looked like a Hells Angel trying to find his lost Harley.

"Mickey, you crazy son of a bitch. Look at you. Mr. Winter Tan. You're back!" his old partner, Danny "Stick" Henrickson, said, embracing him.

"Look at me? Look at you. You look exactly the same, well, except for this," Gannon said, flicking at the dusting of white in Stick's mustache.

"Yeah, I know. It's horrible, right?" Stick said, smoothing

at his whiskers. "You know how vain I am. I was heading to Duane Reade for a new tube of Just For Men when you called."

Gannon smiled as he pounded his old linebacker-sized partner on the back. He hadn't been all that great at keeping in contact with old friends after he moved out of the city, but Stick was the exception.

"So should we sit in the car or hit a Starbucks or something?" Gannon said, shivering.

"No, no. For ancient reunions with old maniac partners, I roll out the full red carpet," Stick said. "Like the hick jacket, by the way. Are you a farmer or something now?"

Stick took out a set of keys and opened up the door of a shop across from where the Chevy was parked. Silver Mine Properties, it said on the door.

"Yeah, I'm a farmer, and you're what? Moonlighting as a broker now?" Gannon said as they came into a cozy office space with some cubicles and a reception area.

"Actually," Stick said as he clicked on a light, "my sister's new husband is the manager of the building here. The last tenant just left, so they're still trying to lease it out. I coop in the office here when I'm downtown."

"Oh, I get it now," Gannon said as he peeked in an inner office and saw the drum set.

Before the cops, Stick had his fifteen minutes of fame as a replacement drummer in Cold Iron Mine, a once famous Staten Island heavy metal band that had toured Europe.

Which actually made sense, Gannon thought, shaking his head at Stick. You had to be heavy-metal-drummer crazy to be an undercover cop.

And Stick hadn't been just any undercover cop either but one of the greatest NYPD narcotics officers of all time, Gannon knew. Though Stick looked like a big dumb white boy headbanger, his mom, a pretty Puerto Rican lady, had raised him speaking Spanglish in the Lower East Side projects. None of the dozens of Dominican dealers he put away could ever believe how well he understood what they were saying.

"You're downtown a lot now, huh, with the feds?" Gannon said. "Your last email said you were still with the JTTF, right?"

"Yeah, well, that was like seven months ago," Stick said as he locked the door. He lay back on a couch in the reception area and put his big Red Wing engineer boots up on a motorcycle magazine–covered coffee table. "I actually had me some second thoughts about it."

"I thought you were all over it."

"I was. The OT was great, but two weeks in, you wouldn't believe the bullshit, Mickey. All the politics and crazy shit. They had us following people who had nothing to do with anything, brother. I mean, it was like gumshoe shit for the politicians or something. I didn't know what the hell it was. I like to do like real cop work against, you know, dealers and crooks and killers. So now I'm back where I was before."

"Up in Midtown North?"

"No, I'm at the One Nine," Stick said proudly. "You're looking at the new detective squad coleader."

"The One Nine? The Silk Stocking District? No way!" Gannon said, grinning. "Your mom must be so proud. Drummer boy makes it to Park Avenue! Must be busy with all the drive-bys up there in rich people land, huh? Let me guess. The butler did it?"

"Ha ha. Keep laughing. You'd be surprised how busy it gets."

"Ever think of this thing, um, retirement, I think it's called, Stick? You have what? Almost thirteen hundred years in now?"

"Screw your career advice, jackass. I thought you said the next time you came back they'd be playing the bagpipes out in Brooklyn at Ascension for you."

"Yeah, I know," Gannon said quietly.

"What the hell is it anyway that makes you darken Gotham's doorstep again? The suspense is killing me."

"I won't even get into the particulars with you, man. Less you know, the better."

Stick shook his head and laughed at that.

"So what can I do for you, then?"

"It's going to sound crazy."

Stick grinned as he put his big palms together.

"Then you've come to the right place, brother."

"There's a guy on the internet on YouTube. His name's Wheldon. Eric Wheldon. He's an alternative news independent reporter. Ever hear of him?"

Stick looked at him strangely.

"Wheldon? Who? No."

"He walks around the city. Talks about government stuff?"

"You're trying to contact some conspiracy theory guy?"

"Yes," Gannon said, taking out his phone and showing him a screenshot. "This is the guy. His name's Eric Wheldon. I know you know everybody. I was hoping you would know somebody who knows him."

Because of his legendary undercover status, Stick knew virtually every cop, FBI agent, DEA agent and district attorney from Yonkers to Suffolk County. In addition to a few Yankees and half the cast of the TV show *Law & Order*, where he used to moonlight as security.

"Ever consider emailing him?" Stick said. "Saves on the hotel and airfare."

"I did," Gannon said. "Several times. But he doesn't answer. This is pretty important. I really need to talk to him. Like now."

Stick squinted as he tapped at his mustache with a knuckle.

"I actually know a few computer nerds in the department that might be of some use. You need to sit down with this guy pronto, huh? Is this about aliens or something? Ancient aliens maybe? On your new farm? No, wait. I got it. Crop circles."

"Stick, I just need your help, okay? I didn't come back up here because I miss the dirty snow. It's important. I'm begging you to help me contact this guy."

"Okay. Relax. Relax. Just wondering."

Stick winked as he took his cell phone out of the leather jacket.

"You just sit back and watch the master at work, Mickey, my boy," he said. "Your wish is my command."

42

At only a little over two hundred flight miles from Washington, DC, to New York City, it took the unmarked government Gulfstream twenty-one minutes tarmac to tarmac to land Reyland and his men at New Jersey's Teterboro Airport.

At five after three in the afternoon, they disembarked into the gray and cold and transferred everything off the sleek white jet into the three black Ford Expedition SUVs waiting along the open tarmac side fence.

By 3:10, they were on the Jersey Turnpike eastbound with all the traffic heading into the city. But they didn't head into the city. Right as the traffic began backing up before the Holland Tunnel, the three dark vehicles swerved onto the litter-strewn shoulder one after the other.

Down at the end of a battered off-ramp was a stop sign they blew past into an industrial area called Kearny. Huge chemical tanks went by on their left. A transmission tower. A looming dark steel railroad bridge.

When they came around a bend, a CSX freight train double stacked with rusty shipping containers was rolling out in the opposite direction.

Getting out, Reyland thought, smiling.

While the getting was still good.

A hundred yards farther south down this godforsaken road, the convoy of tinted-windowed vehicles slowed. The potholed drive they pulled onto had a tall razor-wired fence gate across it with a rusted sign that said KEEP OUT New Jersey State DOT.

Reyland's driver zipped down the window. He fished into his pocket as Reyland listened to the terrific ocean-like roar from the rushing traffic on the turnpike above. Then the driver finally laid his electronic passkey to the fob reader and the rusty gate slid sideways with a rattle and a buzz.

Beyond the gate were salt sheds and stacks of cement highway barriers and columns of road plows that they quickly skimmed past on their way toward a half-dozen construction trailers and shipping containers that were set up in a horseshoe pattern at the truck yard's rear.

Reyland stared at the bristle of satellite dishes and cell tower masts rising from the huge trailers' roofs.

Port New York Center 11, as the site was officially known, was one of the very first federal-to-local law enforcement fusion centers set up in the scramble after 9/11.

He had actually attended the not-so-publicized ribbon-cutting ceremony with Dunning and the former FBI director almost fifteen years before.

Up the stairs and through the door of the huge center trailer a moment later, it looked like a war room. There were columns and rows of desks and computers everywhere.

Reyland looked at the huge screen that took up the entirety of the back wall. It was divided up into smaller ones that showed street traffic and various locales. One screen showed New York City's Central Park. On another was Kennedy International Airport.

Center 11 usually had an alphabet soup of JTTF, FBI field agents, NYPD, Port Authority cops and New Jersey state troopers manning it. But today it was staffed with a small group of hand-selected counter-intel agents and contractors for a special covert counterterror training exercise.

Or at least that was what Reyland was describing it as in the official report.

Reyland turned as Emerson brought over a tall balding Hispanic guy wearing steel-rimmed glasses.

"Robert, you know Agent Arietta, right?" Emerson said.

"Of course. Edgar, how are you?" Reyland said, putting out his hand to the lanky Hispanic.

Arietta, who was rumored to be somewhat autistic, didn't even glance at it or him as he called out, "Bring up array one."

The patchwork grid of screens instantly morphed into one big screen that showed the parking lot of a small brick building on a suburban street somewhere.

"Okay. This is Eric Wheldon's apartment building in Pelham, Westchester," Arietta said.

"Where did Wheldon work again?" Reyland said.

"He rode a Middle East desk at Langley," Emerson said.

"Is that right?" Reyland said. "I wonder how much he's going to like getting rode in a Leavenworth mop closet after we get through with him."

"We've been on it since four in the morning," Arietta continued. "We were about to pop in for a peek around five when he came home alone with no girl. But the good news is we were able to get this with a shotgun mic through the crack in a window."

"Okay. I can meet him tonight if it's legit," came a voice over the overhead speaker. "Okay. Okay. Get me a number. I'll call him back with the location."

"What's that supposed to mean?" Reyland said.

"It means he's meeting up with someone tonight," Arietta said. "The New York office has been watching this joker on and off since his last leak came out at the *Washington Post*. We've been watching him for the last three months. Whenever he meets with people, it's usually one of three locations."

Arietta went to a keyboard and the screen suddenly changed into three side-by-side views of the city.

"Here at the Roosevelt Island Tram on the East Side," Arietta said, pointing. "Or this diner here on Tenth Avenue in Chelsea or this hotel here down from Madison Square Garden."

Reyland looked up at the already-congested pre–rush hour New York City vistas, the crush of cars, the stressed-looking people. The resolution of the images was remarkable. It was like he was standing in the flat-screen section of a Best Buy.

"These camera angles seem high. Traffic cameras, right? Are these live feeds?" Reyland said.

"Yes, it's called the 3RT Retina system," Arietta said, heading over to a keyboard. "It's brand-new. We just got it patched into the traffic cameras a month ago. Watch this."

Arietta went over and clicked some more keys. All of a sudden, red computer-generated squares appeared around the license plates of the cars and on the faces of people in the crowd. The squares followed along with the moving subjects as driver's licenses began to appear along the bottom of the screen. One after another after another.

Reyland looked in shock at the smiling driver's license faces that began to line up along the bottom of the screen. The computer was ID'ing everyone, he realized. He felt a fluttery feeling in his stomach as he watched.

"This is live?" Reyland said. "In real time. You're picking all this up live? And ID'ing everyone live? I've never seen this."

"It's the new video analytics platform coupled with the latest in facial recognition. We have the software tapped into that new Cray at the DOE at Oakridge. They just put it online. With our full trunk-to-block fiber-optic linkup, the speed of the processing is mind-blowing. We're talking two hundred petaflops, which is the equivalent—"

Reyland put up a hand.

"Yeah, uh-huh. It's quick and powerful. Great," Reyland said. "Bottom line, if our little navy friend shows her face in one of these locations, we got her?"

"Her face is already in the system," Arietta said with a nod. "If she shows her face, the computer will know in a fraction of a second."

"Ruiz, what do you think in terms of a setup?" Reyland said.

The short, stocky mercenary stepped forward. He'd been watching everything silently from near the rear of the room among his contingent of men. He pursed his lips and squinted his eyes as he slowly looked from one location on the screen to the next.

"Let's get some printouts of these locales," he finally said. "And we'll take a look-see."

43

Gannon got off the train at Pennsylvania Station at 6:45 p.m. and walked through some corridors and came up a set of stairs onto cold Seventh Avenue. On the dark sidewalk in front of Madison Square Garden there were incredible crowds of commuters, and he had to wade against the flow of the massive herd of them to get to the avenue's east side.

The Arlington Hotel that Stick had told him to go to was halfway down 31st, sandwiched between a luxury wig importer and a shuttered Chinese restaurant called Bamboo Lucky 21. He was a little early, so he passed it and walked the rest of the block over to Sixth Avenue.

He stood there on the corner in the steady rush-hour flow of people. He stepped aside for an Asian woman pushing a double stroller as an ambulance with a blaring siren slowly carved a path through the blocked-up intersection.

Across the street, he watched a messenger chaining up his

bike to a bus stop sign pole. Watching the man bend to secure the lock, Gannon immediately picked up the flat bulge in his jeans back pocket that he knew was a box cutter.

He blew into his cupped hands, grinning in the cold as he thought about his previous life as a beat cop. He had actually loved foot posts. Being a sheepdog out among the sheep looking for the wolves.

After another five minutes, he crossed the street and went back up to the old hotel. He thought it would be crummy inside, but the lobby looked newly redone. There was dramatic diffused lighting and maroon-colored wallpaper and a minimalist chunk of pale limestone for a check-in desk.

The pretty young woman behind it had some kind of Rosie the Riveter retro thing going on with her dark hair. She smiled at Gannon as he sat in a chrome Euro-style chair opposite the desk.

He took out his phone and looked at it and watched it trill as it changed the hour.

"This is Eric Wheldon," a voice said.

"Mr. Smith here," Gannon said. "The Arlington, right?"

"Yes. You have some information for me?"

"Yes."

"What's it about?" he said.

"Is it safe to talk on the phone?" Gannon said, looking at the desk clerk. "I thought we would talk face-to-face."

"It's safe," the voice said.

"It's about Dunning," Gannon said quietly. "He didn't die in Italy."

"Many people are speculating that."

"I'm not speculating. I know," Gannon said.

"Interesting," said Wheldon, unimpressed.

"I saw him with my own eyes."

"Saw him?"

"I actually touched him—his corpse, anyway," Gannon said.

"I would love to believe you, Mr. Smith, but in my business, I need proof. All I have is my reputation for truth. Without proof, I cannot use your information."

"I can prove it."

"How?"

"I have a videotape of Dunning dead. As well as the others."

"The others?"

"Yes. There were six dead altogether. Including the pilots."

"Where is this tape?"

"We should talk face-to-face," Gannon said.

There was a pause.

"Then turn around," Eric Wheldon said.

44

The elevator and the hallway were nicely done like the lobby, but the room itself up on the fourteenth floor had faded beige walls and cheap gray office carpet and Walmart furniture. Gannon looked at the old radiator under the yellow-shaded window opposite the door. It looked like a public school classroom with a bed in it.

"We can talk in here, Mr. Smith," Wheldon said, opening an inside door on the left.

The suite's side room had a table and chairs and a little kitchenette in it. Beyond the table was the bathroom.

"Please call me Pete," Gannon said as he sat at the small table.

"Okay, Pete," the reporter said, sitting down opposite.

Wheldon seemed smaller in person than on his videos and his eyes were bluer. He was in the same nice overcoat he was wearing in the video where he was walking up Park Avenue.

"Now, before we get into this, how comfortable are you about disclosing your identity?" Wheldon said.

"Extremely uncomfortable," Gannon said.

"Okay, so I'll hold off taping," he said. "Now, where did you see Dunning?"

"I saw him on a Gulfstream 550 corporate jet that went down fifteen miles north of Little Abaco in the Bahamas," Gannon said. "They said it was a turboprop plane on the news, but that was completely made up."

"How did you see it?"

"I was out marlin fishing on my boat by myself, and I saw it go down and rip in two."

"Was it on fire or something? What was wrong with it?"

"No, it came in almost gliding very low to the water. I'm not an expert, but I think it had run out of gas."

"Go on," Wheldon said.

"I was right on top of it when it ripped into the water, and I rushed over and saw that the front of it had snapped off and sunk down on a coral shelf. I run a diving business, so I suited up and went down to see if there were any survivors.

"I saw Dunning there inside the plane. He was with two other white guys, one older, one younger. They looked like agents maybe. There was also a fortysomething-looking black guy in a hoodie and jeans as well as two uniformed pilots. They were all dead. As in already dead. Their faces were blue like they had suffocated or something."

"Did you report this?"

"No," Gannon said, shaking his head. "I didn't know it was Dunning until I saw his picture in the paper yesterday morning."

"No, I mean the crash itself. You didn't call anyone when you saw the plane go down?"

"No."

"Why not?"

Gannon looked at him.

"Well, I tried to radio it in at first, but my boat radio antenna was busted. Then I...found the money."

"Money?" Wheldon said, squinting.

"Yes. Diamonds and money. In a suitcase. There were several million dollars in one-hundred-dollar bills and a mother lode of uncut diamonds."

The reporter's calm composure evaporated. His mouth gaped open as he sat up.

"Listen, I know it was wrong," Gannon said. "And I'm regretting it now, believe me. I should have immediately turned it in. And I would have. But no one came. I was out there for an hour, and there wasn't a soul. I had no idea the damn US government was involved. I thought they were all a bunch of dead dopers or something, so I thought why not exit stage left? No harm no foul."

"This money and diamonds," Wheldon said, staring at him with his intense blue eyes. "You still have them?"

"Yes."

"Both?"

"Both," Gannon said. "It was stupid of me. Say the word, and I'll go get them and give them back. I'll do whatever to get this crazy bullshit to stop. That's why I'm here. I want to make this right. Lying about the death of the FBI director is bananas. Just bananas. They can't get away with it. I won't let them. That's unacceptable. People need to know the truth."

"Where is everything?"

"Back in the Bahamas. I hid everything along with the GoPro footage I took from my dive."

Eric Wheldon stared at him with a dumbfounded look.

"This video. You can tell it's Dunning? Clear video?"

Gannon nodded.

"I can't believe this. Is it somewhere secure?"

Gannon thought of the ridge in the pitch-black, unmarked submerged cave a hundred feet underground.

"Yeah, you could say that. Like I said, I had no idea it was the FBI director until I saw his picture in the *Times* yesterday morning."

"I can't believe this," the reporter said again.

"That makes two of us, buddy," Gannon said. "Now it's your turn. What in the green world of God is going on?"

45

"It was a whisper jet," the reporter said.

"A what?" Gannon said.

"A whisper jet. Tell me, were there any numbers or letters on the tail of the plane?"

"I don't remember."

"How about on the jet engines? Sometimes Gulfstream puts the ID tag number on the engines."

Gannon thought about the giant white fishing bob he'd seen.

"No, there was nothing on them."

"That's why they call it a whisper jet. National secrecy and security. It flies anywhere, and no one knows who or, in this case, what's on it. The plane that went down was probably the FBI director's personal jet."

"No! The FBI director gets his own private rock-star jet? A Gulfstream?"

"Oh, but of course. Not just any kind either. An air force

model with aftermarket add-ons like radar jamming. The attorney general has one as well. The least we could do is have our sworn protectors live as large as possible. It's only taxpayer money after all, right?"

"They can do that? Fly around without markings, jamming radar? Aren't there rules?"

"Sure there are. For everybody but the people who make them. Or in this case, claim to be enforcing them. You read the news today? You hear about Messerly?"

"Messerly?"

"The new NSA defector leaker guy stuck at the embassy in Europe."

"Oh, yeah. Messerly. I remember him. From last year, right? The new Assange. What about him?"

"They just blocked all his social media accounts this morning. Just flat-out blocked them. Said he was too hateful. The single greatest whistle-blower of all time who's trying to expose the illegal surveillance of the entire global population is too hateful? They apparently own the social media companies as well as the mainstream media now. They can do anything they want."

"I don't understand," Gannon said.

"Could you excuse me for one second? I need to make a phone call."

"That depends. Who are you calling?"

"It's okay. A source. I just want to confirm something. Just give me a second, okay?"

Wheldon left the room. Gannon could hear him talking in a low voice. He let out a breath and stared at the grimy bargain hotel room. At the little oven, at the half-open bathroom door. He wondered if coming here was actually a good idea.

"You're right, Pete," Wheldon said as he returned and sat down. "Dunning's plane isn't at its usual hangar at Joint Base Bolling in DC. It never returned from Italy. Not only that, there are rumors that it never actually landed in Aviano Air Base in Italy like it was scheduled to."

"What do you make of that?" Gannon said.

Wheldon shook his head.

"I'm trying to grasp all this," he said. "Dunning's supposed to go to Italy but doesn't arrive. Then there's the diamonds. Uncut diamonds. Sounds like Africa. Has to be. Blood diamonds probably."

"You've lost me," Gannon said.

"This is what I think," Wheldon said. "I think Dunning was running what they call a rat line. Basically, it's smuggling using diplomatic cover. They used them in World War II to get the Nazis out of Germany into South America. They've been using them since probably forever to smuggle drugs or stolen valuables. Whatever you want to wherever you want. Hide it in the diplomatic bag. It's one of the oldest tricks in the book."

"But in America? I don't buy it. The FBI director? You're saying he's secretly a smuggler?"

"That's exactly what I'm saying. I bet the stones from the plane are blood diamonds out of Sierra Leone or the Ivory Coast. Instead of Italy, Dunning went there. I wouldn't be surprised if Dunning was facilitating an arms deal."

"An arms deal?"

Wheldon nodded.

"In the interim between when he was deputy director and director, he was counsel for one of the nation's biggest defense companies. Since it's illegal to sell guns to these rebel groups, they love to use untraceable diamonds."

"Like a secret cash-for-clunkers deal?" Gannon said.

"Exactly. Only in this case, it's diamonds for land mines or maybe attack helicopters. But on the way back, something went wrong with the plane and now their ass is hanging in the breeze."

"That's crazy," Gannon said. "That only happens in the movies."

Wheldon shook his head.

"What do you think makes this world go round, Pete? Truth, justice and the American way?"

"Yes," Gannon said.

"Lucky you," Wheldon said, letting out a breath. "It's power, Pete. Power."

46

Gannon made a pained face.

"So they've just gone crazy? At the top? At the FBI? Full-tilt corrupt?"

Wheldon nodded.

"Bought and paid for. An organization is only as good as the people in it, Pete. You ever hear of a dirty cop when you were on the force?"

Gannon squinted at him.

"On the force?" Gannon said, making a puzzled face. "What do you mean? You think I'm a cop?"

"Let's see," Wheldon said. "Face like the map of Ireland, voice like a Yankee announcer and you actually want to return several million dollars of loot you found while fishing out on your boat. Is it such a crazy guess?"

"No comment," Gannon said.

"Anyway," Wheldon said. "The combination of the global

money and influence and no one checking up on them is like nothing ever before seen on the planet. Now you add the technology, the NSA collection of all the global communication data, and now they have a trove of information and blackmail on virtually everyone."

"The NSA collection of what?"

"You need to get out more, Pete. Since one month after 9/11, the NSA has been collecting everybody's electronic sweet nothings and storing them in their computers for a rainy day. It was supposed to be just for checking on the terrorists, but now they don't give a rat's ass about the law. They're using it against everyone. A blackmail Fort Knox.

"And you can't think of the FBI in terms of being a domestic law enforcement agency anymore. After they signed the Patriot Act, the FBI joined the CIA. Almost all of the alphabet soup agencies are now under the same umbrella."

"Like Big Pharma and Big Tobacco, we've got Big Intelligence now?" Gannon said.

"Exactly."

"That can't be right. There must be something in the Constitution, no? Where's the outrage? Why the hell isn't the press doing anything? Isn't that their job?"

"Pete, pay attention. Most media companies are multinational corporations, too. Everybody has secrets, Pete. All you need is a little dirt on some top key people in each of the media outlets, and every story you want tanked gets tanked."

Gannon looked at him.

"Okay, so while I went out fishing, my country apparently turned into one massive corrupt racket. Now what? What do we do now?"

Wheldon drummed his fingers on the table.

"I think there's someone you should meet. She told me the same story you just told me. Well, not exactly the same. But it all fits."

"She?"

"Yes. She's a navy lieutenant, an accident investigator who was sent out to the plane crash site before the cover-up started. At the site, she met a coast guard diver who showed her the video he had filmed of the inside of the plane. That's why when you told me there were six people, I knew you were legit. She told me the same thing last night."

"So there's another video?"

"No. She doesn't have it. She just saw it. And the diver who filmed it is missing now. The FBI tried to grab her down in Florida as well, but she was just able to get away."

"Holy crap. This is real. A full-scale cover-up. This is really happening."

"You said it. Which is why I'd like to interview the both of you and upload it onto my channel."

Gannon sat up straighter in his chair.

"Now, hold up. I don't want to be on a video."

"Don't worry," Wheldon said. "I won't show your face or anything, and I can mask your voice. I could bring her here and talk to her in the bedroom, and you can stay in this room here so you don't even have to see each other."

"That's how it works? Just put it out there? Shouldn't we get my GoPro tape first?"

"No, the more visible the faster the better. The more visible the less likely they'll target you for elimination. If the truth of Dunning's death is out there, their mission will shift from plugging the leak to spin-doctoring the news narrative. Putting you six feet under after the truth is exposed will make less sense for them."

"Say that last part again?"

Wheldon stared at him steadily.

"There is no organization more deadly than a covert intelligence service. A politician tells a group of government workers to work hand in hand with violent military men to do unaccountable things in secret. Outside of the light of scrutiny, these men are told to eliminate people or to sell arms to foreign militaries. Without inventory or receipts. Without any way to check up on them.

"The National Security Division of the Justice Department is not allowed to be inspected, we are told, because the inspectors don't have the intelligence clearance. You see the problem here? What do you think happens?"

Gannon shook his head.

"We need to do this now, Pete," Wheldon said. "The more hits we get, the better our chance of exposing this corruption to the public."

"You think this will go viral?"

"It should, Pete," Wheldon said, wide-eyed. "This is the biggest bombshell I've ever heard."

47

For how on the ball and techy Agent Arietta seemed, his bare windowless trailer office looked like something out of one of those cable shows about hoarders.

It had a cheap white plastic folding table for a desk and a couple of old gray metal file cabinets in the right-hand far corner. Instead of having a computer, the desk was covered in a mountain of paper, and in the corner opposite the metal cabinets was a big plastic trash barrel filled to the brim with greasy take-out containers and Dunkin' cups.

Reyland was sitting at the paper-covered desk reading the file on Eric Wheldon's daughter away at William & Mary when Emerson popped his head in.

"Boss, we got something."

When Reyland went back into the war room, the lobby of the Arlington Hotel was blown up on the big wall screen. He gazed up at the gold-lit sconces on its brown walls and the people standing by the white marble check-in desk. The feed was coming from one of their agents who'd gone in with a pin camera.

"What's up?"

"The girl on the right. Brown hair. Might be her," Emerson said.

Reyland walked over closer and looked up at a girl in profile there at the check-in desk. He studied the photo that the surveillance team had taken of Ruby Everett in Times Square the day before.

"Didn't the outside camera with the facial recognition see her?" Reyland said.

"Well, actually, only if she came in walking from the Seventh Avenue intersection where the camera is," Arietta said. "If she got out of a taxi in front of the hotel, it's probably too far for the camera to see."

"Now you tell me," Reyland said, rolling his eyes at Mr. Geek Squad.

"What do you think?" Emerson said.

Reyland made a sour face as he stared back at the screen.

"I don't know," he said. "Same eye shape, same nose, but the video quality is garbage. It's too hard to tell. Tell them to get closer."

"You need to get closer," Emerson said into his phone.

They waited. The live feed camera wobbled and swung around the other side of the target.

"Wait a second, Arietta. What the hell are we doing?" Reyland said. "Can't you get this feed into your damn supercomputer ID software to tell us if it's her?"

"Yes, of course. I didn't think of that. Give me a second," he said.

If you want something done, you have to do it yourself, Reyland thought, rolling his eyes again.

He placed his hands behind his back as he watched the target head for the elevator. She was pressing the button when she turned, and the red computer box appeared around her face.

"Okay. We're linked into the computer now. Matching up," Arietta said as the door rolled open, and the woman got on.

"Should they follow her? Get in the elevator?" asked Emerson.

"No. Hold up, hold up. Don't spook her. Take it easy," Reyland said.

The elevator door had just closed when a ping came from Arietta's laptop.

Then Reyland smiled as Ruby Everett's military ID appeared up on the screen as clear as day.

48

Ruby came out of the elevator onto the fourteenth floor into a hallway that smelled like weed and furniture polish. As the elevator door rolled closed behind her, she took out her phone. She checked the room number on the text Wheldon had sent her against the plastic plaque on the wall. Then she made a left down the dark-walled hallway.

She'd just been dropped off by Eric's friend Rebecca. She'd crashed at Rebecca's apartment in Inwood the night before, and her hostess had explained that she had worked with Eric in the CIA when she was younger.

Since then, she'd put up several of Eric's whistle-blowers as they came into town. There were more and more these days, she'd said.

Ruby counted the doors. Making a turn at the far corner of the narrow corridor, she suddenly heard the pornographic sound of a woman coming from somewhere.

She shook her head as she zipped her fleece hoodie up to her chin. She still wasn't sure about any of this. About being up in New York. About going underground like some kind of anti-government nut.

Under normal circumstances, she liked to consider herself a good citizen. She always honestly paid her taxes, always voted, always went to jury duty whenever she was called.

She would have gladly turned herself in to the FBI to work this all out, she thought as she came to the end of the sleazy hall, if it weren't for the fact that it seemed to be the FBI itself that was the problem.

14H was the very last door of all. It opened as she was about to ring its doorbell.

"If it isn't Mrs. Smith," Wheldon said. *"Entrez-vous?"*

The room inside was large but drab. Besides the bed and desk, there were two chairs, one just beside the door and another at the foot of the bed facing the desk. On the desk, there was a smartphone in a little tripod with its camera pointed at the bed.

"I thought you said you weren't going to film me," Ruby said, looking warily at the phone as Wheldon locked the door.

"Don't worry. I'm not. Cross my heart," Eric said. "You're going to sit here by the door. I'm going to sit in the chair in front of the bed with the camera taping just me the whole time. I promise."

Wheldon thumbed at an almost-closed door on the room's left-hand wall.

"Now if I could direct your attention, Mrs. Smith. Like I texted you, there's a man in the sitting room who's also going to be part of this conversation. We'll call him Mr. Smith. Say hello, Mr. Smith."

"Hello," said a man's voice through the crack in the door.

"This is weird," Ruby said, wincing at the almost-closed door. "Honestly, I don't know, Eric. I don't even know if I should do this."

"I know. You're right," Wheldon said. "All of this is an incredibly silly way to do anything. Unfortunately, these are some desperate times we're living in, aren't they? And if we want to get back to a semblance of sanity and normalcy and justice for our families and kids, it's up to regular people like us to do the job.

"Because the FBI apparently isn't in the fidelity and bravery and integrity business anymore, is it? Or even the mainstream media when you consider how they're covering everything up. I think it's important that more and more people know that. But with that said, I can't and won't force you. You're free to go whenever you want."

Ruby sighed.

"You'll disguise my voice like you said?" Ruby said.

"Of course," Wheldon said. "Your own mother won't know it's you once I get done editing."

"Okay, fine," Ruby said, finally sitting in the chair by the door.

Wheldon took his seat.

"We're going to keep it casual and just talk like we've been doing," Wheldon said. "Nothing fancy. I'll ask you guys questions and you answer them to the best of your ability, okay? I just need to set up my laptop, and we'll be ready. Sound good? We're all on the same page?"

"Okay," said Ruby.

"Okay," said Mr. Smith through the crack in the door.

49

Outside in the fusion center's truck yard, the MH-6 helicopter's red running lights pulsed like a campfire ember against the dark.

In the high nails-on-chalkboard turbo whine, Ruiz adjusted his butt on the chopper's ice-cold exterior running board bench and gave a last tug on his safety harness. Then he gave a knock on the curved glass canopy, and he and his men were up, up and away with their feet dangling off the helicopter's skids into the pitch-black freezing open January air.

Ruiz felt his stomach get left behind as the aircraft went out from under the turnpike overpass. Still gaining altitude, they skimmed smoothly up over a traffic-filled road, over a junkyard, then over a river.

On the river's other side was a lightless golf course, and as they turned to the left north over Hoboken, the magnificent sparkling sprawl of Manhattan's night skyline came into view.

Ruiz looked at the lights in the high black towers, the water of the Hudson below them like a plain of brushed steel.

"Look, Paw. Them building scrapers are even bigger than our silo," one of Ruiz's commandos said in a hick drawl.

"Can it, Boyer," Ruiz said.

"Less than ten," the pilot called over the comm link.

Ruiz smiled around the chaw of chewing tobacco in his mouth as they choppered east at about the height of the observation deck of the Empire State Building.

He actually loved this shit. He had always been a daredevil. He was from the South Side of Chicago and used to train-surf the Loop along with his ghetto buds when he was a kid. Twelve years old, speeding out in the cold, holding on for dear life at the curves.

Faster than a speeding bullet, he thought, chuckling as he spit. *Able to leap tall buildings in a single bound.*

There was another crackle on the comm line as they flew over a tourist boat on the Hudson a thousand feet below.

"Where now? That circular building?" the pilot called out.

"That's it," Ruiz said, looking down at Madison Square Garden between his legs as they approached it.

"Why do they call it a square garden when it's a damn concrete circle?" the pilot said.

"Beats the shit out of me," Ruiz said, spitting down at the boat. "Remember, go in high then drop down to about thirty or so midbuilding at the back."

"Hover above the alley in between. Got it, bro. I can see it now."

Ruiz looked down at the old gray brick hotel as they swung downward toward it. He would have loved a fixed position shot at a distance, but Room 14H was in the back opposite a windowless warehouse. At least the FLIR body heat infrared scope on his rifle would be sharp as a razor out here in this cold.

They went even faster as they lost some altitude.

The comm line crackled again.

"Okay, we're a minute now. One minute."

Ruiz held up a finger to his three men beside him on the skids in the buffeting wind like an infielder reminding his teammates that it was one out.

The pilot glanced at Ruiz through the bubble of glass between them and gave him a Tom Cruise smile.

"You guys do realize you're all out of your minds, right?" he said.

The wind snapped at the cloth of Ruiz's black tactical pants as he tugged at the harness and the rappelling rope.

"Just keep the black egg in the air," Ruiz said as he clicked his M4's selector off Safe with his gloved thumb.

50

"Okay. Hello, everybody. Welcome to the latest. What is this episode? Number 352, I believe," Gannon heard Eric Wheldon saying.

Gannon sat there in the side room beside the slightly cracked-open door, fidgeting in his kitchen chair. Even though it wasn't TV and his voice would be disguised, and it wasn't even live, he was still nervous about saying something stupid and screwing it up. A memory of being an altar boy came to him. Standing next to the priest, wide-eyed up on the bright altar with the eyes of the entire parish staring at him waiting for him to trip over his feet.

"Tonight," Wheldon said, "I have a really great info drop for all of you that relates to your favorite new subject and mine. The oh-so-mysterious death of—"

In the suite's little sitting room, Gannon sat up in his chair waiting for Eric to continue.

Then there was a heavy thump through the crack in the door.

"Eric?" he heard the Mrs. Smith woman say. "ERRIICC!"

Gannon went to the door and pulled it open and saw the screaming Mrs. Smith down on the carpet. Eric Wheldon was down on his back beside her with the back of his neatly combed head half gone and the scarlet mush of the inside of it dumped out on the floor.

Even over the woman's screaming, Gannon suddenly heard a slight yet distinct sound in the air on his left.

He'd heard it before.

It was the soft yet unforgettable slight click that a high velocity bullet made when it just missed you.

"Down, down, down!" Gannon yelled and immediately dropped to the carpet as the window above the radiator came in with a crashing rain of glass.

A muffled clatter of silenced automatic fire made a constellation of ripping holes grow across the yellow shade as Gannon crawled low alongside the bed. He reached out and seized the screaming navy lieutenant by the back of her plaid shirt, and she screamed even louder as he yanked her around the other side of the bed away from the window.

A corner of the bed's headboard exploded into toothpicks as he dived with her into the sitting room. As they landed, a dotted line of bullets popped instantly through the Sheetrock wall just above them. Gannon kicked closed the door. Then he flipped the cheap table and propped it against the wall with his back.

In the next room outside the broken window, Gannon could hear the high turbo whine of a helicopter hovering close above the hotel. Then he heard a sound at the window itself. Something was smashing at the glass.

It was a boot! Gannon realized.

Holy shit! There was somebody at the damn window! They must have been on a rappelling rope or something. They were coming in!

Gannon folded into the fetal position as the gun started up again blowing more holes through the wall. Bullets whined and pinged off the small two-burner stove across the room.

Gannon suddenly stared at the stove. He quickly crawled over and turned up the two gas burners as high as they would go. More bullets burst in through the shower tile as he speed-crawled low into the bathroom. He grabbed toilet paper rolls from under the sink and some towels and crawled back out.

The paper wrapper on the rolls caught immediately as he threw all of it up onto the clicking blue-flame stove burners. Then one of the towels began to burn.

The hotel fire alarm that went off a split second later was unspeakably deafening. There were two earsplitting blasts of what sounded like a circus clown slide whistle and then a recording began shouting.

"THE SOURCE OF THE ALARM SIGNAL YOU ARE HEARING IS NOW BEING INVESTIGATED. THE SOURCE OF THE ALARM SIGNAL YOU ARE HEARING IS NOW BEING INVESTIGATED."

As the siren blast whooped twice again, Gannon glanced over and saw that all of the towels were burning now. He crawled over and grabbed one and opened the door into the bedroom. Keeping low, he thrust the burning towel under the edge of the bedspread and set it alight. It caught up immediately in a horrid chemical stink, and there was immediate thick black smoke. He threw another burning towel onto the desk.

When the bed was going pretty good, he peeked out around the burning bottom of it. The entire end of the room by the shattered window was covered in smoke, and the wall behind the desk was catching fire.

Gannon got to his knees, coughing, and grabbed the metal frame of the bed and hurled the whole burning mess of it up and at the window. Then he reached into the sitting room and grabbed the young woman by the hand.

He thought he was certainly going to get shot in the back as they leaped over the murdered reporter a split second later.

But the bullets didn't come, and Gannon got the front door flung open, and they were out in the hallway with the black smoke chasing behind them.

51

They ran down the hall in the terrifying alarm squeal. Very confused-looking people were standing in some of the doorways of the other rooms.

"What the hell is going on?" said one of them, an old hairy guy in a bathrobe.

"The hotel's on fire! Run!" Gannon yelled as he dodged past him around a corner.

On the other side of it was a pretty thirtysomething woman standing beside the stairwell doorway.

In midstride, Gannon registered three things about her almost simultaneously.

She had fear in her face. There was a phone in one of her hands and a semiautomatic pistol in the other.

Gannon didn't break stride as he let go of the navy lieutenant's hand. Instead, he tucked down his shoulder and hit the armed woman a lick at the upper chest that leveled her off her feet and sent both of them into the stairwell and down the stairs.

Gannon rode the woman down the stairs like a toboggan and landed his two-twenty hard on top of her at the bottom of the half-flight floor. As he got up, he could see that the nice-looking honey blond–haired woman wasn't holding anything now and her face was showing pure shock. She was gasping and staring at where one of her broken left forearm bones was sticking up between her elbow and wrist, almost through the skin.

Gannon saw her phone there on the concrete beside her, and he stomped it with his new construction boot in a shatter of plastic and then lifted her fallen gun.

It was a Smith & Wesson stainless-steel .45, the single-stack stippled beavertail grip small in his big hand. He racked the slide and saw that there wasn't even a round in the chamber. Gannon checked the eight-round magazine with a click and put one in the pipe with another. Then he cocked the bobbed hammer all the way back with his calloused thumb as he tucked it into his waistband.

He went back up the stairs into the corridor. For a split second, he gave serious thought to returning to the burning hotel room and killing the son of a bitch in the window who'd murdered Wheldon. Instead, he grabbed the navy lieutenant's hand again and brought her down past the fallen woman.

The alarm was still clown whistling, and there was a pandemonium of people in the lobby when they arrived downstairs two and a half minutes later. Without looking at anyone, Gannon led them behind the empty check-in desk into the back. There were some desks and cubicles there and an emergency fire door in the corner with a push bar that Gannon immediately kicked open.

The eggbeater churning of the low-hovering helicopter above

them was incredibly loud as they came out into the garbage alley on the east side of the building.

Then Gannon pushed through another gate, and they were out on 31st Street in the cold air, heading east down the sidewalk toward Sixth Avenue, running as fast as they could.

52

Reyland, in the fusion center, stood before the war room screen in a frozen rictus of wide-eyed baffled rage. On the screen above, smoke was pouring into what looked like a stairwell as a voice repeated, "The source of the alarm signal you are hearing is now being investigated. The source of the alarm signal you are hearing is now being investigated."

"Emerson, you said we had a team on the floor."

"We did," Emerson said, typing into one phone as he cradled another with his shoulder and chin, "but they split up to cover both sides."

"Who's down?"

"Sanderson."

"You put a rookie there on this!" Reyland yelled.

"No, you did, Reyland," Emerson said, glaring at him. "I told you she wasn't ready for our New York team, but she's your buddy the senator's niece!"

Reyland stood there infuriated. He looked back up at the screen. You could hear feet running somewhere in the distance, the sound of pounding.

"Fire! Fire! Fire!" someone yelled as an unseen door boomed open and closed followed by the bedeviled clown whistle again.

"Which one of you assholes did it?" Reyland yelled into the comm link on the desk speakerphone.

"What was that?" Ruiz yelled over the rotor thump.

"Who set the hotel on fire? Did I tell you to burn the place down?"

"It wasn't us. It was the target," Ruiz said over the rotor roar.

"Wheldon?"

"No, he's down," Ruiz said. "The other one. The guy. He lit the room up after we popped Wheldon. Then he dipped with the girl."

"What guy? There's a guy? Who?" Reyland screamed. "Where's the girl? Where's Everett?"

"She's with the guy who set the room on fire. They made it out onto 31st heading east."

"Arietta, what the hell is that drone for? Get me eyes on that street!"

"On it, on it," Arietta said.

The screen changed to show the intersection of 31st Street and Sixth Avenue. A man and a woman were rounding the corner turning left, running north up the west-side sidewalk of Sixth Avenue.

The camera zoomed in.

The woman had brown hair.

"Ruiz, get that bird over Sixth Avenue. We see them. They're heading north toward 32nd."

They watched as the couple ran diagonally through the intersection on 32nd Street into a little park.

Reyland slapped a palm down on a desk as they suddenly disappeared under some leafless trees.

"Where the hell did they go?"

"Shit," said Emerson, now standing by a laptop. "They went down some subway stairs into a station."

"No, wait. 32nd and Sixth. That's not the subway. That's the PATH train entrance, isn't it? The Jersey train?" Arietta said.

Emerson clicked at the keyboard.

"Double shit. It's both. There's a corridor that leads to the PATH train and another one a block long that leads to the subway."

"Where the hell is our team from the hotel? Get them over there!" Reyland yelled.

"Wait, wait. No, this is a good thing. We have this… I'm patching in… We have a link to the MTA CCTV system," Arietta said.

The big screen changed to show a tremendous grid of cameras, and Arietta brought up a screen of a platform with the commuter PATH train.

"I don't see them," he said.

"Gee, Arietta, I guess they're not headed out to the Jersey Shore in January. Go figure," Reyland said.

"It's them! Look! Number 23. I just saw them," Emerson said, pointing. "What's that? The corridor. Where's that?"

"It's the two-block underground corridor that runs toward the subway station at Macy's Herald Square," Arietta said.

"Get our team down into the subway station at 34th and Sixth now," Reyland said into the comm link.

"No, no! Tell them to stay on the road," Arietta said, watching the screen where now the man and woman were running past homeless people down a wide gray corridor.

As they disappeared out of the frame, he brought up the next camera and picked them up again.

"We have eyes on them now. They have cameras throughout the entire system. If they get on a train, we'll see them. The teams can follow from the surface."

Reyland rubbed at his chin as they followed the targets across the grid of screens. At the entrance of the subway, they watched as the man paid for a metro card at a machine.

They got a closer look at him for the first time. A stocky white guy, close-cropped sandy hair, about six foot or so, around forty but lean-faced and fit.

Reyland looked at the shoulders on him. Reyland had played Division One college ball, second-string left tackle at Notre Dame, and he thought the guy looked like a running back, a tough, sneaky white boy faster than he looked.

"Arietta, hit this fool with the facial recognition," he said.

A red square appeared around the man's profile. Reyland took in his lean face, his blue-gray eyes. His goatee was the color of the Carhartt jacket he was wearing. *Is he a hick or something? The reporter's friend?*

They waited. After a minute, the square turned purple.

"What happened? Where's his license?" Reyland said.

"Purple means the computer can't find it. Or he's not in the DMV system."

"It just works for the New York DMV system?"

"No, we're tapped into all of them. It's a national database."

"What do you mean? He doesn't have a frickin' driver's license?"

"Maybe he's not American? Or it could be a glitch. Like I said, we're still in the first stages of this thing."

"Is he using a credit card?" Reyland said.

"No, it was cash," Emerson said as the stocky guy swiped himself and the woman through the turnstile.

They watched them go down some steps to a platform. A train pulled in.

"Okay, Ruiz. Coordinate with the other teams," Emerson

called over the comm link. "They're getting on an uptown F. Next stop is 42nd. Bryant Park."

"Is there a camera on the train, too?" Reyland said.

"No," Arietta said, "but there's one in every station. We just need to keep tracking them. As soon as they get off, we'll be waiting."

53

Gannon got off the F train at 59th and Lex with the woman, and they went through the crowded station and down some dirty stairs to another platform and got a connecting uptown 4 train that had just pulled alongside the platform.

As they sat in the half-filled car, he took his first good look at the attractive young navy lieutenant. He saw there was a dazed, stalled-out look in her light brown eyes. She seemed to still be in a state of shock, but at least she was letting him lead her.

"Hey, how you doing?" Gannon said.

She blinked at him and took a breath and started coughing.

He patted her on the back.

"It's just the smoke. I know this is crazy, but stay with me. We're going to get through this. I promise. My name is Mike. What's yours?"

She looked up at him wide-eyed.

"Hey, come on. It's okay. Just talk to me. What's your name?" he said again.

"Ruby," she said, finally looking at him. "I'm Ruby."

He took her hand again and stood with her as the train screamed into the East 68th Street–Hunter College Station.

"Okay, Ruby," he said to her as they came out of the rattling doors. "Stay close. I know a place we'll be safe."

Up the stairs on Lexington the street was filled with moving cars and buses and there was a bunch of people milling around in front of one of the Hunter College buildings beside the subway.

They were stepping onto 68th Street's southeast corner's curb when the speeding SUV came at them out of the traffic on Lexington in a mad-dash diagonal. It was a black Cadillac Escalade with midnight tinted windows and there was a roar of horns as it jumped the curb twenty yards ahead of them and shrieked to a rubber-smoking skidding stop.

Gannon had just registered that its rear left passenger door was already open, when a slim man wearing black tactical clothes and a black balaclava popped out of it. Gannon watched as the man did a graceful crow hop onto the sidewalk and turned directly toward them, hunched over something in his hands.

It was a bullpup submachine gun, and as he leveled up with it to his shoulder to kill them, Gannon, already squared to target with the stainless-steel .45 up to his dominant right eye, shot him twice through the bridge of his nose just below his tactical goggles.

Gannon, moving at the waist to keep his center of mass, put two more in the driver's door glass and two more through the rear windshield.

The slim man Gannon had killed was down against the left rear tire when he closed the distance between them. Gannon dropped the .45 and snatched up his fallen snub-nosed machine gun by its smooth doughnut hole–like grip.

It sounded like a box of dynamite was going off in Gannon's

face as he crouched and fired the unsilenced machine gun full auto into the car. Casings pinged off the inside of the open back door as he raked it back and forth and back and forth.

In the spray of the bullets, he killed the already-wounded driver with a head shot and hit the balaclava-wearing passenger beside him with another.

The last of the balaclava-wearing men was in the back seat. His left hand held a semiauto while his right scrambled at the door latch beside him like a falling man at the edge of a cliff.

He lifted the pistol as he turned.

Gannon put a point-blank burst into the side of his head.

In the ringing silence, Gannon raised the rifle to his right and to his left toward the sidewalk and street. He peeked behind him quickly over each shoulder, checking his spots.

There was a wind chime sound as he dropped the emptied rifle into the gutter on top of the pile of spent brass.

He turned to see Ruby standing there in frozen shock. He took her hand again without speaking and led her back the way they had come. Most in the pedestrian crowd around had also frozen up, but cars and buses were flowing by on Lexington as if nothing had happened.

As they walked away, Gannon turned and saw the second man he had shot haltingly get out of the driver's seat. The whole front of him from head to crotch was completely splattered in blood. As Gannon watched, he sat down on the sidewalk casually with his hands behind him and his head tilted back. Like Lexington was a beach, and he suddenly wanted to catch some rays.

They made the corner of 68th and turned east. The only sound Gannon could hear in his ringing deafened ears was the thump of his heart. Everything felt numb and dull. Like he was underwater. They walked toward Third Avenue slowly. The woman's mouth moved. He tugged at her, nodding.

"Slowly," he said.

It was hard to talk because he could only barely hear himself.

"We need to go slowly," he said again.

They made it half the block. He wondered if he should turn around. He decided no. A quarter block left. Twenty feet. Ten.

Then they hit the Third Avenue corner and Gannon pulled Ruby to the right and yelled "Run!" as loud as he could.

They ran. Hand in hand at first, but then Ruby was getting it, running beside him on his left, matching him stride for stride. They made it to 67th and Gannon turned right again, running back up toward Lexington.

"No," he heard Ruby say as she tugged at him.

"It's okay," Gannon said, heading back toward Lexington. "This is the way. The only way. Trust me. It's okay. I promise."

54

A dark blue evacuation of fired-up cops was pouring out of the 19th Precinct when they arrived at it. Without pausing, Gannon maneuvered around them as he tugged at Ruby's hand, leading her straight in up the steps of the old ornate stone building.

In through the front door, a full-figured cop grabbed at Gannon as he was halfway through the worn vestibule. He was a puffy, pale uniformed sergeant with a pockmarked face. Gannon looked at the man's eyes through his thick glasses.

"Jimmy Farina," Gannon said, smiling widely. "You gotta be kidding me."

"Hey, Mickey. Kidding me? What the hell? Is that really you?" the cop said.

"Hey, hon," Gannon said to Ruby. "You know who this is? It's Jimmy Farina, an old boss from my days on the West Side."

Ruby stood wide-eyed and managed a smile.

"What the hell, Mick? You back now?" Farina said.

"Yeah, Sarge. I'm back. Not a moment too soon, it looks like. What the hell's going on here? You need any help? This a fire drill?"

"Yeah, I'll say. It's a shots-fired drill. Only it's not a drill. There just was a shooting at the college around the corner. Somebody with a damn machine gun, they said. I heard it myself there at the desk or I wouldn't even have believed it. Believe this shit? Probably some Columbine deal with these nutjob blue-hair college kids. It's just all-out pandemonium these days. ESU is on the way."

"Crazy, man. Wow. Maybe you should retire, too, huh? Before it's too late. Hey, is my boy Danny up there?" Gannon said, sliding past him.

"Yeah, Stick's up there minding the store," Farina said, looking at Ruby approvingly as Gannon pulled her with him.

"Doing well for yourself, huh, Mickey?" Farina said, giving him an A-OK sign with his fingers. "When you get back?"

"While ago," Gannon lied, hoping his voice didn't sound bizarre. "Been back for a bit."

"We should go out for a Guinness," Farina said.

"If you're buying. I'm a pensioner now, remember?" Gannon said, grinning like a fool.

"Mike? Is that you?" Stick said from his office doorway as Gannon finally got up the stairs and came through the detective room door. "What in the stone-cold hell are you doing here?"

Gannon brought Ruby past the empty cubicles into the office and sat her down on Stick's couch.

"And this is?" Stick said.

"Close the door, Stick," Gannon said, looking down at the floor, his mind racing.

"What?"

"Close the damn door, Stick," Gannon said, looking at him.

"What is it?" Stick said as he closed the door. "Which one

of you smells like a mattress fire? What the hell, Mick? What's going on?"

"We've got a bit of a situation," Gannon said.

55

"He's dead, boss," Ruiz said over the comm link.

"Daly is dead?" Reyland said, standing before the wall screen.

"Yes. And all of his New York squad guys, too. I just got off the bird in Central Park. I'm at the scene."

"Yeah, okay. We see you on the UAV," Reyland said as he scanned the live feed they had over Lexington Avenue.

"Actually, they're working on Janowski," Ruiz continued. "But it's no use. Three-quarters of his skull is gone. This guy blew everybody away. All pop tops, too. He must have had help, right? These men were no weekend warriors, Reyland. I was in Fallujah with Daly. He was one of the best I ever saw. What the hell is this? Did you see it?"

"No. That doesn't matter. Ignore Janowski. You need to find them."

"We have a problem," Arietta called out.

"What?" Reyland said.

"We just got the feed from the 19th Precinct security camera. The guy in the Carhartt went in there five minutes ago. He's in there right now with Everett."

"Whoa, whoa. What? The police precinct?" Reyland said.

"Yes. They're in the 19th Precinct right now," Arietta said. "On one of the upper floors. I'm not sure which one. Only the ground floor has cameras."

"What!" Emerson said. "The precinct? We're done! This guy who grabbed her must be a cop or something. That's it. We're cooked, Reyland. This is... This whole operation is... We're done!"

"Get a hold of yourself, Emerson," Reyland said as he pressed the comm link to Ruiz. "Our targets are around the corner in the 19th Precinct. We need you and your men to go in, Ruiz."

"Go in where?" Ruiz called back.

"The 19th Precinct."

"Go in? They're cops!" Ruiz said. "How can I go in?"

"I don't give a shit. It doesn't matter. Eliminate those targets. That's a direct order. You need to go in there and do it."

"But they're cops. My freaking dad was a cop," Ruiz said.

"You want to go to jail, Tommy?"

"You can't cover this," Ruiz said.

"I can cover anything. You think this is the first time I've done this? When the well is on fire, you have to use dynamite, Tommy. Now go in."

"How will you cover it?"

"That's my lookout. The entire building is empty. You have to go in right now."

"I can't believe this. You're actually crazy."

"Crazy like a fox, Ruiz. Go in. We're all in here, buddy. You, me and every last damn one of us. We're halfway through, and the other side is paradise. Or you might as well shoot yourself. The graveyard or paradise, Tommy. Which one?"

"Double, then. Double our fee. For me and all my men."

"Done. You're a millionaire now. Congrats. Now go in."

"Fine. Give me a second to think," Ruiz said.

"We're out of those, Ruiz. Get in there and kill them."

56

Stick sat at his desk and Ruby sat on the couch, but Gannon kept pacing.

It was blazingly bright and steamy hot in the old government building office, and as he paced, Gannon began to sweat. He wiped at his brow, wondering if he should take his coat off. But he didn't take it off. He didn't know what the hell to do.

As he paced, the police radio in the corner behind Stick's desk gave out a manic triple beep.

"Crowd control issue at location," cried a fired-up cop at the scene.

"Clear the air," said the female Hispanic dispatcher. "Sector units on the way."

There was a radio break and another cop said, "Where are those buses? We got likelies, four of 'em."

Gannon could still smell the cordite on his hands as he bit at a fingernail.

"En route, en route," said the dispatcher. "Less than a block. To clarify, are the shooting victims police? Over."

There was a beep followed by a screech of feedback.

"We're waiting on that, Central," said the cop.

Boy, are we ever, Gannon thought, wiping at his sweating face with his hand.

"They're feds," Stick said grimly as he got off his cell phone. "My guy on scene just pulled their IDs."

Gannon finally sat down on Stick's couch beside Ruby. He bent over and cupped his hands over his face for a moment then sat back, folding his arms.

"FBI?" Gannon said.

"Two were Department of Energy. One was DEA and one was ATF," Stick said with a hushed tone of awe.

Just as he said this, Gannon glanced over at Ruby on the couch as she started to double over with a greenish look on her face.

He lunged and grabbed Stick's wastepaper basket and whisked it under her just as she began to retch. He knelt down beside her, deftly keeping her hair out of the stream of it.

Can you blame her? Gannon thought, shaking his head.

He was feeling pretty damn sick about the situation himself.

"What the hell, Mick? Feds? Four feds? Four dead feds?" Stick said, folding his arms nervously.

"No," Gannon said, turning toward him. "Aren't you listening? They're not feds. Or they're dirty feds. Hell, screw it. I don't give a shit who they work for. These folks, whoever they are, just blew a reporter's fricking head off, an innocent American citizen's head off, back at that hotel.

"They shot the room to pieces, man. It was a miracle we got out. Then they drew down on me on the street not five minutes ago, Stick. No 'freeze.' No 'you're under arrest.' Just up comes an Escalade and out pops an assassin with a machine gun. I don't know about you, but for me, that's a lot of machine guns for one evening!"

Stick stared at him.

"You need to pick up on the theme here!" Gannon said. "These guys are trying to kill us."

"Four dead feds," Stick said quietly, shaking his head.

Gannon looked at him, looked through him, pacing now, trying to think.

How in the hell did they find us so fast? he wondered.

It was impossible. Pure dumb luck. Or had they tracked them on the subway somehow? That must have been it.

They can do that now? he thought. *Surveillance and artificial intelligence is that good now? To track someone in real time through Manhattan?*

Think about that later, Gannon thought. *Now matters. What does it mean for us now?*

He stopped pacing, his hands coming together as he closed his eyes.

It meant they knew they were in here.

He thought about Wheldon. The reporter's brains staining the bad carpet.

He turned and looked at the pebbled-glass office door.

They would come in, he knew.

It didn't matter that it was a precinct. All normal rules had been cast aside. The gates of hell had been unhinged over this.

They would actually come in.

A fire team was what? Four? There would be two of them. Eight!

He let out a breath.

Eight professionals. Eight elites with a whirlybird. Four would come from the top, four from the bottom. And they'd be in between, stuck in the middle to play the shit part in the shit sandwich.

He thought about the back way out, windows, but they could already be on them.

Then he hit on it. Pacing toward the door, he saw it across the bull pen, leaning up in a corner.

Plan C, he thought.

"Okay, listen up. I know what to do," Gannon said, throwing open the door.

57

"Hey, Sarge, these are the other members of my team," Ruiz said to a pudgy NYPD sergeant named Farina as Shepard and the rest of his men showed up in their tactical fatigues and backpacks.

From the corner of his eye, Ruiz watched Farina give Shepard a thumbs-up. He had already shown the cop his fed credentials that said he was a member of the US Marshals Service. He had given him the vague impression that the dead men in the truck were his colleagues and that the shooting might have been related to some fugitives they were in pursuit of.

Ruiz glanced out on the Lexington Avenue sidewalk behind them. There were four NYPD patrol cars and a fire truck around the shot-up SUV like a wagon train.

And more coming, Ruiz thought with a groan as he saw two more radio cars show up.

"You have a description of your perps yet so we can put out a BOLO?" Farina said.

"I'm still waiting to hear back from my boss," Ruiz lied. "Until then, I was wondering if we could set up a staging area inside the precinct house. Like right now, if that's possible."

"You got it. Of course. Follow me," the doughy cop said, guiding them through the lights and cops and lookie-loos already four deep on the sidewalk.

"Is there a back door to the precinct? The damn press is going to be all over this," Ruiz complained as they turned the corner onto 67th.

"No, but there's a garage just to the left of the front door with a rolling door. You can use it to get in and out without being seen. Will that work?" Farina said.

"Sounds perfect. Show me," Ruiz said, quickly picturing the garage from the blueprints of the precinct that Reyland had already sent him.

They walked east down 67th to the sound of the screaming ambulances. Farina led them down a little alley beside the precinct. He opened a call box and pressed a code. Ruiz kept his head down at the overhead camera. The garage door began to roll open silently.

Inside was a dim and tiny exhaust-reeking garage with three personal cars in it and a row of NYPD moped scooters. To the left of the scooters was a pile of garbage bags and an old gun locker with a peeling American flag sticker on it.

"So do I have this right?" Ruiz said, pointing at a door on the right as they walked in. "Through that door is the patrol supervisor's office and beyond that's the muster room? And the back stairs are in the hall beyond that, right?"

"Yeah, you're right. How'd you know?" Farina said.

Ruiz smiled as he raised his right arm up behind Farina as if he was about to give him a pat on the back.

Instead, he pressed his SIG Sauer P226's long squared-off suppressor to the base of Farina's skull and blew the back of his head off.

58

"How are we looking up top?" Ruiz called into the radio as two of his men dragged the cop's body out of sight between the parked cars.

"They're rappelling in as we speak," Reyland said.

"Okay, inserting now," Ruiz said as the four of them went in through the door behind the silenced H&K MP5 submachine guns they'd removed from their bags.

The dimly lit hallway inside was painted cement block. The four men moved down it in a silent flow, leapfrogging each other smoothly and quickly, keeping both ends of the hall covered at all times.

Ruiz hand signaled at a closed beige metal door on the left-hand side of the corridor and two of his men stopped and crouched along the side of it. Ruiz came forward, crouching low with Shepard behind him walking upright, his MP5 up over Ruiz's head covering their twelve o'clock.

Ruiz checked the door's knob. It was unlocked. He opened it.

Inside was an office space, chairs and desks and cubicles. Catty-cornered from the cubicles was another open doorway that he knew led into the muster room, and beyond that was the back stairs up to the second floor.

As Ruiz leaned in behind his SIG to check the corners, a uniformed female Hispanic cop walked in from the muster room doorway with a can of Diet Pepsi to her lips.

Ruiz didn't think she had even had a chance to notice him before Shepard shredded the can and her face with a tight controlled burst.

Ruiz breezed forward over the dead cop's feet, careful of the pool of soda and blood. He poked his head through the muster room doorway. There was a podium, a TV in the corner. A flyer tacked to a bulletin board beside the TV advertised an upcoming blood drive. He scanned the empty tables.

"Clear," he said.

They pressed forward through the empty muster room and pulled open a door in its corner into a back concrete stairwell. There was a low whistle from above and they filed upward and linked up with the top-down team already waiting on the next landing.

"In, in, in," Ruiz said, pulling open the detective room's side door.

Inside was a surprisingly beautiful, high-ceilinged room. Paneled in old dark oak, it seemed formal, like a library. It was filled with cubicles, all empty now. Along the back wall was a row of old-fashioned pebbled-glass–doored offices.

Ruiz hand signaled at the one farthest left.

It was the only one with a light on inside of it.

The commandos hurried in a silent column, going low past the desks. Two men flanked the lit office door as Ruiz and his backup man came forward again.

Ruiz put a couple of pounds of pressure on the short reset trigger of the SIG and turned the knob and pushed open the door.

"Oh, shit," he said, immediately letting off the trigger as he saw the bricks and rubble and dust on the carpet.

In the left-hand wall of the office, there was a hole. It was three feet high and three feet wide, and from it poured in cold air and the sound of loud sirens.

Before the hole on the dusty carpet were a couple of sledgehammers. Ruiz lifted one. *NYPD Anti-Crime* was written on the yellow handle in Sharpie.

Ruiz crouched and clicked on the flashlight on the bottom of his SIG's barrel and turkey peeked his head and shoulders out of the hole. He looked left and right. The hole led out onto a one person–wide breezeway that separated the precinct from its neighboring building to the west. The thin alley at its bottom was blocked off on the 67th Street side, but the other end of it led north into what looked like a backyard for the adjoining building.

"Bad news, boss," Ruiz said into the radio after he crawled back inside.

Shepard helped him easily up to his feet.

"They freaking mouse-holed us," he said.

"What?" Reyland said.

"They busted a hole in the outside wall of the building on the second floor. They went out of the building into an alley to the west. It looks like it might lead out onto Lexington."

"What are you waiting for? After them, Ruiz. We can still get these bastards," Reyland said.

"They've got eight, ten minutes on us," Ruiz said, looking at his watch. "It ain't gonna happen, Reyland. We lost this round. They're gone."

PART THREE

IT'S DEADER IN THE BAHAMAS

59

Around five in the morning, after their second truck stop somewhere in northern Virginia, it started snowing heavily.

Wired tight on panic and bad gas station coffee, Gannon, at
the wheel, cracked the window and clicked the seat up straighter.

The very last thing they needed at this time, he thought,
blinking in the cold bracing air, was to spin out or to hit something or to get stuck.

They'd left New York at a little after midnight over the
Goethals Bridge in a Subaru Baja crossover pickup truck they
borrowed from Stick's cousin out in Staten Island. They stayed
on 278 until it ended in Elizabeth then drove backstreets through
there and Plainfield until they got onto 78 West.

An hour later, they crossed the Jersey state line into Pennsylvania. Then just before they reached Allentown, religiously
following the speed limit, they swung south on I-81.

He looked at Stick sleeping in the back. He felt terrible dragging him into this. *But what a friend, huh?* he thought, smiling, as he heard the big galoot start to snore.

He'd shown up at his office with the minions of hell at his back and his old crazy partner hadn't batted an eyelash, had he? Not only that, five seconds later he was actually swinging a sledgehammer, helping Gannon bust a hole through his own office wall.

Gannon's smile left as he blinked out at the rushing highway. He couldn't stop thinking about the four men he had killed in the Cadillac. He thought about their wives, their kids. The phone ringing to tell them Daddy wasn't coming home.

The men had probably been decent fellas, decent cops. The jackasses behind all this corruption had probably said he was a terrorist or something, lied to them.

Then he thought about Wheldon blown across the hotel carpet.

He wasn't going home either, was he? he thought. *What about his wife? What about his kids?*

What an unholy mess, he thought.

"Hey," Ruby said, suddenly sitting up in the passenger seat.

"Hey," Gannon said.

He turned the bad wipers up higher and glanced over at her. She seemed different now. Normal. Calm and alert.

Incredible what just a few hours of not being shot at could do for one's general health and demeanor, Gannon thought.

"You okay?" she said.

"Me?" Gannon said. "Never better. I thought at first that this government-trying-to-gun-you-down stuff wasn't really my cup of tea, but now I have to say, it's really getting my blood pumping."

"You, too, huh?" Ruby said with a small smile. "Even so, you look beat. Let me drive."

"No, I'm fine," Gannon said.

"C'mon. You need some sleep," she said.

"So do you," Gannon said. "I got this shift."

"No, for real, Mike. I've slept. It's your turn. Pull over, and we'll switch."

Gannon smiled at her.

"You're pretty stubborn, huh, Lieutenant. Are those navy orders?" he said.

"Yes," she said after a yawn. "Navy orders."

"In that case," Gannon said with a yawn of his own, "aye, aye, Captain. Next exit, I'll pull off, and we'll switch."

60

The snow was starting to turn to rain when Ruby got off the highway. It was just before the Tennessee border, and they took back roads west into hilly southern Kentucky, following the instructions Stick had typed into the Garmin GPS on the dash.

It was still raining at around noon when they finally found the address down a rolling hill in the middle of a tree-filled nowhere. Ruby pulled over onto the shoulder before an old rusty mailbox. Gannon turned and shook Stick's leg in the back seat.

"Hey? This it?"

Stick blinked and looked around.

"This is it," he said with a yawn.

"And your uncle won't be home. You're sure?"

"Positive," Stick said. "The lucky son of a gun owns several beer distributors along the Jersey Shore. He's got hunting cabins all over the country."

"Any chance he'll be here?"

"No," Stick said. "He leaves for his elk-hunting place in northern Arizona day after Christmas."

"Okay. Here goes nothing," Ruby said as she pulled off the old road onto a muddy driveway.

The steep slope of the drive leveled off, and then about another half football field in off the road was a double-wide trailer beside a barn the color of driftwood.

Best thing Gannon could say about it straight off was that there wasn't another neighbor in sight.

Ruby parked behind the trailer, and they sat listening for a moment to the rain drumming atop the car.

"Looks deserted. Good," Ruby said, finally killing the engine.

The trailer was actually all right. It was furnished with Ikea stuff and had a pellet stove that warmed up the space quickly. Stick turned on the water and the propane tank beside the house that powered the water heater and the stove.

Gannon peeked out the living room blind as Ruby went into the back bedroom to take the first shower. There was an empty field across the narrow road, and in the distance stood a sole old leafless oak tree that was dark and ominous against the gray of the rainy sky.

Staring at it, Gannon tried to gauge his thoughts and feelings about all that had just transpired. What it meant. How he felt. What to do about any of it.

He stopped after half a minute. He'd have to try again later.

He blew on his cupped hands and rubbed them together and stamped his feet.

The only thing he could think about was how much he missed his son.

61

"What do you hunt down here?" he said to Stick, who was turning on the TV.

"Quail and turkey," Stick said, turning up the volume. "What in the—"

Gannon walked over. On the news channel, there was a helicopter shot of the black Cadillac Escalade he'd shot up, now sitting sideways on the Lexington Avenue sidewalk. It looked like the carcass of a large dead animal that had been brought down. There were half a dozen cop cars around it. A fire truck. Gannon felt like he was going to be sick.

FOUR FEDERAL OFFICERS GUNNED DOWN, it said on the screen crawl beneath.

"And in further developments," said some male talking head, "to those of you just tuning in, as if the shooting of four federal officers wasn't shocking enough, we have just learned that three officers of the nearby 19th Precinct, Sergeant James Farina,

Sergeant Carla Diaz and Detective Daniel Henrickson, seem to have gone missing during the shooting."

"What?" Stick cried.

"Investigators are looking into it, but there are some still unconfirmed rumors that the police department coworkers used the emergency to ransack the precinct's evidence locker of a drug cache and have fled to places unknown."

Stick started actually laughing.

"Me and Diaz and Farina just became the Jesse James gang or something?" he said, wide-eyed. "That's what they're trying to sell?"

"They're both dead, Stick," Gannon said.

Stick turned to him wordlessly.

"They shot them when they came in to get us, and then they took the bodies with them," Gannon said. "You can't think of these guys as just bad cops, Stick. This was a military operation with highly trained soldiers and helicopters. This was straight-up covert urban guerrilla warfare."

Stick was silent for a moment.

"We're like Fallujah now, Mick? Or Somalia? Except instead of crazy warlords, the FBI is gunning after the NYPD?"

"No, it's not the entire FBI. Just a rogue group within it. Hell, the guys I shot might not even be Americans. They've got multinational mercenary contracting companies now."

"Government special forces murder American citizens now," Stick said, nodding, absorbing this new reality. "Reporters and even cops. Then the press spins it. These damn feds. Top secret, my ass. Makes sense now why I quit the JTTF. Politicians and all that corporate cocktail party news network anchor reporter bullshit. Money, money, money. Pack of pencil-neck jackasses. I knew something wasn't right."

Gannon went into the kitchen. There was some instant pancake mix in a cupboard, and he poured it into a plastic mixing bowl with some water. He began beating it with a big fork he found in a drawer.

"This is some pretty unacceptable shit, Mick," Stick said, following him into the kitchen. "Farina was kind of a jerk, but he was our brother, man. And the Spanish kid had just started. I'm not sitting still for them getting whacked. I need to...I need to call people."

Gannon looked at his friend.

"No, Stick," Gannon said, shaking his head slowly. "They know from the precinct video they scrubbed that we were in your office, that you helped us and left with us. Your house phone, your cell phone, all of it is tapped now. You try to contact someone, hell, you put your battery back into your phone, they'll be here in an hour."

"What the hell are we supposed to do, then?"

"Nothing," Gannon said.

"Nothing?" said Stick.

"Not yet. We rest up for a while. Stay hunkered down. They'll be looking for a moving target," Gannon said.

62

When Reyland woke up at his house, it was eight in the evening. He went down into the empty kitchen and put on some coffee. A note on the granite kitchen island said that everybody was at Sadie's clarinet performance. His knuckles cracked as he balled the paper into his fist.

Two hours later, he had his driver let him off at the Hoover Building's 10th Street side.

"Evening, Deputy Assistant, or is it Director now?" Harry Naylor, the most veteran of the FBI security cops on the night shift, said quietly as he came into the lobby.

Reyland stopped and looked down at the mustached veteran's poker face. Like everyone else there at the puzzle palace that was FBI HQ, even the damn security guards were coy and cryptic masters of innuendo and rumor.

"When I become director, first order will be purging the

deadwood," Reyland said coldly as he passed the desk. "So believe me, Naylor, you'll be among the very first to know."

Off the elevator on seven, instead of making a left down the long corridor toward his office, Reyland immediately made a right.

He came around a deserted corner and key fobbed himself in through an unmarked gray door.

Five feet from the hall door inside stood a white steel box that almost looked like a small shipping container. There were thick beige-colored electronic cabinets attached to the front of it, and to the right of the cabinets was a small shiny silver metallic door.

The antiseptic white walls and fluorescent light inside the box gave it a look of a doctor's examination room. In its center was a rolling office chair surrounded by three computer terminals and two huge black flat screens.

The room inside a room was called a SCIF, short for Sensitive Compartmented Information Facility. Sound-baffled with electromagnetically sealed steel plate walls, it thwarted even the most sophisticated remote electronic eavesdropping methods.

He wouldn't have come in to the office at all except that he wanted to return a call from London. Technically, it had been a text message. One with three long-awaited, very intriguing words.

Very Good News, it said.

He closed the door and typed the required coding into one of the terminals. The closest of the two screens blinked on a moment later, and a short sixtysomething woman with overdone glamour-puss makeup and big owl-like spectacles was staring at him.

"Well, you're looking cheery, Robert," the woman said.

The woman's name was Brooke Wrenhall, and she was his contact at MI6. He had worked with Wrenhall several times over the last fifteen years and liked the feisty, extremely sharp, bitchy Brit.

"It's this wonderful lighting," Reyland said.

"Long day?" she said.

"Long career," Reyland said. "Just trying to keep it going. Getting harder and harder these days."

"Well, hopefully my tidings will help on that front."

"News?"

"The doctor picked up our package."

Reyland fell back into the office chair as if he'd been shot.

"No!" he yelled.

"Would I lie to you, Robert?" Brooke said, smiling.

"When did this happen?"

"Six hours ago."

"And everything is in there?"

"Yes," she said. "All of it. He took it back to his apartment. He stared at it for quite some time. There was some crying. When he put it away, he hid it in his closet in an old suitcase."

"So the wife doesn't know?" Reyland said, pumped.

"Presumably."

"That is very good news. He's committed. He's really going to do it."

"It certainly looks like it."

Reyland found himself suddenly smiling.

"So we're still on."

"Yes. Full speed ahead. We seem to have him on the hook now. Congratulations. I knew you'd be pleased. How long have you been planning this? A year?"

"And a half," Reyland said.

Reyland, still smiling, shook his head at the white walls as he pondered the ways of fickle fortune. Even after everything. Even after the disaster with the plane and Dunning's death, the last phase of the operation had just clicked into place.

They could still pull it off, Reyland thought. They really, really could. They just had to seal up everything.

"Okay. Very good. But don't pop the champagne yet, Brooke."

"I know full well. We still have what? Six days?"

"Yes. We just need to keep everything under wraps for six more damn days," Reyland said.

"How's things on your end with the crash management?" Brooke said.

Reyland looked at her. She obviously hadn't looked at the news in a while.

"Still not one hundred percent, but we're getting a cover on it."

"I thought you said you had eyes on the issue," Brooke said, raising an eyebrow.

"We did but..."

Reyland thought of Mr. X factor, the way he took out his contractors. The fact that they had completely lost the trail on him and Everett.

"But what?" Brooke said.

"Don't worry about it, Brooke. Don't spoil my good mood. We'll sew everything up on this end. Especially now that the good doctor has shown his fresh new commitment to the cause."

"Shall I give word to our special friends of the latest happy developments?" Brooke said.

"No," Reyland said as he glanced at the text on his encrypted phone. "Please allow me, Brooke. I'm actually meeting with them in the morning."

63

Gannon didn't know what time it was when something woke him.

He was in the trailer's living room on an air mattress they'd found, and it squeaked as he sat up in the complete darkness.

"What is it?" Stick said from the couch.

"I don't know," Gannon said, standing.

He crossed past the kitchen into the hall. He knocked on the back bedroom door and waited a moment then opened it and turned on the light.

The bed was empty. The pillows and blanket were gone. He crossed past the bed and checked the bathroom. Ruby wasn't there either.

"What's up?" Stick said as he came back out into the hall.

"She's gone."

"Gone?"

Gannon lifted Stick's Glock off the kitchen table as he pushed out the door.

He'd been sleeping in his clothes, and he stepped down the stairs in his boots into the yard.

He scanned the cold, open, dark outside and glanced over at the truck. She wasn't in the cab. It was dead silent. There were no cars on the distant road. No lights anywhere.

"Please," he said.

He was quickly crossing the yard for the barn in the starlight when Ruby stood up from where she'd been sitting in the bed of the pickup.

"Oh, hey," she said.

"What the hell? Are you okay?" Gannon said, rushing over.

"I'm sorry. I'm fine. I didn't mean to wake you."

"What are you, um, doing?" Gannon said, slipping the Glock into his coat pocket as he arrived. He could see she was fully dressed in her hoodie and boots and had brought out her blanket and pillows.

"I woke up to get a glass of water, and I saw all the stars, so I came out to take a look."

"The stars?"

"Yeah," she said, smiling. "See for yourself. They're really incredible here."

The screen door creaked.

"Mike, what's up?" Stick called over.

"I'm sorry," Ruby said. "Now I've woken everybody up."

"Nothing. It's fine. False alarm," Gannon called back. "Ruby was just getting something from the truck. It's all good."

"I can go back to sleep?" Stick called.

"Yep," Gannon called back.

The screen door creaked again.

"I'm sorry," Ruby said again.

"Nothing to be sorry about. We were just a little worried for a second. So you're into astronomy, huh?"

Ruby nodded, looking up at the sky.

"From my father. He was a high school science teacher, but space was his passion. Every summer we'd camp at stargazing places all over Ohio. My little sister about died with boredom, but I actually started to get into it. It's all about getting away from light pollution from cities and highways. There's hardly any here. It's pretty perfect."

Gannon looked up at her, at the light in her eyes as she gazed up.

"Don't you need a telescope?" he said, watching her.

"Actually, no. I mean, it's good to have one, but you don't need one. To me, it's more exciting with the naked eye. More, I don't know, old-school."

She looked at him, almost blushing.

"I know what you must be thinking. 'The whole world is after us, and she's out gazing at the night sky. This chick has lost her marbles.'"

"If anyone has lost their marbles, it's me," Gannon said as he helped her down out of the truck bed. "I got myself into this by taking that money. What did you do? Just your job?"

"Not even," Ruby said as they walked in the cold. "They wouldn't even let me near the plane."

"Exactly," Gannon said. "You're on the run for the seditious crime of wanting to do your job."

Gannon looked up at the sky.

"You ever see them from way out in the ocean?" he said.

Ruby shook her head.

"Come on. You were in the navy, weren't you?"

"They started me in the Office of Naval Safety straightaway. I've never been assigned to a ship."

Gannon looked up.

"This is nothing," he said. "You should see them thirty, forty miles out in the Atlantic off Eleuthera."

"Yeah?"

Gannon nodded.

"It's like outer space. Tell you what. If you ever get down to the islands, I'll take you out. I'll teach you how to swordfish. You can give me an astronomy lesson."

He held the screen door for her.

"Are you putting me on?" she said.

"No," Gannon said. "I'm serious. Once we get this garbage sorted out, we'll go out on my boat. We'll have ourselves a whistle-blowers' night cruise."

Gannon watched Ruby's face brighten for a moment as she thought about it. Then her expression collapsed.

"You mean *if* we get this sorted out," she said quietly as they stepped out of the cold back into the warmth of the trailer.

64

It had started snowing when Reyland left the house at 10:00 a.m. that morning, and by the time he made it to Annapolis and finally pulled to a stop before Griffin Island's one-car bridge, a square of snow fell in one piece from the gatehouse's sliding window.

He gave his name to the guard. Then he looked over the water at the snow falling gently onto the misty trees.

He had grown up a navy brat in Annapolis nearby and always thought Griffin was more like a resort or a private country club with its own zip code than an actual town. Most of its small body of land was taken up by its world-renowned golf course, for one thing, and there were exactly zero businesses or stores. Even the island's narrow roads were like golf cart paths, and in the summer, there were more golf carts in the circular driveways of the mansions than cars.

When the booth's stick went up, he drove to the other side

of the causeway and made a left into a zillion-dollar neighborhood they called Cherry Hill Forest. Down on the other side
of it was the island's East Shoreline Road, and he sat for a moment at the stop sign.

Across the road was the island's famous country-club boathouse and there was a huge peace sign lit up with Christmas
lights hanging upon its clapboard side. In the pale yellow glow
beneath it was a Crayola box–colored row of flipped-over ca-
noes peeking out of the snow.

Reyland often fantasized about buying a Griffin Island bayside vacation villa one day, and as he sat there, he closed his eyes,
imagining it was summer. Breathing deeply, he thought of him
and Danielle and the kids walking a canoe across the boathouse
dock in life jackets as their goofball hound dog, Charlie, barked
excitedly, trying to catch up.

He thought of three hundred–yard drives pin straight down
the fairway, martinis at sunset, cookouts with fireworks. Tow-
headed toddlers collecting fireflies in mason jars. In his mind,
he saw himself at exclusive parties where all the wives were
blonde and thin and pretty, and all the men were lean and tan
and wore dinner jackets with Bermuda shorts.

After a few more deep breaths, he opened his eyes and looked
at himself in the rearview mirror.

"Now go and get your future back, you son of a bitch," he
said as he put the Audi back in Drive.

The driveway that Reyland pulled into two minutes later was
the only one on the shore road with wrought iron perimeter
fencing and a solid gate. There must have been a hidden camera somewhere because the gate opened inward as he slowed
for the call box.

The gatehouse he'd been told to park at was a whimsical
fieldstone-and-glass castle-like building with a pointy Roman-
esque roof. Up the stairs on the cold, windy porch stood two
large hard-faced security men in black overcoats who asked for

his cell phone. There was another security team inside on the first floor who wanded him before he was guided to the stairs.

Up on the dimly lit second floor, it looked like an arcade at an amusement park. There were pool tables and poker tables and a foosball machine and a pop-a-shot basketball court. There was even one of those dance machine games with the floor squares that lit up.

Beyond it were the men he was there to explain himself to.

They didn't seem like they were in the mood for any boogying, Reyland thought, taking a deep breath as he stepped over.

65

By the huge water-view window, the three old men sat side by side silently at a poker table.

The man on the left side was wiry and buzz-cut and pointy chinned and had a professorial air about him. The one farthest right was quite fat and had tortoiseshell eyeglasses.

In between them, the eclectic owner of the bayside estate gave Reyland a pleasant nod, which Reyland immediately returned.

He was small and handsome and blue-eyed and had backward-swept steel gray hair and baby-soft skin so pale and white it looked powdered.

That the pointy-chinned man and the fat man were midlist Forbes 500 billionaires would have been quite impressive had it not been for the striking ghostly blue-eyed man sitting between them.

He was from one of those old European banking families

whose whispered-about wealth was so vast and unfathomable, it never showed up on any lists at all.

Without prompting, Reyland stood up as straight as his six-foot-six height would allow and delivered his full report to them. He left out nothing. He didn't try to minimize his role.

When he was done, there was no yelling or outrage from the three highly intelligent worldly men sitting at the table. What mattered blame at this point?

Reyland stood calmly in the silence, waiting for their reply. Like a baseball manager who had put in his best pitcher yet still lost the World Series, he stood by the logic of his decisions. Given another chance, he would have done it exactly the same again.

The fat man spoke first, and when he did, his Texan's voice was unexpectedly deep and gruff and buzzy with what linguists call vocal fry. It could have been the voice of a drill sergeant who smoked three packs a day.

"And is there any trace of them now?" he said.

Reyland was about to tell him the difficulty of the task, to tell him how many analysts they had at this moment sitting in front of computer screens, devising new algorithms and looking for anomalies and clusters in the data mine.

He was going to tell him how thorough a proctology exam they were giving to the life of Ruby Everett and the mysterious, now-missing NYPD detective Daniel Henrickson. How several of his staff would literally be living at the office until they were found.

Instead he said simply, "No."

The old men pondered that some more.

The pointy-chinned man spoke next with an East Coast lockjaw voice that was high and almost effeminate.

"Damage control aside for the moment. What is your recommendation for moving forward on Director Dunning's initial mission?" he said.

"Glad you asked me that, sir. London is a green light. I just got off the phone last night. Despite everything, we're still looking very good. Our asset is ready to operate as scheduled."

"So it's just a matter of discretion, then," the ghostly white blue-eyed man beside him said with a pleased surprise.

"Yes, sir," Reyland said. "We just need to keep it all under wraps for five more days."

The old man looked down at the table, his striking eyes half-hooded. There was a strangely amused look on his face, like he was about to tell the punch line of a funny joke. Reyland watched him. This mysterious man who collected CEOs and senators and Congress people like baseball cards.

When he suddenly smiled, it was like the whole dim room lit up. He flashed deep dimples, and his soft multibillion-dollar Dodger-blue eyes twinkled like the lights on the Chesapeake Bay Bridge out the window behind him.

"Then by all means I think you should continue, Robert," he said with his plum-in-the-mouth British accent. "Plug this potential leak. We'll handle the media. You leave that to us."

"Still with no parameters, correct?" Reyland said, staring at this famous secretive man who many said had economically devoured his first country, a small South American one, before he was thirty.

"Correct," the blue-eyed man said.

"With all available resources at my command?" Reyland said.

The elegant old man's amused, ever-playful smile didn't waver one iota.

"By any and all means necessary, Robert," he said with a slow wink. "How could we have it any other way?"

66

Happy to have the situation somewhat stabilized and still have his head attached to his shoulders, Reyland was turning from the table when the infinitely rich old blue-eyed Brit stood.

"Robert, wait. I'll walk you out," he said.

Oh, boy, Reyland thought. An audience with His Serene Eminence. *What now?* he thought as the rich man stepped over.

The old man put his arms behind his back in a formal, almost military posture as they walked slowly alongside the arcade games.

"Tell me, who is your contact on the London end? That Watkins fellow?" he said.

"No, Wrenhall," Reyland said. "Brooke Wrenhall."

"Ah, yes. Ms. Wrenhall. She is quite good. Sharp. Yes. Quite sharp. Her father worked for me once years ago. Or was it her grandfather?" the billionaire said, wrinkling his brow.

They continued walking.

"I'm sorry to further burden you, Robert, but I have a question concerning the director's plane."

"Of course," Reyland said, stooping to listen.

"I was told that this Mr. Biyombo individual brought a package with him out of the Congo. Is that true?"

"Yes," Reyland said, nodding. "He did."

"May I ask how you know this?"

"I was on the phone with Dunning before they took off," Reyland said. "Biyombo showed him the case. The director told me there was what appeared to be a very large amount of diamonds inside of it."

The rich man nodded.

"And your report said this case is still missing?"

"Yes. Along with the money. We're still looking. As I mentioned, we still have a team down in the islands working solely on that," Reyland said as they made the top of the stairs.

The ghostly blue-eyed man nodded again.

"Now, this is just an ancillary matter, Robert, but we believe Biyombo's diamonds were actually stolen from a convoy out of one of our mines on the Zaire border three years ago."

Reyland blinked as he thought of whom the rich man meant by the word *our*.

"If you come across these diamonds in your travels, Robert, I would be forever in your debt if you brought them directly to me."

Forever in debt to a man with an infinite amount of money, Reyland thought, looking into the icy blue of the man's eyes.

It was here, Reyland realized.

The opportunity that he had always dreamed of but was hesitant to ever actually expect, even to himself.

He would be a player. That was what he was being offered here. World-Class Player Status.

If he retrieved Biyombo's satchel, he would get his own golden passport into the sky city.

He thought about the boathouse again, about the fireflies.

"I'll make it a priority, sir," Reyland said with an impossible-to-hide smile as he started down the steps.

67

Gannon woke up at around five thirty in the double-wide's small bedroom. When he went into the living room, Stick and Ruby were sitting silently watching the news.

"Are we still the lead story?" Gannon said.

"Yes," Ruby said. "But at least they're not showing photos of us yet."

"Is there anything about Wheldon? About the fire at the hotel?" Gannon said.

"No," Ruby said. "Not a thing."

After the news was over, the only thing to eat was more pancakes, so they had them for dinner along with some bacon that Gannon defrosted from the otherwise empty freezer.

After they were done eating, they stared at each other in silence. Then it was Stick's turn to do some pacing. Ruby and Gannon sat at the small kitchen table, sipping instant coffee as they watched Stick walk the length of the small living room to the pellet stove and back.

"Hell, I need a drink. Is there anything to drink?" Stick said.

Gannon got up and looked in the pantry where he'd found the pancake mix.

"You're in luck. There's beer," Gannon said, kneeling down. "No, no. Wait. Sorry. False alarm. It's just that O'Doul's non-alcoholic stuff."

"Screw it. Bring it out," Stick said, making a gimme gesture with his big hand. "I'll take even a pretend beer at this point."

They watched him crack the bottle open and drink while he continued to pace.

"Okay, so there's obviously something there about the plane," Stick said. "Something about the director and the people there with him that is so unholy, there isn't anything they're not going to do to cover it up. So what the hell could it be?"

"Before he was shot, Wheldon was speculating it had something to do with the uncut diamonds," Gannon said. "He said maybe they were illegal blood diamonds from some war-torn African country and that the exposure of the FBI director on the plane with the diamonds would expose some kind of Iran Contra–type deal with African warlords."

"Maybe that's true," Ruby said. "The range on a G550 is transcontinental. They easily could have traveled from Africa to the East Coast of the US."

"Or maybe the dead guy in the hoodie was some kind of African terrorist or something?" Stick said. "And they were doing some kind of off-the-books deal with him? Sneaking him into another country or something?"

"Awful lot of maybes and somethings to go on there," said Gannon.

"You're right," Ruby said, letting out a breath. "We can't really say what it is."

"So what do we do?" Stick said.

"I think we need to do what Wheldon said before they shot him," Gannon said.

"Which is what?" Stick said.

"Get the tape out there," Gannon said. "We need to go back to my place and get the video. Get it out to the world. It's the one thing they don't want."

"That actually makes a lot of sense," Ruby said. "They're willing to kill us to cover it up, right? But if the truth gets out, it's out. The reason to kill us suddenly disappears."

"Plus, at the very least, we're going to need money and plenty of it to keep staying under the radar with these jacks hunting us," Gannon said.

"Just one little detail," Stick said. "How do you plan on getting us from here to the Bahamas with the FBI and probably every cop in the United States out looking for us?"

Gannon smiled as he thought of something.

"We'll take the back roads," he said.

68

They were just over the border of Kentucky the next morning when they saw the gas station.

They were on a two-lane strip of desolate Tennessee hill country road heading downward into a valley, and Gannon saw it ahead on his left off by itself in the middle of nowhere.

It was a blue-and-white Marathon station with a little mart attached to get doughnuts and Gatorade and lottery cards. Behind it was a tree-filled hill edged with a small cliff of striated brownish-gray rock.

"Guys, what do you think? Stop for gas?" Gannon said.

In the back seat, Stick lifted the binoculars they'd brought with them from the hunting trailer.

"Do it," he said. "There aren't any cameras that I can see."

It was cold when Gannon stepped out by pump number one. He looked up at the dawning overcast sky. The forecast called

for rain, but snow made more sense. He stepped past the cigarette ads and the propane cage and opened the door.

There was a middle-aged couple inside, a heavyset lady with
silvery blond hair and a skinny man with a mustache and glasses.

"Forty bucks on pump one, please," Gannon said, putting a
couple of twenties on the counter.

He saw the cruiser straight off as he came back out the jin-
gling door. It was a Tennessee state trooper Dodge Charger de-
tailed in cream and black with a yellow stripe. Gannon had the
pump clunked in and had just squeezed the handle as it pulled
to a stop right behind them.

Just bad luck, Gannon thought, trying to calm his breathing.
Just full-out bad luck.

The trooper who climbed out of it was pale and square-jawed
and about thirty. He was medium-sized, five-nine or so, but
bulked up wide with muscle from working out. Gannon, seeing
the no-nonsense expression on his lean face beneath the green
Smokey the Bear hat as well as the shine to his patent leather
cop shoes, did what he could only do.

He smiled and nodded.

"Morning," he said.

The trooper looked at him, looked at Ruby, looked at Stick,
and gave him a fake smile back.

"Taking a trip, huh," he said.

"Yeah, how'd you know?" Gannon said. Then he laughed.
"Oh, right. The plates. Yeah, my old lady's idea. Got a vacation
week off from work, and two nights ago, out of the blue, she
says she needs to see Graceland. Bucket list thing."

"Happy wife, happy life," the trooper said, peering into the
back. "Got a buddy with you?"

"Kinda," Gannon said.

They both looked out at the road as a rattling dump truck
went by tugging a backhoe on a trailer.

"How's that?" the trooper said.

"That's her brother," Gannon said.

"In-laws," the trooper said, nodding knowingly as he stepped for the mart. "I get you there, partner."

Gannon heard the door jingle.

"Let's get going," Stick said, rolling down the window.

"Shit," Gannon said as he clicked the nozzle back into the pump.

"What is it?" Stick said.

"It's only thirty-four."

"What does that mean?"

"I got change coming."

"Screw it. Let's just go," Stick said.

"Relax," Gannon said, turning for the mart. "Take it easy."

The trooper was coming out with a coffee in one hand as he was going in. He gave him a look as Gannon held the door for him but said nothing as he passed.

"Looks like I overshot it a bit," he said to the heavyset lady behind the counter.

She smiled, opening the register.

Shit, Gannon thought as he looked out at the trooper where he was sitting in the cruiser typing at his terminal now.

69

"You know he's running the plate," Stick said as Gannon got back behind the wheel.

"I know, I know. Just take it easy."

"You keep saying that, but it's getting harder and harder," Stick said as they pulled out.

Gannon watched the trooper in the rearview as he slowly accelerated. He was on his radio. Then Gannon saw him move the cruiser just as they hit the bend in the descending road ahead.

"He's following us," Stick said, glancing back, "and he's on his radio now. They've got a BOLO on the truck. Has to be. What do we do?"

"Nothing," Gannon said. "Just hold on. Let's not get too hasty, okay?"

"But you know he's calling for backup."

Gannon looked ahead. Far below down the slope of the road

they were descending, there was a car. It was coming up, heading toward them at some speed.

"Dammit! It's another cruiser!" Stick called, pointing the field glasses over Gannon's shoulder. "I knew it."

Gannon looked ahead where some high voltage lines bisected the road at a high-to-low diagonal. He looked at the rusted red transmission towers over the trees on his right where the lines went down. They were a hundred yards from the utility cutout.

"Put on your seat belts! Now!" he called out.

"You have got to be shitting me," Stick said as Gannon wheeled to the right off the road.

There was the snap of fallen tree limbs then a crunch of flying gravel as they swooped down an embankment onto a tire-track dirt path. Thirty feet from where they caught the path, there was a fenced-in stand of electrical equipment at the base of one of the transmission pylons, and the back end of the Subaru clipped one of its corner poles smartly as they skimmed headlong past it.

Coming down the cutout was like riding a bucking bronco down a ski slope. Dirt showered off the hood as they seesawed into the hill face and crunched over tree stumps and slid over gravel.

After a few hundred terrifying more feet, they suddenly hit a flat of concrete that supported another of the electrical pylons. Then they were off-roading again, zigzagging left and right as they bounced up and down hard over the rough descending terrain.

Gannon managed to halt the truck with a high screech at the cement base of the next pylon, and he rolled down his window and looked back up the slope.

Not surprisingly, the cruiser hadn't followed them.

Of course not, Gannon thought. The guy was young, took care of himself. He didn't want to die just yet.

"Mike, there's an access road. See it?" Stick said, pointing another thirty feet below.

"Hallelujah," Ruby said when they were finally on asphalt again.

The access road ran alongside a river onto an actual road.

"We need to ditch the car," Gannon said as he gunned it past an old farmhouse. "Get a new one. They're going to have every cop in the state looking for us now."

They came to an intersection and hooked a right. They'd just crossed a bridge over the river when Ruby grabbed his arm.

"Wait, wait. Slow down."

"What's up?" Gannon said, easing off the accelerator.

"Turn left here. See?" she said, pointing at the road they were coming up on.

On the corner, there was a little green sign with an arrow on it.

Hollytree Airport, it said.

"Yeah?" Gannon said.

"Trust me," Ruby said.

70

The road curved up a wooded hill for about a mile and a half before they came into the small airport's parking lot. There were a half-dozen cars there that they sped past as Ruby guided them toward a utility road that ran parallel to the tarmac fence.

After twenty feet down the road, they came to the back of a long white metal hangar that fronted into the airport.

"Stop right here. Right here," Ruby said, pointing at a little set of stairs that led to a door at the hangar's end.

Ruby had her door open even before they stopped. She flew up the stairs and rattled at the little black box that hung from the door's knob.

"Good. See, it's just a key holder like real-estate agents use. I knew it. Is there a crowbar in the truck?"

Gannon took the Glock out of Stick's leather jacket pocket and stepped up the stairs and shot the lockbox with a sudden loud pop.

"That'll work, too, I guess," Ruby said as she grabbed the key from the grass and opened the door and clicked on the lights.

The hangar inside was pristine. On one wall hung a huge American flag, and under the fluorescent lights in its center gleamed a new-looking cream-and-white single-engine prop plane.

"What do you mean to do?" said Stick.

"What do you think?" Ruby answered. "We're flying the hell out of here."

"You can fly?"

"No, I just thought I'd suddenly give it a shot. How hard can it be?" Ruby said as she went to the plane and threw up the pilot-side batwing door.

"Of course I fly," she said as she climbed in. "Since I was in high school. You need a pilot's license to even join Naval Safety."

They stood watching as she checked the instrument panel and clicked some buttons.

"Gotta love rural airports," Ruby said, looking down at them. "The key's already in it."

"People just leave the damn keys in?" Stick said.

"Of course," Ruby said. "You know how much trouble you get in for stealing a plane?"

"What's the plan?" Gannon said.

"The power is good to go, and there's half a tank of gas. On a six-seater, that's a range of about five hundred miles. I get this Beechcraft up and run it dead open for fifteen or twenty minutes to the south. She'll go two hundred knots, and I'll keep it low, under the radar. By the time they figure it out, we'll be over the state line in Georgia."

"Where are you going to put it down?" Gannon said.

"On a rural road," Ruby said. "Or a field even. The tires looked pretty good."

"Then what? Hitchhike?" Stick said.

"We'll call a cab."

Gannon laughed.

"That's hilarious. But that just might work, sailor."

"Hurry now. Get the gate," Ruby said.

Gannon hit the button beside the roll-up gate and ran back as it started to rise.

Ruby turned over the engine and the propeller began to spin as Gannon and Stick climbed in.

The radio crackled on as they were outside on the taxi road about to get on the runway.

"This is tower. You are not authorized to take off. What the hell are you doing?"

"Tower, we have a sick child aboard. We need to take off now. Clear the air," Ruby said.

"You are not authorized!" cried the radio.

"We have no choice. Divert all aircraft. We're coming out," Ruby said and turned down the radio volume.

They hit the tarmac and turned and began to pick up speed.

"I can't believe we're actually doing this," Stick said over the rising roar of the engine.

"Yep," Gannon said as he crossed himself and began a quick "Our Father."

"I never should have let you into my office," Stick yelled as they suddenly left the ground. "I knew you were trouble, but I had no idea this chick was as crazy as you!"

71

In the gilded mirror, Reyland held his right hand over his chest like he was about to pledge allegiance.

Then he tilted up his chin and slowly drew the razor up his shaving-creamed throat.

As he clicked the steel against the rim of the full washbasin, they hit enough turbulence to make the water slosh.

As the rattling subsided, there was a change in light at the porthole window above the commode and Reyland stepped over and looked out.

The clouds they had been in had thinned out, and now seven miles down beneath the Gulfstream, he could see the bleached-salt white line of the North Florida coast.

The G550 they were on now belonged to the attorney general. Reyland had heard that the AG tried to block his use of it. Well, at least until he heard the nosebleed height from which the request had originated.

Reyland went back to the mirror and paused again with the razor as they hit some more bumpy air. He squinted at the back of Emerson's head where he was sitting with a PowerBook on the jump seat just outside the restroom's open door.

"Hey, you didn't tell the pilot I was shaving, did you, Emerson?" he said.

Emerson swiveled and smiled.

Reyland kicked the door shut and finally smiled himself.

Now that they actually had something to smile about.

They had finally found the mystery man.

His name was Gannon. Michael Gannon. He was a diving instructor who lived on Eleuthera Island in the Bahamas with a boat registered in the Bahamian database called the *Donegal Rambler.*

Even with all the technology at their disposal, it was sheer unadulterated shoe leather that had finally broken the logjam.

They had taken screenshots of their pesky unsub off the MTA closed-circuit system in New York City and had them sent to their team of agents still down in the islands.

Their agent on Eleuthera had just lost hope when a guy in a bar said he knew the man in their picture, had fished with him. The agent had asked him where they had fished. The man had said they had gone marlin fishing in the Atlantic falloff thirty miles out north of Little Abaco.

It was this Gannon who had found the money. Reyland was sure of it. Gannon had come across the plane and had taken the money. Since he was a diving instructor, he had probably even dived down for more loot and had seen the director dead in the plane.

Which was the reason why, like Everett, he had apparently come up to NYC to talk to that puke, Wheldon, to blow the whistle about it.

Oddly, Gannon was an Irish national. Or at least he had used an Irish passport when he flew into the States from Eleuthera Island. He had flown to Tampa and then to Phoenix, of all places, and then on to New York City.

But besides that, all they knew about Gannon apparently was his name, address and boat. He had no social network presence. No credit cards at any major banks.

They had even hacked the Irish government records to see if there was any clue to his origins, but no dice. Not only was the Irish database a primitive, disorganized nightmare, there were actually thirty-seven bog-trotting Irish Michael Gannons running about in the world.

No matter, Reyland thought. He and his team were now on the way to Eleuthera right now. When they got there, they would go to Gannon's house and hopefully find him there with his pants down. If not, they would tear his place apart and find out everything they could about him. Pick up his computers, any physical files he had.

Who knows? Reyland thought pleasantly. In their search, maybe they might even come up with the items the man had stolen.

Done shaving, Reyland let the warm water out and turned on the cold and splashed some on his face. When he glanced up, the electronic in-flight display board to the right of the mirror said that they would be arriving at Nassau in forty-seven minutes.

He patted at his face and neck with a fluffy cream-colored towel that smelled like a scented candle. As he did this, the ETA on the screen suddenly changed to forty-one minutes.

How do you like that? Reyland thought, smiling. They were making even better time now. Things were coming up rosy all fricking over.

72

Coming on 3:00 a.m., Sergeant Jeremy was out at the Coral Castle Resort in Charles Bay.

He was sitting in its lobby, and beyond the arched opening in front of him he could see the bartender turning off the lights of the straw hut bar beside the elaborately lit pool. To his left on the bench beside him sat a man. He was a large white man with a bad sunburn and a prodigious gut that protruded through the curtain-like gap of his unbuttoned Hawaiian shirt. The man's eyes were closed, and he was sweating profusely.

Sergeant Jeremy sat beside the big man patiently, listening to his breathing. He had caused quite a ruckus forty minutes before, and Sergeant Jeremy, always reluctant to make an arrest, was hoping that the drunken tourist was about to finally fall into a restful slumber. He was beginning to edge away when the big man snorted himself awake.

"Where is she? Where is she?" the man said with German or maybe South African–accented English. "Is she back?"

"Not yet, but I am sure you will see her soon," Sergeant Jeremy said with soft encouragement.

"Why aren't you taking me seriously?" the man said, punching on his own thigh. "She was kidnapped, I tell you. Kidnapped!"

"Yes, I know. I remember," Sergeant Jeremy said quietly.

Sergeant Jeremy nodded as the man mumbled to himself incoherently. He had been called to investigate such kidnappings before. It usually happened after the rum began to flow. Boyfriends and girlfriends and sometimes, as in this poor man's case, even spouses would disappear. But in almost every case, such disappearances were the result of the victim voluntarily heading into the bedroom of another inebriated guest.

"Then why aren't you doing anything? Shouldn't we fill out a report or something?" the large man cried.

"We were just about to, sir," Sergeant Jeremy said, lifting the clipboard in his lap.

He had taken out his pen and was about to click it when he finally heard the best possible resolution to the situation. Incredibly loud snoring. The man had slumped over with his sweating head against the palm pot beside him.

"Is he okay there for now?" Sergeant Jeremy asked, walking over to the desk clerk.

"Is he really asleep this time?" the clerk asked.

"Out for the count, I would say."

"Not so fast," the clerk said, tossing a chin.

Sergeant Jeremy turned to see a skinny middle-aged blonde woman come in off the beach. He thought there would be some fireworks as she started shaking at the large man. But he was wrong.

"Another kidnapping successfully solved," Sergeant Jeremy said with a click of his pen as the two tourists stumbled off down the corridor together, singing and laughing.

He was heading back up Sherman's Highway near Tarpum Head in his Jeep when he came up on his friend Michael Gannon's cul-de-sac turnoff.

He found himself putting on his clicker. There had been some break-ins in nearby Rock Sound and on White Road Beach to the south, and he thought he'd do a quick spin past.

He was approaching the second-to-last old bungalow when he saw the light in the window of Michael's house. It was blue and flickering, his friend watching TV perhaps.

Home early? Sergeant Jeremy thought, rolling up.

He had parked the car in front of the house and was coming up the path when the blue light suddenly shut off.

That was strange, he thought.

He stood there in the darkness for a moment waiting, listening. The clicking sound of some kind of bird in the distance had just started up when the door to the house opened silently. A man appeared in the threshold. A tall man. He was smiling serenely in the moonlight.

Michael's son?

Then Sergeant Jeremy saw the pale bald round head and a sudden sense of panic rattled through him.

"You," Sergeant Jeremy said in utter confusion.

"Yes, it's me, Sergeant. Funny meeting you here," said the FBI man with the wolf's eyes.

"I should say the same thing," Sergeant Jeremy said. "This is not your house!"

"And whose house might it be, Sergeant?" the FBI man said. "In fact, why don't you come in here, Sergeant, and talk to us. We're all friends, right? Colleagues, fellow law enforcement officials. Perhaps you could help us with the investigation we're conducting."

Sergeant Jeremy stiffened as something cold touched his neck at the back of his collar. A short muscular man in black tactical clothes and some kind of goggles over his eyes was standing there with a gun pressed to the back of his skull.

"After you, Papi," the soldier said.

The blow to his chest that came when he set foot into the house was like a sledgehammer. Sergeant Jeremy went back off his heels onto his ass with his breath gone. He actually skidded a little down the short corridor before he came to a stop against the wall.

It took him a second to process that the FBI man, Reyland, had kicked him. The huge bald man had just stomped him in the chest with the heel and sole of his big dress shoe.

"There you go. Have a seat, *mon*," the FBI man said. "You sit right back and get real comfy, you little lying sack of shit."

73

It was eight thirty in the morning, and out on the faded sunny South Florida concrete, the Beatles' iconic song "Day Tripper" died down from the speaker above to be replaced by some driving steel drum Bahamian dance music.

For the twentieth time.

Gannon sipped on the dregs of his iced coffee as a yellow forklift loaded with pallets rumbled by on the quay.

They were in Fort Lauderdale now at the busy Port Everglades Harbor. The terminal they were sitting outside of was for a US-to-Bahamas daytrip high-speed ferry service called Raytrippers.

Gannon's son, Declan, had taken it a few times because it was cheaper than flying and only a driver's license was required to get through customs if you told them you weren't staying overnight.

Gannon smiled as Ruby came out from the lounge inside and sat beside him.

Forty minutes after they had taken off she'd landed the plane as pretty as you please in a hayfield in a little town called Dalton, Georgia. Since then, they'd been heading stealthily south via local taxis.

"You must speak Bahamian by now. What do they keep saying?" said Ruby, who was dressed now in a maxi dress with a ridiculously garish sunset on it.

On their way south, they had stopped outside of Jacksonville and bought some beach stuff at a Dollar Store that didn't have a camera out in front of it. With Gannon's new madras shorts and a seagull T-shirt and floppy golf hat, they could have been a blue-collar couple doing a second honeymoon on the cheap.

"What do you mean?" Gannon said, thumbing his cheap sunglasses up the bridge of his nose. "What does who keep saying?"

"In the song," Ruby said, pointing at the speaker.

Gannon bopped his head to the steel drum rhythm, listening.

"Party in the backyard," he said with a grin. "I tink, mon."

Ruby smiled.

"Any word?" she said, checking her watch.

She was talking about Stick. He had headed down to Miami three hours before. In his younger days, Stick had worked on loan from the NYPD as an undercover with the Miami DEA, and he had gone down there to ask an old criminal informant for a favor.

"No, not yet," Gannon said, glancing at his burner phone, "but don't worry—he'll make it."

"You know," Ruby said, looking at him intently. "I was thinking about what you did back in New York."

"What do you mean?" Gannon said.

"How you got us out of the hotel, took down that agent and those other armed men. Opening the wall of the precinct? Not to mention your expert work with the wastepaper basket."

Gannon laughed.

"So what about it?"

"What was it that you actually did in the NYPD?" Ruby said.

As Gannon opened his mouth, a huge cruise ship from the nearby Princess terminal let off its departure air horn. Just as it stopped, Stick came out of the terminal door behind them. He looked even more ridiculously touristy than they did in his surfer jam shorts, golf visor and yellow T-shirt that said California Dreaming on it.

"So did you get it?" Gannon said.

"Did I get it?" Stick said, flicking their new fake Florida driver's licenses across the outdoor table's white metal top like a blackjack dealer.

Gannon thumbed the waxy paper and looked back at the Walgreens picture of himself that had been taken this morning. He nodded, impressed.

"These are good, Stick. They look real," he said.

"They are real, or so my guy claims," he said. "There's a guy in the DMV who he gets them from."

"Even the DMV is corrupt, huh," Ruby said. "Is nothing sacred?"

"How much? Five hundred apiece?" Gannon said.

"Six actually," Stick said with a nod.

"I'll pay you back when we get down to my house. Hope hundreds are okay," Gannon said.

"Sure," Stick said. "Hundreds are cool."

"Or diamonds. We could do diamonds," Gannon said.

"Diamonds? Hmm. I know the ladies like those things. Let me think about it," Stick said.

"Wait, Jessica Roberts?" Ruby said, annoyed as she squinted at her license.

"What do you want?" Stick said. "You kinda look like Julia Roberts to me, so I went with it."

"She was a movie star back in the olden days of the eighties," Gannon explained.

"Duh," Ruby said. "I'm thirty-five, Mike, not ten. *Steel Magnolias, Mystic Pizza*. I've heard of her. But Jessica? Ugh. Jessica?"

"Hey, you're lucky. Look at my new name," Gannon said, showing her his ID.

"Burt Clancy," Ruby said. "Stick, really? Burt? That's the worst name in the history of names."

Stick suppressed a grin.

"What are you talking about? Burt is a tough name. It's making a comeback," he said.

"Oh, sure. What's your new name?" Ruby said. "Let's see it."

He passed it over. She showed it to Gannon. He looked at it and laughed.

"Wow, you're an idiot," he said.

"Steven Van Damme?" she said.

"What?" Stick said with a smile. "I always wanted to have a real kick-ass name."

74

The high-speed ferry left Fort Lauderdale at nine on the button and landed at a marina dock near Princess Beach in Freeport on Grand Bahama at a little before noon.

It was an uneventful crossing except for some choppy water as they came through the Gulf Stream. The seesawing of the ferry had woken Stick from where they'd been napping in one of the inside lounges and sent him green-faced into the bathroom.

Standing in line at the deck rail to get off, Gannon searched around nervously until he turned and saw the *Donegal Rambler* waiting at the other end of the dock behind them. He waved back to Little Jorge standing in the stern.

"More boating now. Oh, and a smaller one now, too. Super," Stick said as they got off and headed down the dock toward the *Rambler.*

"All gassed up, stocked and ready to go, Captain Mike," Little

Jorge said as they stepped aboard. "You said we were in a hurry, so I grabbed you guys lunch. Should we just get going, then?"

"You took the words out of my mouth," Gannon said, untying the line and giving Little Jorge a high five.

Tourists were already being tugged around on banana boats out in front of the pink-and-white stucco hotels as the *Rambler* pulled out of the marina. When they'd cleared the bay, they went dead southeast with the throttle open.

They put Great Harbour Cay and the Berry Islands behind them and kept going out into the open water. It was a gorgeous day, temperature in the low 70s and hardly any wind.

At around five, Ruby came up into the flying bridge, where Gannon had just relieved Little Jorge. She had her hair pulled back and her sunglasses on and was smiling as the breeze ripped at her maxi dress.

"How's Stick doing?" he said.

"He's asleep."

Gannon laughed.

"Hey, good news," he said. "I saw the weather report. It's going to be a crystal clear night tonight."

"Oh, yeah?" Ruby said.

Gannon smiled.

"For our cruise, remember? You're not getting cold feet, are you?"

Ruby laughed. She looked out at the water through the rushing wind.

"What do you think is going to happen, Mike? I mean, this is a level of nuts never seen before. The FBI is making people disappear? Killing reporters and cops? That's hard to even say, let alone believe. I mean, is it even possible to straighten this out?"

Gannon looked at her, looked out at the water.

"Anything can be straightened out," he said.

"Do you really think so?"

"Anything," Gannon said.

"You're unbelievable," Ruby said.

"How so?"

"How the hell are you so confident?"

Gannon shrugged.

"I don't know. Good genes? A happy upbringing in the home?"

Ruby laughed.

"You know, I almost believe you."

"Believe what?"

"That you're not shitting bricks, too."

It was Gannon's turn to laugh. Then he pointed out through the breeze.

"Hey, look," he said.

There was an island, faint in the hazy blue up ahead.

"You see there? That's Pimlico Island. That's at the tip of Eleuthera," Gannon said.

"Home?" Ruby said, smiling.

"Yep," Gannon said, smiling back. "We're almost home."

75

Instead of going straight to his berth in Davis Head, Gannon had Little Jorge go a few miles farther south down the beach on the island's Caribbean side.

The dock they finally chugged in toward was very old and had several missing boards. It belonged to a place called the Ocean School that was just a two-and-a-half-mile walk to Gannon's house.

"Are you sure you want to go in alone?" Ruby said.

"Don't worry," he said, smiling. "You guys go back up with Little Jorge to Davis Head and get some dinner. I'll come up to get you in my truck after."

"No, really, Mike. Why don't I come with you? Hell, why don't we all just go?" Ruby said.

Gannon looked up at her from where he was throwing a couple of things into a knapsack. She'd gotten some sun on the crossing, her skin glowing. He remembered holding her hand as they ran through the cold dirty subway what seemed like a lifetime ago. And how cute she looked in the headset she'd put on in the prop plane.

Pretty Woman, he thought.

"No, Jessica," he said. "I got this."

"But," she said.

"No buts. You head to dinner. Naval orders," Gannon said.

"Wait," Ruby said. "I thought I gave those."

"Only in the US," Gannon said, holding up a finger. "We're in the Bahamas now. You heard Little Jorge, right? I'm the captain down here."

Gannon watched until they made the wide turn in the water before he came in off the beach toward a cluster of low one-story buildings. A gypsy cab came around a bend as he came out of the school's driveway onto Sherman Highway. It was dark enough now to notice the glow of its brake lights as it slowed. But Gannon waved it on, and its brake lights went off, and it kept going.

When he got to his cul-de-sac, the first thing Gannon did was to go off into the brush. He reached into his bag and stood scrutinizing his house and the other three of his neighbors' houses with binoculars.

Two of the bungalows belonged to American families that only sporadically came down and were often deserted. The last of his neighbors was a cranky retired Canadian doctor who was usually around, but he'd gone back to Toronto to take care of a sick relative two months before.

Gannon knew he was probably just being paranoid as he scanned the front and side of his house. He didn't think it was possible for them to catch up with him this quickly.

But then again, he hadn't known they could track people through the NYC subway in real time either.

He came farther down his street in the twilight and stopped beside one of the absentee neighbors' houses and stood looking at his place. At the dark windows. It was a very nice evening. There was a rose-gold quality to the evening light.

There were no vehicles except for his truck. Everything seemed in order.

"Okay," he said and took a breath and came out of the shadowed brush.

He closed the final couple of hundred feet and hurried across his front yard and keyed open his door. He stood for a moment, looking at the dark inside. He sniffed at the air.

Was there a hint of something? Cologne? Or was he just being paranoid?

He was still standing there, still wondering, when quick as a weasel, a man with a gun popped his head around the side of the house at the carport.

He was a heavily muscled black man in a blue Hawaiian shirt and silver mirrored aviator sunglasses. The gun looked like a .45. The squarish silencer on the business end of it was pointed directly at his face.

"Go on in, friend," the man said in his American voice.

He smiled, showing very white teeth, as he tilted his head and the gun at the door.

"I insist," he said.

76

Gannon stood there frozen in the evening twilight as the man in sunglasses stepped up onto his front yard path behind the gun. He was about six foot three, in his early thirties, trim-waisted as an athlete, moving easily.

Through the heavy thumps of his heart in his ears, Gannon turned and looked through the dim doorway.

How stupid could you be? he thought.

The guy stopped three feet away.

"What are you? Hard of hearing?"

Gannon looked at him.

Run? he thought with desperation. *Fight?*

Gannon looked back at his dark doorway. He definitely did not want to go in there.

Still not moving his feet, he glanced back at Sunglasses, his vision tunneling in on the steel of the .45 in his hand as the guy thumbed back the hammer with a loud click.

"You hear me now? Get in that house or I'll blow your brains out," he said.

He had thought he'd been prepared for something like this, but now that it was right here before him, moving too quickly for him to get a handle on it, he realized he had thought 100 percent absolutely wrong.

Gannon finally took a step forward toward the door. As he did it, he suddenly felt exhausted, his body heavy and slow and weak, as if he were slogging through wet mud.

No, it wasn't mud, he realized from a distant memory.

It was sand, he thought, as he stepped over his threshold into his house.

It was wet sand and then a voice from long ago violently yelled in his head, "Get in the game, puke! You even think about checking out, I will personally drown your damn scrawny ass in this surf!"

The memory evaporated with the heavy thunk of the door closing behind him.

77

There were two more men inside of his house sitting in his living room.

They were both lean and clean-cut and wearing business attire.

They actually looked the way FBI agents were supposed to look, Gannon thought. In their crisp khakis and polos and Top-Siders, they could have been a couple of finance guys down to the islands for a corporate conference.

The one sitting in his leather recliner was older and taller and completely bald. There was a crackle of plastic as he reached into the bag of shelled peanuts that was in his lap. He had stolen them from his cupboard, Gannon realized.

As Gannon watched, the man cracked one of the peanuts open and picked out the nut and let the cracked shells spill from his palm almost playfully to the floor. He must have been doing this for some time because the Spanish tile between his size-thirteen new boat shoes was completely littered with shells.

"Well, well, well. If it isn't Mystery Man," the bald agent said, cracking open another peanut and licking it out of his palm.

"Mike, I'm FBI deputy assistant director Reyland," the bald man said with a grin after he had chewed and swallowed. "And on the couch over there is FBI special agent Emerson."

Emerson gave him a wave from the couch. He was dark-haired and younger and metro preppy. There was an open Apple laptop on the couch beside him.

Gannon looked back at the bald man. Then he looked back at Sunglasses, at the large bore of his Smith & Wesson trained three feet from his face.

"You're not an easy man to catch up to," Reyland said. "And we'd love to ask you a few questions. How are you doing this fine evening?"

Gannon watched as Reyland slapped bits of peanut shell off the lap of his slacks. After he was done, he smiled broadly as he crossed his long legs and placed his big hands onto the ends of the chair's armrests. He settled back and raised his bald head high with a relaxed, ready-to-be-amused expression on his face. A king on a throne ready for the jester's performance.

"Cat got your tongue?" Emerson said.

"Can I help you?" Gannon finally said.

"Oh, you've helped enough, I think, haven't you, Mike?" Reyland said. "First by taking what didn't belong to you. Then by killing our friends. Or maybe we have the wrong house? Tell me, you weren't around Lexington Avenue this week, were you? With a gun in your hand? Killing four US federal law enforcement agents?"

Gannon looked down as a flash of the inside of the Escalade suddenly came to him. The reek of cordite and smoke and the three men shot to pieces with their blood splatter up on all the shattered windows.

He shook the memory away as he put a knuckle to his lip as if he were trying to remember.

"Around what time would this have been?" he said.

Reyland smiled.

"Oh, around seven Friday last."

"Oh, yeah, now that you mention it," Gannon said after a pause. "As a matter of fact, I was out on Lexington that night. But I didn't shoot any law enforcement people."

"Is that right?" Emerson said. "Are you sure?"

"Positive," Gannon said, looking at him. "That night I was only killing reporter-murdering scumbags."

Reyland smiled even wider. He had nice clean white teeth. Dimples.

"Funny," he said, swiveling to and fro in his chair. "Now for something not so funny. Agent Emerson, if you would do the honors."

"It would be my pleasure," Emerson said, smiling as he stood in his razor-creased khakis. He walked past the small kitchen into Gannon's back bedroom. A moment later when he came back out, he was dragging something heavy.

It was a man.

A short naked black man, and he was covered in blood.

78

Emerson dragged the little black man over among the cracked shells.

It took a full thirty seconds of looking at the swollen, broken face to verify it was Sergeant Jeremy.

The bald man laughed as he dumped out what was left of the peanuts over Sergeant Jeremy at his feet.

"You sons of bitches!" Gannon said, wild-eyed, stepping forward.

As he did this, Sunglasses clocked him hard with the gun in the temple. As Gannon put his hands to the spot, his right leg was kicked out from underneath him and he fell backward. He landed hard on his ass, banging the hell out of the back of his head against the tight hallway's Sheetrock wall on the way down.

Gannon's lower lip split as Sunglasses kneed him explosively in the face a few times. Then the barrel of the gun was jammed painfully in his ear.

"You have a choice here, Mike," Reyland said, standing as Emerson dragged Sergeant Jeremy back into the bedroom.

"An end-of-life decision actually," he said as he crunched over the shells.

He crouched down until they were eye level.

"We can either take you and your friend back into that bathtub of yours and get busy slowly lopping you into pieces small enough to wash down the drain. Or you can tell me where our property is."

Gannon stared down at the tile. A drop of blood from his split-open temple plopped down onto it. Then another drop from his lip followed it. One of his lower teeth was loose. He could actually move it with his tongue.

He looked up at Emerson as he returned from the bedroom alone.

Then he finally played the only card he had left.

"I have a video of the people on the plane," Gannon said, looking up into the bald man's gray eyes. "I had a GoPro camera when I dived down. It shows the FBI director, the black guy, and the other two white guys. It shows their faces. All close-ups. That's what you want, right? That's what all this is about?"

In the silence, Reyland peered at him poker-faced.

"And let me guess," said the younger agent, Emerson. "If you're not back somewhere by the right time, it gets released by a lawyer or some other bullshit?"

"No," Gannon said, shaking his head. "I didn't make any copies of it. The tape's still in the camera, and I can get it for you. Right now."

Reyland continued to peer at him.

"What about the missing items? Don't lie and say you don't know what I'm talking about. We found the empty case."

"It's there, too. I hid everything together."

"Who the hell are you, anyway?" Emerson said. "You're obviously NYPD or something. Except your fingerprints aren't in the NYPD database. You have no Social Security card, but you have an Irish passport? You don't even have any records here in the Bahamas except for your shitty boat."

"A New York cop? Me?" Gannon said. "Okay, fine. Guilty as charged. I was a cop. But I've been clean for a few years now. Don't ask me about the records. The Irish passport thing was because my old man was from Donegal. I registered for dual citizenship because I didn't want to pay taxes back to the States. I'm just a retired cop who happened to see a plane go down. I want to work with you here, okay?"

Gannon turned to Reyland.

"Listen, I have what you want. I'm just going to need my diving stuff. I hid the video nearby underwater in a blue hole."

"You hid the video in a what?" Emerson said.

"It's an underwater cave," Gannon said. "They call them blue holes. It's about half an hour south from here."

"Well, Mike, I'm glad you're cooperating," Reyland said, putting an arm over his shoulder. "I'm on a pretty tight schedule, and I'm overjoyed at least that you're not being a deaf-mute pain in the ass like your stupid stubborn old friend back there."

"Let me just go get it," Gannon said.

"A man of action, Mike. I like that," Reyland said. "But do me a favor and go to the front door, would you?"

Sunglasses opened the door for him. The barrel of the .45 stayed rammed in his ear as he pulled him up to his feet.

On the other side of his lawn, a sky blue painters' van with ladders on its roof was pulling up at his curb. There was a short, stocky Spanish guy in the front passenger seat, and there was an extremely jacked black-bearded guy with a lot of tats behind its wheel.

The Spanish guy got out and opened the van's side door.

Inside, Ruby and Stick and Little Jorge were all down on the floor next to each other. Their hands and feet were secured with zip ties, and they had duct tape covering their mouths.

"Please," Gannon said to Reyland as his front door was slammed shut. "I'll get you everything you want. You can't hurt them. They have nothing to do with this."

"First he's a wise guy. Now it looks like Mike, the cop, here wants to make a deal all of a sudden," Reyland said as they all laughed.

"Why the hell are you doing this?" Gannon said, looking at him. "What the hell is this even for?"

Emerson stepped over and put a hand on Gannon's shoulder again and leaned in. Fatherly. The way a coach would in a close basketball game.

"We couldn't even tell you if we wanted to," he whispered in Gannon's ear. "It's a matter of national security, Mike. Strictly need-to-know."

79

When they went outside into his warm backyard, the sun was completely down, and it was raining slightly. With the help of the mercenaries forming an assembly line over the scrub grass from his storage shed to the carport, it took almost no time at all to load up his truck with the Gator and the diving equipment.

Gannon watched as they clunked several more tanks than necessary into the truck's bed.

"You don't need to do that. Two tanks are more than enough," Gannon said.

"Good one," the short, cocky Spanish thug from the van said. "You think you're going anywhere by yourself, think again."

Gannon looked at him. Like the rest of them, he was an American. He reminded him of a guy he once knew, a little all-state wrestler at his high school in the Bronx. What had they called him again? El Mighty Mouse, Gannon remembered.

Sunglasses zipped Gannon's hands behind him hard and tight

with some plastic ties and put him into his pickup's crew cab. Gannon watched as he went over to the van with Blackbeard. A moment later, El Mighty Mouse got in behind his truck's wheel with Agent Emerson riding shotgun.

"Pardon me for stating the obvious," El Mighty Mouse said as he sorted through Gannon's key chain, "but your truck here's a real genuine piece of shit."

"Well, now we know why he took the money," Emerson said as he rolled down the window.

Gannon stared at the blue van with Ruby and Stick and Little Jorge in it. After a minute, the big bald son of a bitch, Reyland, came out of his bungalow's front door.

At least they were getting away from the house, Gannon thought. He wondered how long they'd had Sergeant Jeremy for. Over a day at least. His wife, Emmaline, had to be crazed. He was badly beaten, but he was a tough old codger. Maybe someone would come by looking for him.

Reyland walked over to the truck.

"Ruiz, if you would," he said, gesturing toward the house.

Ruiz grinned back at Gannon before he climbed out and walked across the lawn.

"What the hell is he doing?" Gannon said frantically as El Mighty Mouse went in through the open front door. "What's he doing in there?"

The FBI men said nothing. They all stared at the house.

No, Gannon thought, biting his lip. There was no way.

Gannon reared back in his seat as if he'd been Tasered as the two shots boomed.

As El Mighty Mouse walked out of the house whistling, Gannon's gaze slid down onto the inside of his truck floor. There was an empty Gatorade bottle there. It was next to an old sky blue kid's flipper from when Declan was young.

He felt dizzy as El Mighty Mouse, still whistling, climbed back into the truck and turned over the engine.

The sergeant had five kids, Gannon thought. Twenty-something grandkids.

As the engine revved and they began to pull out, Gannon remembered Sergeant Jeremy's invitation to his sermon.

He closed his eyes.

There would be only one way out of this now.

80

Two hours later it was full dark, and they were all back behind the pine woods on the rough rock shelf above the blue hole.

Along the ridge of the water hole, the mercenaries made an actual campfire, and there were chairs and a folding table with coffee and radios on it. Behind the table was Gannon's Gator as well as another 4x4 quad they had in the back of the van.

It looked almost like they were on safari or something.

They had done a better job of setting up shop than he and the Aussie geology professor had done, Gannon thought as he sat there. And they had been there for over two weeks.

Beside Gannon sitting on the uncomfortable rock were Ruby and Stick and Little Jorge. Reyland was seated to their right about five feet away on one of the camp chairs.

As they sat silently in the firelight, Gannon busied himself by vividly wondering how the skin of Reyland's neck would feel in the palms of his bound hands.

He was still quietly staring and imagining when there was a sudden loud splash from the water below.

"He's right. It's like a damn maze under there, boss," Blackbeard suddenly called up from the hole's pond-like surface. "There are tunnels at every damn turn. We could be here for months. Shit, years!"

Reyland turned in the campfire's light.

"You sneaky little prick," he said, flinging the dregs of his coffee thermos at Gannon across the firelight.

"You're wasting your time," Gannon said as he chinned coffee off his face onto his shirt. "Just send me down already. I know exactly where it is."

"I think this cop is playing games, boss," he heard Blackbeard call up from the water hole. "There's so much silt in the water you can hardly see even with a flashlight. I think he's lying. I don't think there's shit down there."

Gannon took a relieved breath as he heard this. Twenty minutes before as the mercenary suited up and went under alone, Gannon had started worrying that maybe the son of a bitch might actually come across the bag by sheer luck.

Guess not, dumbass, he thought.

"You hearing me, boss?" Blackbeard called up.

"Shut up," Reyland said, staring at Gannon.

"I know you have a map. Where is it?" he said.

"I already told you. I had a map, but I burned it after I hid everything," Gannon explained. Which was actually true.

Reyland wrinkled his large brow as he leaned back in the folding camp chair, thinking.

In the silence, the only sound was Emerson sitting at another chair behind Reyland, typing at his computer.

Gannon looked across the limestone rim of the hole to where Sunglasses and El Mighty Mouse stood strapping what looked like fully automatic M4 military rifles. They carried them with a casual ease up before them in the position known as high ready. Butt tight to shoulder, elbows in, trigger finger against the receiver.

Textbook, Gannon thought, watching them. Professional.

"What are you looking at?" El Mighty Mouse said to him as Reyland finally nodded.

"Boys, new plan," Reyland said, pointing at Ruby. "Take the woman and take her clothes off and tie her to that palm tree there."

"Wait for me, fellas," Blackbeard yelled from the water. "Toss me another rope. C'mon. You can't start the fun without me."

"If you touch her," Gannon said, calmly shaking his head, "if you touch any of us, you never get it back."

"Who are you kidding?" said Sunglasses. "Your girlfriend will be squealing so loud, you'll tell us the moon is made of queso dip to make it stop."

"The only thing you'll get out of hurting me or my friends," Gannon said, squinting at Reyland, "will be the joy of me making sure you never find what you're looking for. Ever."

"Oh, listen to this, boys. Supercop here is going to stand up to torture. We've got a tough guy here among us," Sunglasses announced.

Gannon's smile was almost wistful in the firelight.

"I'm not that tough," he said, staring at the water.

Gannon's smile evaporated as he stared at the man level in his aviator sunglasses.

"I'm just tougher than you," he said.

"Sit your silly ass down," El Mighty Mouse said to the mercenary as he started to come around the rim of the hole at Gannon.

Gannon turned to Reyland.

"I said I would get what you need. Untie me, and I'll go get it."

"Maybe this information is time sensitive," Reyland said. "Maybe I don't care as long as it stays buried."

"And all those diamonds?" Gannon said, staring at him. "Are they time sensitive, too?"

"Diamonds? What diamonds?" El Mighty Mouse said.

Gannon looked over at him and then back at Reyland and smiled.

"You didn't tell him?" Gannon said. "Oh, wow. You didn't, did you? He doesn't know. And here I thought all you guys were friends."

"What diamonds?" El Mighty Mouse said again.

"I mean, the money is nothing," Gannon continued. "Two point eight million. What's that? Chump change. The stones down in that cave are worth ten, twenty—who knows, maybe thirty—times that."

El Mighty Mouse looked at Gannon, then back at Reyland.

"Is that true?" he said.

"No. I don't know. Maybe," Reyland said, putting up his hands. "You think they tell me everything, Tommy? Was I on the damn plane?"

"It's true," Gannon said. "There's a fortune down there."

Gannon strained to hide his elation as El Mighty Mouse walked over and knelt. There was a quick metallic snick of a knife and then the zip ties were cut from his wrists.

"You win," he said to Gannon. "We won't touch the girl. Put your shit on. You're going down with our boys to find it."

81

Blackbeard stroked across the surface of the blue hole as Gannon came down the rope, lugging his tanks and vest. Gannon looked at his tattoos. There were plenty to look at. In fact, from his bull neck on down, there seemed to be virtually no uninked skin at all.

He tensed at the playful expression on the mercenary's face as he arrived.

"Hey, boss," the huge killer said, smiling widely.

"Hey," Gannon said.

"C'mere. Let me show you something," Blackbeard said, swimming up close.

As Gannon watched, the commando grabbed his rope. As he did this, he drew from somewhere a machete-sized black knife. It had evil high-tech lines and a silvery razor-sharp scimitar-like edge that glittered in the firelight as he laid it none too gently up under Gannon's jaw.

"Hey, it's cool, man," Gannon said, trying to hold the rope and his heavy gear and stay very still all at the same time.

"I don't give two shits about recovering anything or whatever they said up there," he said, staring in Gannon's eyes. "You mess with me when we go down, you're going to be the world's first recipient of underwater open-heart surgery."

"No problem," Gannon said, swallowing carefully. "Gotcha, man."

As the blade was withdrawn, there was a tremendous splash. When Gannon turned, he saw Sunglasses was there in the water behind them.

Gannon winced again as the man smiled at him. He was without his sunglasses now, and where his left eye should have been was a hole you could have putted a golf ball into.

Where did Reyland get these people? Gannon thought as he began to strap up.

Three quick minutes later, Gannon adjusted his mask, popped the regulator's gummy rubber piece into his mouth and let go of the rope. He went down first with Blackbeard following almost at the end of his flippers and Sunglasses close behind him.

He had been walking it all through in his mind, so as they got to the floor of the blue hole's bowl, he softly tapped the BCD valve to get the horizontal perfect and went easily and immediately into the corridor-like passageway to the east.

He turned around for the first time when he got to the limestone stairwell with no stairs about a minute later.

Shit, they were actually good divers, Gannon thought. Still Blackbeard was right behind him, shining his light in his face, and his buddy Sunglasses was close behind him.

It didn't matter, Gannon thought as he turned and began to descend lower and lower into the darkness.

There was no other choice. No other play.

He breathed in deeply through the hissing regulator and

slowly let the air bubbles flow out behind him. He closed his eyes and listened to the silence. After a moment, he began to hear his heartbeat pulse faintly against his eardrums.

He would just have to get everything done in the eyeblink of time that he would have.

82

"How long has it been now, Emerson?" Reyland called into the radio.

"Twelve minutes," Emerson called back over the Motorola.

Ruby glanced over at Reyland.

Emerson had just left on the Gator quad a minute after they had gone under. Ruby had overheard him say he was having trouble getting a cell signal for the laptop and wanted to try to get better service out closer to the road.

Ruby looked back across the depression at Ruiz standing there with his rifle. As they sat there, from way up the beach or perhaps from a boat moored out at sea, there was the faint sound of music. It was a slow mariachi song, some sad guitars and lamenting trumpets. Then just as suddenly, it cut off.

"How long can the tanks go for?" Reyland called into the radio after another minute.

"I don't know," Emerson called back out of the radio. "Doesn't Ruiz know this shit?"

"Don't ask me," Ruiz said to Reyland. "I was army, man. Delta. Shepard is the one who was in the Marine Raiders. I can hardly even swim."

Ruby looked at Stick, who looked at Little Jorge.

"Yeah, right," called Ruiz, looking over at them. "Like I can't see you stupid fools eyeballing each other. You want to get a good look at your bone marrow in this romantic firelight, please, by all means, try something funny."

Ruby looked up at the sky. She suddenly remembered what Gannon had said about taking her out on his boat.

She looked down at the black water where Gannon had gone.

There were no stars out tonight after all.

83

The blue hole's corridor-like passage began to close in narrower and narrower. As Gannon got to the extremely tight pipelike end of it, he suddenly put on the jets and swam hard into the tiny entrance of the cathedral.

He felt his right shoulder slice open on a sharp rock as he squeezed through the pipe, but that didn't matter. He ripped himself inside into the huge space, swam straight in for ten feet, dropped his light and left it there on the chamber's floor. Then he turned and swam upward and back over the opening where he had just entered.

Gannon floated there, probing with his hands. There was nothing and still nothing, and he almost went into full out-of-body panic mode, trying to remember where he put it, thinking maybe someone else had found it.

Then his hand found the old duffel fishing rod bag.

MICHAEL LEDWIDGE

Gannon's heart rate and breathing came faster and faster as he pulled the bag to him and unzipped it.

The yard-long piece of metal he pulled out of it looked like a spear gun except instead of a spike at the end of it, there was a short squat length of steel tubing that almost looked like the coupling for a water hose.

The device was called a powerhead, and it was a one-shot underwater firearm that was triggered by making jabbing contact with something.

Due to the retarding density of water, a bullet shot from a regular gun at a distance under water was virtually harmless. But a powerhead set off by spring-loaded direct contact ripped into a target no differently than any other firearm round fired into something from point-blank range.

Already loaded with a waterproofed shotgun shell of double-aught buckshot, the powerhead Gannon pulled from his bag was the kind that spear fishermen used as a backup to protect themselves from sharks.

Gannon pulled out its safety pin and placed its shaft between his teeth like a pirate's knife and took the second powerhead from the bag.

He'd just pulled the second one's pin and was turning down toward the entrance of the cathedral double-fisted when Blackbeard's head emerged into the chamber through the opening just below him.

Floating unseen in the dark two feet above, Gannon waited until he saw the commando's tattooed bodybuilder shoulders.

Then Gannon swung the powerhead down at the base of the big son of a bitch's unprotected skull with every single solitary fiber of fear and fury and life force he possessed.

84

Everyone turned to Reyland's radio as it suddenly began to sputter out static. There were several frantic clicks followed by a short loud beep.

"Emerson? What is it?" Reyland called into the Motorola.

"Holy shit! Reyland!" Emerson called out in a loud, suddenly very clear panicked voice.

"What!" Reyland said.

"The email I was waiting for," he yelled. "Holy shit! I knew it!"

"What?" Reyland said.

"You have got to be kidding me!" Emerson yelled.

"WHAT!" Reyland screamed back into his handheld.

"This guy, Gannon. The report just came in on him. I had Rayne cross-reference his fingerprints with the covert database, and it popped. It popped. We got a hit! You're not going to believe this."

"What are you trying to say?" Reyland called on the radio.

"Reyland, stop interrupting him!" Ruiz yelled from across the hole, sounding suddenly nervous. "How many times I gotta tell you? Every time two people key a mic at the same time, it kills the signal. Keep the line open!"

"Come in, Emerson. Over," Reyland said into the radio.

There was another crackle and then Emerson said clearly:

"I have the report on Gannon. Listen, he was NYPD, but before that, he was DEVGRU, Reyland. Top echelon. Task Force Blue."

Ruby's mouth dropped open as she sat there.

Being navy, she knew that DEVGRU was short for the Naval Special Warfare Development Group.

The special operations organization previously known as SEAL Team Six.

She thought about Gannon. His diving skills. The way he had handled the SWAT team in New York. His preternatural calm.

Gannon was a SEAL! she thought, wide-eyed.

"He's a SEAL?" Reyland said.

"Yes. Listen to this record. Navy SEAL Buds training, 1995, at age twenty-one one of the youngest ever to go through. SEAL Special Sniper School, San Diego, California. SEAL Covert No Contact Urban Environment Recon Course at Fort Gordon in Georgia."

Ruby beamed at the growing dread on Reyland's face.

"He's also done covert ops, boss. Ninety-six, he was Special Actions Division in Africa. In ninety-eight, he was South America with the same group. In twenty-oh-one, he was deployed to Afghanistan with the CIA first expeditionary force in search of Osama bin Laden."

"Shit, shit, shit!" Ruiz said.

"After that he switched to the DIA. Iraq and Afghanistan ops. Year after year after year. Eight tours, Reyland. Eight! This guy's killed more people than fentanyl. He must have joined the NYPD after cycling out of the SEALs."

Ruiz looked down at the water in panic.

"I knew it," he said. "This guy is a seasoned hunter-killer recon cowboy, and my guys don't know!"

"Emerson, listen to me. Are you sure about this? Are you sure?" Reyland said into the radio as he sat up straight.

They all listened. There was the scratch of empty signal. The sound of the wind.

"Emerson, come in. Over," Reyland said.

Reyland crackled the thumb piece again but there was just more fuzz.

"Emerson, come in. Over," Reyland said again.

They listened, but there was still nothing but the sound of crickets from the darkness and the soft rustle of wind in the fronds of the palms.

85

Across the rim of the depression, Ruiz suddenly crouched and backed away from the firelight. His M4 glistened as he shifted it up to his shoulder, pointing it up the path Emerson had gone.

"Reyland, listen to me," he called across the sinkhole. "Where the hell is the other gun? The one with the FLIR heat scope?"

"It's in the Gator. Emerson has it," Reyland said.

Reyland lifted the radio and keyed it again.

"Emerson. Emerson, come in. Over," he said.

"Emerson is dead," Ruiz said, not taking his eyes off the trail.

"What the hell are you talking about?" Reyland said.

"I don't know how, but this script has shifted," said Ruiz. "This SEAL has pulled a fast one on us. We need to get out of here and I mean now, Reyland. Get on that quad and turn it over and drive it over to me here. Do it now."

"You're crazy," Reyland said. "Emerson's battery died or something. This guy's still under the—"

The radio dropped from Reyland's hand as a sharp crack of scratchy signal feedback suddenly sounded out of it.

"Hello, Reyland," said a new voice from its speaker where it lay between his feet.

Ruby looked up at the dark sky, smiling as she felt her heart soar. It was impossible. But yet there it was.

It was Gannon's voice.

"Reyland. Come in, Reyland," Gannon said with a sharp whistle. "Come in, Assistant Special Deputy Agent Reyland, you bald ugly bastard. What? You don't want to talk to me now?"

Reyland stood up out of the camp chair slowly.

"No sudden movements, asshole," Gannon said from the dropped radio. "I have a bead on you right now with this rifle's beautiful FLIR scope. What did you think? I'd hide everything somewhere where there was no back door? Welcome to my house, shit for brains.

"You have a choice here, Reyland. You lie the hell on the ground, you get to live. You don't, I'm going to blow that big ugly Charlie Brown head of yours clean off your neck. Tell El Mighty Mouse same goes for him. Tell Short Shit to lay down his rifle or I will grease his spunky little ass."

There was a scuffling sound, and when Ruby looked up, Ruiz was running full sprint along the rim of the depression.

The rifle crack that came from the trees behind them a moment later seemed inconsequential, a car door closing. Ruiz screamed out mournfully as he went sprawling across the rough limestone face-first.

When he slowly regained his feet, he was clutching at his lower back with one hand like an old man in an aspirin commercial. Using his rifle like a kind of crutch, he began moving again much slower now, his feet shuffling, kicking up rocky dirt along the blue hole's rim.

The next shots from the trees came in a louder cluster. A kla

kla kla—ing burst of fire that made Ruiz's baggy yellow guaya-bera shirt billow outward as he stopped dead in his tracks.

When he turned slowly, you could see the dark blood splat-ter like huge ink stains all down the front of the shirt. He was attempting to lift his rifle to his shoulder when there was an-other shot that took him through the hollow of his throat just above the breastbone.

Then Ruiz teetered over headfirst into the depression and fell from sight.

His heavy little body had just hit the water with a cannonball-like splash when Ruby was suddenly yanked to her feet.

Gripping at her bound hands and the back of her hair, Rey-land ducked in behind her. He swung her hard between him and where Gannon's fire was coming from.

"You keep backing away with me," Reyland said in her ear as he began to pull her backward past the campfire, "or, by God, I will snap your neck clean in two."

"Let her go, you son of a bitch," Gannon called from the radio as Reyland shoved her to the right beside some palm trees where the other 4x4 quad was parked.

As she tried to pull away, Reyland swung her hard by her arms off her feet. The air was knocked out of her as she landed stomach first into the metal side of the quad.

She was still gasping to catch her breath, still in a daze, when Reyland kicked her away from the vehicle and leaped on top of it.

Reyland got the four-wheeler started. As he revved the throt-tle, the palm tree trunk just beside the left side of his face ex-ploded.

But Gannon's shot had just missed him, and Ruby screamed as Reyland crouched his pale bald head down between the handle-bars and tore off into the woods, the engine wailing.

86

Shirtless and soaking wet, Gannon ran top speed out of the shadows into the firelight beside the blue hole, carrying the M4 carbine he'd taken off Emerson.

He peeked over the rim of the depression and saw Ruiz floating facedown there in the water. Then Ruiz's head blew apart as he clacked another tight burst of 5.56 NATO rounds through the back of it.

Gannon squinted down at the cocky little prick who had killed Sergeant Jeremy.

He only wished he could bring Ruiz back to life. So he could kill him all over again.

"Mike! Over here," Little Jorge called.

Over the rim of rock, Stick was laid out on the stone on his side with Little Jorge kneeling beside him.

"Everybody okay?" Gannon said as he arrived and began slicing off zip ties with Blackbeard's knife.

"Yes," Stick said, smiling, "thanks to you. I never doubted you for a second, brother."

"Really? Then why did you keep saying 'we're dead, we're dead,' over and over again?" Little Jorge said, giggling, hugging Gannon after he helped him up.

Gannon ran over to where Ruby lay on the ground.

"You okay?" he said, kneeling down.

When he sliced off her zip ties, Ruby doubled over, clutching her stomach.

"Hey, are you hurt?" Gannon said, pulling at her baggy dress. "Let me see. Maybe you broke a rib or something."

"No, no. It's okay," Ruby said, immediately shoving him away. "It's better now. Much better. I'm fine now. Perfect, in fact."

"Suit yourself," Gannon said with a wink as he pulled her to her feet.

He led Ruby back to the others and crossed over to the other side of the campfire and started dumping out bags the mercenaries had left. In the second one, he found his truck keys. In the third one, two full magazines fell out and bounced off the rock.

"Little Jorge, listen," Gannon said as he tucked a magazine into the back pocket of his wet madras shorts. "You get everybody back to the Gator and go straight to your place. I'll meet you guys there."

"Where the hell are you going?" Stick said.

Gannon listened to the rip of the quad's engine getting fainter and fainter in the southern distance. He raised the M4, punched out the half-shot magazine, inserted a fresh one and ran the smooth-oiled action with a loud snick.

"To end this bullshit once and for all," he yelled as he began to run.

PART FOUR

THE ONE THAT GOT AWAY

87

It took Gannon under a minute to run back down the forest trail. His Sierra was parked there on the dirt road they drove in on, and he turned it over with a roar and laid the rifle down into the passenger-side foot well and opened the crew cab door.

When he came around to the tailgate, he saw Emerson on the other side of the dirt road. He was unmoved from the spot in the grass beside the Gator where Gannon had sneaked up behind him and choked him out.

He saw he was semiawake now, groggily staring at him from above the wraps of duct tape he'd tied him with.

"On your feet, you damn weasel," Gannon said, grabbing him by his hair. "We're going for a ride to find your boss."

A ragged column of trailing dust rose behind the speeding truck as Gannon hauled it up the dirt drive. When they hit Sherman's Highway, he was doing close to eighty, and the Sierra's spinning back tires gave out a long, high scary bark off the asphalt as the rear end fishtailed.

He went flat-out south as fast as he could for another mile. Then he let off the throbbing engine and rolled all the windows down, listening.

When the ripping sound of the quad came ahead through the trees on his right, he quickly pictured the terrain in his head.

Reyland was along the water now on the Bahama Banks–side beach. South of him where he was headed was Lighthouse Point, where the island ended.

The truck's V-8 throbbed to life again as Gannon buried the accelerator.

"I got you now, you son of a bitch," he said.

A quarter mile to the south the road began to dogleg to the left. When he saw the palm trees on the far side of it, he realized they actually rimmed the beach Reyland was currently driving on.

Gannon reached over and grabbed his seat belt.

"Bump!" he called back to Emerson as the Sierra bucked up off the road and plowed through the brush.

The speeding pickup just fit between two palm trees and then there was a crunching sound as it bottomed out on some jutting rocks. Beyond the rocks there was a descending sand dune, and Gannon felt his stomach drop as the truck's front end got sudden air.

He was rocketing down the curve of the dune, frantically pumping the brakes, when Reyland blew past at incredible speed from left to right across the beach right in front of him.

Gannon spun the wheel and locked his eyes on the quad's cherry-red running light and gunned it down the beach. He was reaching over to grab the rifle a split second later when the quad suddenly zoomed out of his headlights to the left.

"No!" Gannon screamed as he watched the red light disappear from the beach up a dune of sand that sloped up toward the ridge on their left.

He was halfway up the slope after it a moment later when the truck's tires began to slip.

"No!" he screamed again as the rear end swung back and forth in the loose sand as he revved it.

But it was no use.

Gannon slammed the stuck truck in Park and grabbed the rifle and bailed out the driver's door. He sprinted up the dune between the quad's tire tracks past the island's abandoned old gray concrete lighthouse and then came running down the ridge's other side.

He'd just made the flat sand of the Atlantic-side beach when he saw a spot of red to the north.

He halted and brought the infrared scope of the rifle up to his eye.

The quad had stopped. He could see Reyland's heat signature light up white against the dark as he stood beside it. He seemed to be talking on his phone.

Gannon blinked in the scope, gauging the distance. Four hundred yards, he thought. Four-fifty, tops.

Gannon hurried to his left. He braced himself in against the rough trunk of a jutting palm tree trunk and clicked the scope's range selector to four hundred and tucked the butt of the rifle tight into his shoulder.

He'd steadied the cross of the scope's reticle on Reyland's brainpan and had just begun pulling the trigger when he heard the chopping rumble behind him.

Gannon let off the trigger and turned with a mind-boggled expression on his face.

Back over the lighthouse ridge he'd just come down was the unmistakable metallic churning sound of a helicopter flying low.

A *bup-bup-bup-bup-bup-bup* sound of gunfire started up a split second later.

Gannon's eyes almost bulged out of his head.

The six-round burst was followed by another.

Bup-bup-bup-bup-bup-bup.

It was the rattle of a chain-fed machine gun.

"No," he whispered.

It was a gunship, Gannon realized.

A helicopter gunship had arrived now, and it was shooting up his truck.

88

Gannon immediately strapped the M4 on his back and began scrambling up the rock and through the heavier vegetation of the ridge beside him as fast as he could. He was halfway up the promontory when the helicopter roared in over the tree line twenty feet to his right.

It was a gunship all right, Gannon saw as he pressed himself dead still against the shadowed rock with his breath taken. It was a large Bell helicopter like a news chopper, and there was the long black barrel of an M240 bristling sideways out the side of its open sliding door.

As it crested the slope toward the Atlantic-side beach, a blinding white spotlight shot out of the far side of it. The light was probing at the silver palm he'd just been hiding behind when Gannon finally reached the top brow of the ridge.

He was on his hands and knees tucking in under a rock overhang he'd found in the promontory about three minutes later when he heard the helicopter come back over to the Bahama Banks side again.

He crawled out from under the rock and stood and listened to it getting fainter and fainter. After thirty seconds, he saw its lights heading way to the north and west out over the water.

He was terrified that it might head back to attack Ruby and the others, but he realized that Reyland was evac-ing off the island.

Heading where? he thought, tracking the aircraft as it went west. To Nassau? Where else? Had to be.

He hurried quickly south to where he had left the truck.

He shook his head in wonder as he climbed up the sand toward it a minute and a half later. He'd been right. All the windows were shot to shit and the hood and bed had been Swiss cheesed.

But for all that, its engine that he'd left running was miraculously still chugging.

"And they called you a piece of shit," Gannon said as he climbed in over the broken glass and clicked on the dome light.

There was a sound of ragged breathing behind him. He winced as he glanced back into the crew cab thinking surely Emerson must have been turned into a bunch of bloody rags.

But no. Emerson, wide-eyed and very much alive, sat on the floor of the crew cab staring back at him.

He leaned in closer and looked him over. There was blood on the right leg of his khakis. He took out Blackbeard's knife and slit open the pant leg and looked at the gunshot wound.

Emerson had been shot through his right thigh. Gannon turned him to the side. The exit wound was nasty.

But at least it was off center on the outside of the leg. It didn't look like the bullet had hit any bone or arteries.

He slipped Emerson's belt from his khakis. He cried out as Gannon tightened it into a tourniquet above his thigh.

He rolled him back over and checked his pulse.

He was in a bit of shock, but what do you know, Gannon thought with a shake of his head as he clicked off the dome light.

Like the truck, Emerson was still kicking, too.

Gannon brushed the glass off the seat and sat and put the truck into Reverse. When he let off the brake, gravity began immediately rolling them back down the hill of sand.

After he got the truck turned around, he had to stick his head out the door window to see past the shattered glass.

After a moment over the hiss of the radiator, he heard Emerson begin to cry softly behind him.

"I know, right?" Gannon said. "Shoot up a fine vehicle like this. How could they? Make a grown man cry."

89

"Emerson, enough already. Wake up," Gannon said, softly slapping the young agent on the cheek.

"What's going on? What the hell?" Emerson said weakly from where he sat taped to a kitchen chair.

Gannon watched the young agent's eyelids flutter open. Then Gannon smiled as he watched them shoot wide as he took a good look around at the windowless rusty Quonset hut they were now in.

It was three hours later, coming on midnight, and they were in the northernmost opposite end of the island in an area known as Lower Bogue. They were behind the razor-wired fence of a business called Island Safe Storage that belonged to an associate of Little Jorge.

Gannon gave Little Jorge and Stick and Ruby a thumbs-up through the glass of the office behind them. They were drinking soda and eating pizza as they went through the money and diamonds they'd already taken from the recovered sea bag.

Gannon loudly dragged an old kitchen chair over the battered concrete floor and sat before the one Emerson was now duct-taped to.

"I know you're still a little groggy from the painkillers, but it's time we started talking, Emerson. Bad news. Turns out, you're not doing so hot."

Emerson moaned as he looked down at himself where he sat shirtless and in his underwear. There were bloody bandages all over him, at his shoulder, at his crotch, at his right thigh where the tourniquet was still cinched.

"What is this? What's going on?" he cried as he shook in the chair. "Untie my hands. Untie my hands."

Gannon leaned forward and lifted one of the incredibly bloody bandages off Emerson's abdomen.

"Emerson, stop. Get a grip," Gannon said, showing him the bloody rag. "Your stupid friends shot you in the truck back at the beach, remember? One of the bullets came in through your shoulder here, see, and went down your torso doing who knows what to you before it came out here next to your hip."

"Nooo!"

"It's true. I'm worried about you. Your lungs, your major arteries. You were shot with a 7.76. That's a very large fast-moving piece of lead, son. Do you feel hot? Like you have a fever? You're in incredibly serious need of medical attention."

"Then get me to a doctor!" Emerson cried.

"I want to, bro. I really do. And I will," Gannon said as he placed the bloody rag back onto Emerson's stomach.

"But I need to find out what in the living hell is going on first. What the hell is going on?"

Emerson looked at Gannon in complete horror. He looked down at his shirtless self, at all the blood and rags.

"This can't be happening," he said.

Gannon folded his hands in his lap as he sat there. He crossed his legs as he calmly bit at a thumbnail.

"You're wasting time, Emerson. Precious seconds. But hey, it's your life. Not mine. I didn't get shot. My heart and arteries and internal organs are intact and working fine."

Emerson took a deep breath and held it. Then he let it out in a loud rush. His eyes were huge as he stared at Gannon.

"It's about Messerly," he said.

"Messerly?"

"Yes, Messerly. The NSA defector at the embassy in London. The entire operation. It's all about him."

"Oh, that Messerly," Gannon said. "Assange 2.0. How is it about him?"

"He's about to release a trove of classified emails that will rip the roof off the Western global intelligence apparatus. It reveals all of our black ops, our black sites. It also reveals some very questionable Bitcoin financial transactions between some very nasty people around the globe and members of US and British intelligence. Many people, especially a lot of higher-ups in the NSA and CIA and FBI, will go to jail for treason if it comes out," Emerson said.

"I see," Gannon said. "You guys are fighting to stay out of jail. I can buy that. That actually makes some sense considering your recent behavior. But what the hell does Messerly have to do with the FBI director's plane?"

"Our mission was to stop Messerly from releasing the information. But he and the information he has are secured behind the walls of the Chilean embassy in London, where he was granted asylum. Since then, we've been scouring the Chilean embassy staff for a turncoat. Someone with enough bad habits to be blackmailed or possibly bribed."

"Cut to the chase, Emerson. Clock's ticking, remember?" Gannon said.

He took a deep breath.

"But the problem is that Messerly is very well protected even in the embassy itself. A guard is staffed 24/7 outside his room, and only a handful of people are actually allowed to come into his tiny windowless third-floor suite. That's why we finally homed in on the embassy doctor, Raphael Santos, who has routine access to Messerly. We looked for a way to blackmail him into knocking out Messerly and retrieving his data, but it turned out that we were digging a dry hole."

Emerson took another deep breath.

"So that's why we kidnapped the doctor's kid," he said.

90

"You kidnapped his kid! *His kid?*"

Emerson blinked at him.

"Isn't the FBI supposed to solve kidnappings?" Gannon said. "Now you commit them?"

"His name was Scott. He was a college kid. He went to Cambridge. He was nerdy but real smart and caring and socially aware. We learned that he had an internship with the French refugee relief group, Cesse de Pleurer, that was going into eastern Gabon for the summer. The CIA had contacts in the rebel groups just across the border in the Congo. So we hired one of the Congolese warlords down there to grab him."

Gannon shook his head, dumbfounded.

"So the young guy with the headphones on the plane was the embassy doctor's son? That was Scott Santos?"

"Yes," Emerson said.

"And the dead black man was your African warlord?" Gannon said. "He was the kidnapper you hired?"

Emerson nodded.

"Yes. His name was Biyombo. Terrence Biyombo. After he grabbed Scott, he read from the script we gave him. At first, he asked the doctor for money like in a regular kidnapping. But after three million dollars was delivered, he called Santos back and told him that he had learned who the doctor was and where he worked and the Russians he bought his weapons from now wanted something else."

"Messerly's data," Gannon said.

"Yes," Emerson said. "Messerly's data."

"Why was the FBI director involved?" Gannon said.

Emerson looked up at the rusted ceiling.

"For a bunch of reasons. Dunning was neck deep in Messerly's data, for one. Also, Dunning worked with MI6 during the tail end of the Cold War, and we needed him to smooth things over with the British intel people in London who were helping us in the operation.

"But most of all, we needed his radar-jamming G550 to smuggle Scott and Biyombo out of the Congo. The area where Biyombo was holding Scott was in a war zone, and it was becoming increasingly unstable. So Dunning agreed to stop there covertly in the jungle on his way to an Interpol conference in Milan."

"That's where they were headed when the plane malfunctioned? To Italy?" Gannon said.

"Yes. The cabin pressure failure problem must have happened as soon as they got to altitude. The plane was supposed to make a turn to the north, but it never did. It kept going west out over the Atlantic."

"Until it ran out of gas," Gannon said.

"We had no idea where it was until it crashed," Emerson said. "We couldn't track it because the radar-jamming device was on."

"Who was the other guy on the plane? The other stocky white guy?"

"His name was Oliver Buchanan. He was an undercover MI6 agent working with us. He was posing as a hostage negotiator working with the doctor's family for Scott's release."

"Wow, quite an elaborate production," Gannon said. "A cast of thousands."

"Are you familiar with the term *parallel construction?*" Emerson said. "It's standard operational procedure in a case like this. We needed to put the doctor in a moving box, cover every angle."

"You certainly seemed to have accomplished that," Gannon said. "You must have had him coming and going."

"Yes. Please, now you know everything. I've told you everything. Get me to a hospital now. Please, I'm begging you," Emerson said.

Gannon stood and started pacing back and forth behind Emerson.

"Not so fast. I don't think you're telling me everything," Gannon said.

He walked over to a computer on a desk in the corner. He shook the mouse, brought up Google, typed into the search bar and hit Enter.

"I knew it," Gannon said, looking up from the screen. "It says here Messerly's big info drop is in two days' time. This operation is still on as we speak, isn't it? Dr. Santos is still about to take out Messerly for you. He still thinks he can save his son."

"I don't know," Emerson said.

"You don't know? Okay, fine," Gannon said as he came over and started peeling off Emerson's bloody rags. "Are you familiar with the term *bleeding out?*"

"Stop!" Emerson screamed. "Okay, okay! Yes, you're right. The doctor is still in the dark. He picked up a package in London we sent him three days ago. It contains sedatives and a drone he's to use to get all the data out of the embassy for us. That's why the diver was renditioned and the reporter killed. All the potential leaks needed to be plugged in order to keep the doctor in the dark."

"Because if Messerly delivers the truth," Gannon finished for him, "then all you corrupt rotten filthy pieces of money-grubbing shit go to jail."

"Yes," Emerson said. "That's really it. That's all of it. Now please just drop me off at a hospital. I don't care if I go to jail. I'm twenty-nine, man. I just don't want to die!"

"Relax, bro. You'll be fine," Gannon said.

"But the internal bleeding!"

"There isn't any," Gannon said. "You were only shot in the leg. It's a through-and-through. I just covered you in some of your own blood. You think you guys are the only ones who can make shit up?"

"You son of a bitch!" Emerson said.

Gannon nodded.

"You better believe it," he said. "I'm about as nasty a son of a bitch the friendly neighborhood psychopaths of the Naval Special Warfare Command and Joint Special Operations Command and the theater of combat ever created."

Gannon shook his head as he laughed.

"And what do you know? You and your genius boss just pulled me out of retirement," he said.

91

The most important briefing in Reyland's life took place at eleven thirty in the morning off-site in a ruddy brick antique furniture warehouse in the Camden section of London.

Reyland rolled into its rainy cobblestone courtyard with his new team in two Range Rovers at eleven fifteen. There were eight men in his new British operational detail. He thought they looked much like his old American team only they were paler and better dressed.

He left his new men on the ground floor and came up the warehouse's creaking stairs alone. Coming along the grim and grubby walls, Reyland thought the massive furniture-filled space looked old enough to have stored the tea bags that started the Revolutionary War.

He took a breath and sneezed. It even smelled old. There had been a consignment shop just down the road from where they'd summer sometimes with his grandparents in the rural hick kingdom of southeast Indiana, and it smelled like that. Like old church ladies' coats that had been sitting up in a hot, dusty attic.

Reyland was standing by the window when his MI6 counterpart arrived with her people at twenty past. Reyland smiled as he watched her clop over between the old sideboards and rolled-up rugs in her ridiculous heels. Brooke Wrenhall was shorter in person than she had seemed in the SCIF screen, and her makeup was even more garish.

For a moment, they watched the rain pissing into the green water of the Regent's Canal outside the dusty old arched window.

"Ah, another sunny day in London," Reyland said.

Wrenhall took a fat file folder out of her bag and slapped it onto the top of a tarp-covered desk they were standing beside.

Reyland didn't even have to look at the title beneath the national security designation to know it was Michael Gannon's covert military records file. He had just read some of it himself on the plane. He'd actually asked the Pentagon for a completely unredacted version and had straight up been denied. There was no love lost between them and the DIA.

"Doing a little light reading?" Reyland said.

"I just got off the phone with a friend of mine in California about this Gannon. This Michael Gannon," Wrenhall said.

Reyland lifted his chin.

"Interesting conversation, was it? How's the weather out there?"

"Do you know Bill McKendry?"

"The recently retired head of JSOC? I've met the admiral," Reyland said, nodding.

Wrenhall patted the fat file folder.

"Bill says this Michael Gannon was a legend among legends in the SEAL community and was nice enough to send me some of his records. He's been through the CIA's Farm, did you know that? He has tradecraft."

"I vaguely remember hearing that."

"What's especially interesting for me personally, Robert, is the title of the special forces program he helped start at Fort Gordon in Georgia. The Covert No Contact Urban Environment Recon Course. He virtually wrote the textbook on infiltrating, hiding and surviving in a city. And what do you know? Here we are in a city. My city."

"Stop being paranoid," Reyland said.

"And," Brooke said, ignoring him, "some of these covert military ops in which he was involved are quite familiar to me. They were SEAL-SAS joint operations, which means it's probable that Gannon might have actual contacts here in the UK."

"We'll find him," Reyland said. "Santos is in a box. NSA is in complete control of his communications now. There's no way to make contact with Santos by phone or text or fricking carrier pigeon."

"How much time do we have on that end?" Wrenhall said.

Reyland looked at his phone.

"We have T-minus eleven hours and eight minutes."

"You knew this Gannon was involved. His background, his training, and yet you failed to mention it?"

"I found out five seconds ago, Brooke. I had no idea," Reyland said.

"You know what McKendry said about this? Do you know what he said when I suggested Gannon might be at loggerheads to our operation? He said, and I quote—"

"Brooke," Reyland said.

"And I quote," Brooke repeated. "'You folks just opened yourselves up a box of hell.' End quote."

"A box of hell?" Reyland said, wincing.

"That's what the man said," Brooke said.

"Even so, Brooke, what should we do? Abort? And what then? Shoot ourselves? We're in this completely, and there's only one way out. We either pull this off or…" He trailed off.

Out on the water, a low canal boat went by, the wood roof glossy like the lid of a coffin.

He tapped at the glass.

"Or that, Brooke, that right there. Only over a waterfall and on fire."

She looked with him out at the coffin-like boat and took a deep breath.

"You're right, Robert," she finally said. "Of course. Tell me what you need."

92

"Taxi, sir?"

Rolling his carry-on into the drizzle out the front doors of Heathrow, Gannon shook his head.

"No, thank you. I'm waiting on a ride," he said.

Twenty-four hours before, Little Jorge had smuggled Gannon into the Dominican Republic near the port of Bajos de Haina just west of Santo Domingo.

The Dominican Republic was the center hub of Caribbean drug smuggling, and with a little help from some friends, Little Jorge was able to get Gannon everything he needed in quick order.

They had found a very accommodating Venezuelan bank to open up a two-hundred-fifty-thousand-dollar account in cash, and Gannon had put the rest of the money along with the diamonds in a safety-deposit box in a large Canadian bank across the street.

The stolen Canadian passport Little Jorge had scored for him six hours later had cost five grand, and Gannon had flown first-class out of Puerto Plata on an overnight Eurowings flight.

Stick and Ruby had wanted to come, but they could score only the one passport, and there was no more time.

Being an international fugitive wasn't that difficult, Gannon thought, as he removed his burner phone from the pocket of his new raincoat.

All you needed were extremely heavy-duty criminal smuggling contacts and an unlimited amount of money.

"Yes, hello?" a voice said when the phone picked up. It was a little boy's voice in an almost whisper.

"Hi. Is Callum there?" Gannon said.

"Yes, but Daddy can't talk to you. He's driving."

"Oh, okay. My name is Mike, and I'm a friend of your dad. Could you tell him I'm outside of the airport?"

"Daddy says don't worry—we're on our way. We'll be five minutes."

"Thank you," Gannon said, smiling as he hung up.

It was more like three minutes when the beat-up white Volkswagen Golf pulled out of the busy traffic to a stop in front of him.

"Mickey! Screw me sideways! Mickey! How ya been?" his tall lanky old buddy Callum said, wrapping him in a bear hug as he leaped out.

He'd lost most of his sandy hair, Gannon could see. He was also thinner than he remembered him and was wearing glasses. He almost looked like a professor now.

Gannon remembered where they'd met. Some shithole outside Kirkuk where Callum and his SAS guys got cut to ribbons trying to free some brain-dead Brit tree huggers who got kidnapped by al Qaeda. Callum had been shot five times, and the bad guys were pulling him into the back of a technical when Gannon and his boys had shown up.

"I'm really sorry to bother you, man," Gannon said, frowning at him. "I didn't know who else to call."

"Sorry? Get stuffed. Here, give me that," Callum said, grabbing his carry-on and going to the trunk.

There was a strawberry blond–haired kid of four or five in the back seat playing a game on an iPhone.

"Are you an American?" the boy said as Gannon put on his seat belt.

"Yes. Born and raised."

"Did you know Daddy when he was a soldier?"

"Yes, I did," Gannon said. "That's when we met."

"Were you there when he got his scar?"

"Just after, son," Gannon said, smiling.

"He's the one who gave me the ride in the dune buggy," Callum said, slamming the driver's door.

"Oh, with the camels! When you saw the camels, Daddy!" the freckle-faced boy said, his eyes as big as saucers.

"Yes. Now play your game with the headphones," Callum said.

"But—"

"Play!" Callum yelled.

"I wish I had a dune buggy," the little boy mumbled to himself as he pulled on a pair of headphones.

Gannon laughed as he looked out at the traffic.

"I forgot about those camels," he said as they pulled out.

"I didn't," Callum said, smiling, as he pushed his glasses up his nose with a thumb. "Nor the ride."

93

The farm was in Wycomb in the Midlands about an hour west of London.

Callum listened patiently, and when Gannon was done, he put down his tea mug with a clack on the kitchen counter. He folded his arms.

"Lying about the dead FBI director. They're all mad now. Just mad. They'll do and say bloody anything. And even the press doesn't care? I knew it was heading this way. I worked for a contract company for over ten years, but it just got to be too much. Just bedlam on every level. Anyway, ready to see the stuff?"

They went out the front door of the damp little stucco house and walked along a field with two fat red cows in it toward a concrete barnlike building. As they came around its corner, Callum's son was kicking a muddy soccer ball off the side of it.

Inside, there were milking stalls and an office with a window. Callum led them into the office and clicked on the light and closed the door. He opened a large steel locker in the corner.

"I think I was able to get everything you asked for."

Gannon looked at the night vision goggles. The two Heckler & Koch MP5 submachine guns.

The oiled black pistol he lifted looked almost like a Colt M1911 .45 automatic but the barrel was too small.

"MAB?" Gannon said, squinting at the markings.

"Yes, it's a French company. Fifteen in the mag and one in the pipe. A *pistolet automatique très bon*."

"What is it? A thirty-eight?" Gannon said.

"Nine millimeter," Callum said.

"Ah, of course, the metric system," Gannon said. "And that was the box truck we passed on the way in?"

"Yep. Rented on the sly just like you requested. So it's all good, yes?" Callum asked.

"Yes, it's good, Callum," Gannon said with a nod. "Very, very good."

Callum went to the computer on his desk and clicked at the keys.

"Screw me, you're right. Here it is in the *Daily Mail*," he said. "'Messerly announces newest leak is a major one. Tomorrow night, the people of the Western world will learn what their governments are supposedly doing in their name.' End quote. Listen. They're speculating there's evidence of illegal arms trading, drug smuggling, satanic shite, pedophilia, you name it. And that many brand-name multinational corporations might be involved. A bunch of major banks."

"I told you Messerly's about to blow the sewer wall," Gannon said. "And fifty years of the rankest filth and corruption the world has ever seen is going to come a' flooding down Fifth Avenue and Downing Street and the Champs-Élysées."

"And you're saying your FBI friend, Reyland, is going to try to grab Messerly's data tonight to prevent it from coming out?" Callum said.

"Yes," Gannon said. "That's why I'm here."

"You're going to stop him from stealing it."

"Yes."

"How?"

"I'm not exactly sure," Gannon said. "I haven't thought that far ahead. But I'll think of something."

"But why?"

Gannon thought of Sergeant Jeremy. His starched shirts. His kindness. What he had done for him.

Hair actually stood up on the back of his neck as he suddenly remembered the title of the sermon the good sergeant had never gotten to deliver.

God Has a Mission for You.

"Because I have to," Gannon said.

"But you have that bag of money," Callum said. "Why not take off? Why not go fishing forever?"

Gannon laughed. Ruby had said almost the same exact thing to him at the airport in the Dominican.

Before she had unexpectedly kissed him goodbye.

He gave Callum the same answer.

"But I am going fishing," Gannon finally said with a smile.

He thought of Reyland.

"Tonight, I go for Moby Dick," he said.

94

Two hours later, at ten o'clock, everything was ready.

Reyland, with all his notes memorized, turned from the window at his agents and analysts. He smiled at the buzz in the air, smiled at his security men standing at the back of the room with their blunt, hard faces.

All the king's horses and all the king's men, he thought.

There was a blown-up map of the city of London on the whiteboard behind him, and in front of him on the conference table was a 3-D cardboard mock-up of two buildings, one marked EMBASSY and one marked WORK SITE.

Reyland took out a pair of reading glasses and a laser pointer as he cleared his throat.

"Ladies and gentlemen, this," he said, waving the laser pointer across the shorter side of the box marked EMBASSY, "is Upper Belgrave Street.

"This," he said, pointing the laser between the boxes to its shorter side, "is Wilton.

"Our setup is at this work site here across Wilton, which we will infiltrate from Wilton Mews here to the north. Our agent in the embassy will open a window here on the Wilton side of the embassy in the back. Once the exchange from the window to across the street to the work site is complete, we will exit here down the work site scaffolding on Upper Belgrave into a waiting vehicle here. Once in the car, we will go in a protective convoy back here in the route that you've all been given. So far so good?"

He looked at the faces. Everyone was nodding.

"Any questions?"

"What about the foreign service security at all the embassies on Upper Belgrave? What if we're spotted?" asked an agent.

"You don't have to worry about that. We will be jamming all communications," Reyland said.

"In addition, all pertinent staff at surrounding allied embassies have been briefed. The whole area will be on stand-down," Wrenhall added.

"What if there is resistance from the Chilean embassy security or another intel force? Do we have permission to engage?" said another ops agent.

"The sensitivity of this operation could not be greater," Reyland said. "With that said, the acquisition and protection of this asset supersedes everything, and I mean everything."

"Engage anything that jeopardizes the mission?" said the security man.

"Yes, treat Upper Belgrave as a battlefield. Engage and remove all threats," Reyland said.

"Robert, if I could?" Brooke Wrenhall said, standing from the table.

"By all means," Reyland said.

"As you all know, this operation is in no way, shape or form authorized by any local police, so use the highest levels of stealth and aversion at all times," Wrenhall said.

"But remember," she said. "There aren't any words to explain exactly how important this mission is. I've been working in intelligence circles for almost forty years, and what we are seeking to recover is the most important piece of actionable intel I've ever come across.

"This mission is tide turning, ladies and gentlemen. History making. Or breaking. We all know our jobs. Let's do them."

95

Belgravia in London was a neighborhood that seemed to consist solely of large white bank-like buildings.

From the box truck's front passenger seat, Gannon looked out at the perfect columns and pristine arches, the stone balconies, the high dark windows.

"Ritzy," Gannon said as he went around a double-parked Rolls-Royce.

The Chilean embassy at 14 Upper Belgrave was on the northeast corner of Wilton. As he passed it, Gannon surveyed its security cameras, its twelve-foot-high thick wrought iron gate. The heavy black metal door behind the gate was as featureless and formidable as a bank safe's.

No wonder the intel services had gotten so desperate, Gannon thought. No one was getting in there without a wrecking ball or a five-hundred-pound bomb.

He passed the embassy and made a right onto a tree-flanked

road then another onto Belgrave Place, and then twenty feet up past a road called Eaton Square he pulled over.

Gannon got out and went to the back of the box truck that now had telephone company markings along its side. He popped the doors and put on a hard hat and orange traffic vest. There was a telephone company manhole just in off the corner, and he took out some traffic cones from the back of the truck and placed them around it. Then he lifted a crowbar off the floor of the truck and bent and popped the manhole.

After he dragged the lid aside, Gannon stood on the street glancing nonchalantly at the passing traffic. Then he went down into the hole with a flashlight and a pair of bolt cutters.

There were four old lead-covered phone cables and five fiber-optic cables leading into the block of buildings he was parked in front of, and it took him less than two minutes to cut every single one of them.

When he was done, he climbed out of the hole and slipped on a large backpack from the rear of the truck and lifted the crowbar. There was a work site there at the first building of the block he'd just blacked out, and he ripped open its plywood door at the hinges.

Inside was a completely gutted hollowed-out building with just a staircase left. There was no alarm clang even after a full minute, and he closed the plywood door and quickly went up.

It was three flights to its roof, and he came out a little attic-like door and stood up on the tar paper roof in the cool air looking north over the chimney caps. From Eaton Square to Upper Belgrave were fourteen separate town houses that butted up against each other so tightly they looked like the same building.

Gannon hefted his bag and walked north to the first terra-cotta roof edge and quietly stepped over it and kept going.

Two minutes later, he stood near the northern edge of the last building overlooking Upper Belgrave directly across from the embassy. There was a large air-conditioning unit there about the size of a minivan and he pulled himself on top of it and unstrapped the knapsack.

Of all people, Gannon knew exactly how ballsy it was to just walk into the middle of an intel op.

But also of all people, he knew what such an op was like from the inside.

He'd been on manhunts before. All eyeballs involved were now Krazy Glued on Messerly and the embassy and whatever the hell was going on in there. The last thing any of them would be thinking about was someone coming up on their six.

He zipped open the pack and opened the first flap and began laying everything out on the metal roof of the A/C unit.

The barrel of the sniper rifle came first. Then the bolt. Then the suppressor. The lower part of the rifle was under the second flap and he lifted it out and extended its bipod. He turned on the FLIR scope that was already attached and then slapped in the magazine of ten .338 Lapua Magnum rounds and slipped in the bolt with a click.

He played with the FLIR scope's settings until the contrast was just right, and then settled in flat on his belly.

It took only five minutes before he saw one of the white panel-like coverings on the third floor of the construction site across from the embassy on Wilton Street open up.

Someone appeared in the gap. Someone with binoculars, pointing at the embassy.

Gannon checked his watch and smiled.

"Thar she blows," he said.

He'd guessed right. Small smartphone-powered drones had limited ranges. He'd studied the map around the embassy. The work site was the only logical place for Reyland to wait to receive it.

As he focused in the FLIR's zoom, he saw that the figure in the work site flap wasn't Reyland but a woman.

But that didn't matter, Gannon knew. Reyland was up there.

He'd known men like Reyland. Psychopaths. He'd met his share of them.

Reyland wouldn't miss being front row center for the grand finale of his sick little play for all the world, Gannon knew.

Gannon tilted the rifle right and eyed the embassy.

"Shit!" he suddenly said.

His plan was to shoot the drone as it came out of one of the windows and knock it down safely behind the embassy gates.

But as he lay there, he realized a problem he hadn't anticipated.

There was a damn Chilean flag flapping on a pole at the top corner of the Wilton side of the embassy.

If the drone came out from one of the back windows on the other side of the flag down Wilton, he wouldn't be able to see it until it was too late. At best, he'd only be able to knock the drone down into the middle of Wilton Street, where the bastards could still retrieve it.

"Shit!" he said again, taking his eye off the scope.

What the hell was he going to do?

He was thinking of maybe laying fire on the embassy itself, shattering some windows to raise the alarm, when out of the corner of his eye he caught movement, and he turned.

A piece of scaffolding sheet on the Upper Belgrave side of the work site where Reyland and his team were now hiding was wafting back and forth in the breeze.

"Screw it," Gannon said to himself as he suddenly leaped up.

He left the sniper rifle where it was and started running with everything he had back across the rooftops the way he'd come in.

96

Up on the third floor of the construction site, Reyland squatted by a concrete mixing tray as a muscular female MI6 agent slit open another piece of the white plastic construction scaffold wrapping.

She turned and handed him the binoculars.

From where Reyland peeked out, it was a level clear lane straight across Wilton to the embassy's rear stairwell window where Dr. Santos would make the drop.

Reyland checked his watch. It was 11:25 a.m. Any minute now.

He looked at the dark window of the embassy, thinking about the doctor. What he had to be going through. The despair of betraying his patient and possibly going to jail warring with the hope of getting his son back.

Yes, that one hope, that tiny beam of light, was guiding him toward Messerly's room at this very moment.

Reyland's phone vibrated. He looked down.

It was an empty text from the good doctor. The signal.

He was by the window now.

"Keep your eyes peeled. It's on," Reyland said to the agent beside him.

In the end, it was almost ridiculous how easy it was. There was a sound of a window opening across the street, and then out of the window came a quad drone the size of a radio-controlled plane.

Then Reyland heard the embassy window shut as the agent leaned out of the panel slit.

"Gotcha," she said.

"Are they there? Are they there?" Reyland said, and then his eyes lit up as the female agent dropped the thumb drives into his palm.

He gazed on them, three little smooth white slabs of plastic each no bigger than a gum eraser, *Toshiba* written on their sides.

Over this? he thought, shaking his head.

A year's work. Millions spent. Lives lost. Over a gram of plastic and silicone?

"Time to go," he said.

The line of his British security commando men waved Reyland west over the construction site roof like coaches at an obstacle course. He passed some aluminum framing beams, a pile of steel rods, a rolled-up hose. There was a stepladder that went up over the roof wall to the scaffolding on the Upper Belgrave side of the building, and Reyland went over it and started down the nine-story scaffold's steps.

They were coming down the seventh-story flight of stairs when Reyland heard it. There was the high scream of a car engine on Upper Belgrave, and all five of them stopped on the stairs and went over to the street-side railing.

At first Reyland couldn't see because of the plastic sheeting, but then he pulled at the plastic until he got it to part like a curtain.

Then he turned to the right.

Down Upper Belgrave came a huge white work truck flying like a runaway train.

It was a phone truck, Reyland could see, as it jumped the curb onto their block and came roaring up the sidewalk directly at them.

"Back! Back! Back!" Reyland cried.

Then the truck smashed somewhere down below into the scaffolding they were standing on, and Reyland yelled as he felt the stairs jolt and heave beneath his backpedaling feet.

97

The fifteen-thousand-pound truck's speedometer was hovering around the eighty mark when Gannon plowed it into the base of the scaffolding.

The rapid-fire bongs of the ripped-free galvanized steel pipes blasting off the speeding hood and grille sounded almost festive, like wedding bells.

He ducked down as one of the pipes jumped up sideways and shattered the windshield. Another pole came into the cab itself a split second later like a spear where his head had just been.

Gannon kept his foot pressed down on the accelerator in the fantastic gonging as support pipe after support pipe after support pipe popped free.

The runaway truck had just torn loose the last of the supports at the end of the block when one of its front tires exploded like a bomb blast. Gannon closed his eyes as he felt the truck wobble crazily toward the right. It was actually on two wheels when it came off the sidewalk into the street again. Gannon hugged the steering wheel to brace himself as it toppled over completely on its right side and went skidding through the intersection in an incredible screech of metal and clanging support pipes and spitting sparks.

Reyland and the rest of his team were still scrambling up the stairs between the sixth and seventh floors of the scaffold when the heavy ninth-story transom of the compromised structure suddenly ruptured.

They were still running as the ninth floor pancaked into the eighth floor and the eighth floor into the seventh, and then the heavy wooden seventh floor slammed down onto them like a giant textbook onto the heads of a half-dozen scurrying ants.

The entire superstructure of the scaffolding ripped completely free from the building a split second later and tipped over into the street.

The screams of the dying and the mangled among Reyland's party were lost in the banging as pipe upon pipe rained down mercilessly onto the sidewalk and asphalt seventy feet below.

Along with the pipes, lethal arrows of rebar, pallets of bricks, and boards flew down by the dozens. A falling construction dumpster went through the roof of a street-parked Mercedes like a knife through warm butter as half a dozen fifty-pound bags of concrete shattered off Upper Belgrave street all around in reverberating, bursting clouds of gray dust.

The critically collapsed scaffolding was still clanging and splintering and exploding into the narrow street even as Gannon pulled himself up out of the knocked-over truck's passenger-side window.

He hopped down into the street over the hood of the cab and looked around and saw that he had come to a stop in the street almost directly in front of the Chilean embassy's wrought iron gate. As he leaped down off the toppled truck, he saw the embassy front door open and some confused-looking men emerge from it.

"What happened? Are you okay?" one of them yelled as Gannon headed into the cloud of silvery dust that now almost completely obscured Upper Belgrave on the other side of Wilton Street.

The first human he came across in the thick mist was one of Reyland's commandos. He was on one knee, coughing. Gannon saw the machine gun on a strap at his back and lifted a broken two-by-four up off the asphalt as he came in behind him, brought it down with a bonk over the guy's head and took his gun.

A moment later, there was the rev of an engine through the dust, and Gannon walked toward it.

"Hey, hey, hey! Over here, Reyland!" called out a man's voice with a British accent. "Where are you? Where is everyone? What bloody happened?"

As Gannon got closer, he could see the man, some stick figure—skinny English guy. He was standing beside the open door of an idling black Range Rover.

Gannon put the bead of the Heckler & Koch between the guy's suddenly hugely wide eyes as he approached.

"Get away from the car!" Gannon yelled then let off a clacking burst at the guy's feet to give him some incentive.

Gannon found Reyland thirty seconds later ten feet from the Range Rover.

He was under a sheet of plywood between a couple of parked cars, and as he stood over him, the FBI agent moaned sorrowfully.

Then Gannon saw why.

There was a pole sticking out of him. It was a piece of galvanized steel pipe about three feet long and it was jutting from his torso just below his chest. It had sliced cleanly through his windbreaker, which was now completely drenched in blood.

Ouch, Gannon thought when he saw the rest of the galvanized pipe sticking out of Reyland's back. The pipe he was skewered with was actually leaning sideways against one of the parked cars, and it was kind of propping him up in a seated position as he sat there in the gutter.

"I'm hurt. What is this? What happened? I'm stuck. Why am I stuck?" Reyland suddenly said.

It was a miracle that Reyland was still alive, let alone conscious, Gannon thought as he shook his head.

Gannon knelt and patted and then reached into Reyland's bloody windbreaker pocket and removed the three thumb drives there.

He pursed his lips as he thought of what to do with them.

"What are you doing?" Reyland said as Gannon pulled off one of Reyland's boots.

"It's okay. Everything's okay, big man. You just sit tight," Gannon said as he peeled off Reyland's sock and put the thumb drives into it and tied the sock up into a ball.

He was going to throw it back over the Chilean embassy fence. But as he jogged back across Wilton, he actually encountered one of the burly guards he had seen by the door. He was now standing out on the sidewalk on the corner.

"Here," Gannon said as he untied the sock and poured the thumb drives into the startled guard's hand.

"These belong to your guest," he said. "Dr. Santos dropped them out the window. You should probably talk to him about that. Also, you should probably check on Mr. Messerly."

"And you are?" the guard said with a Spanish accent.

"No one at all," Gannon said as he started running back toward the destruction.

"Help," Reyland said as Gannon got back to the idling Range Rover.

Gannon stopped and looked down at the deputy assistant director as he began making loud huffing and puffing sounds.

"There's something stuck in me. Pleeeeeease! I can feel it," Reyland said. "It's between my ribs! It's stuck. Stuck."

Gannon peered at the shaft of blood-slicked metal sticking out of Reyland's guts and suddenly smiled as he thought of what he had told his buddy Callum about going whale fishing.

How do you like that, he thought.

It looked just like a harpoon.

"You must help me," Reyland said. "I have a family. My wife. I'll give you anything."

In the distance, Gannon could hear the first sirens approaching. He thought they would have that weak *weee aw, weee aw* Euro sound from the movies, but they sounded just like American ones.

"Sounds like you need a doctor, Reyland," Gannon said as he got behind the Rover's wheel. "Maybe Dr. Santos over at the embassy could help you out."

Gannon slammed the door and zipped down the British luxury car's window.

"But on second thought, probably not," Gannon said as he slammed the gas into the floor.

EPILOGUE

When Gannon finally appeared out of the sliders onto the upper terrace, he was wearing a new pair of cargo shorts and a black T-shirt with a neon blue barracuda on it that he had bought at the airport.

It was coming on seven in the evening, and he was back in the Dominican Republic now at a gated vacation villa in the La Costa Brava neighborhood of Santo Domingo up in the hills high above the bay.

He walked to the rail and looked out on the sea, then down at the lower terrace where Little Jorge and Stick were laughing and drinking beer. They were grilling steaks beside the infinity pool with some reggae music bopping out of a speaker beside the grill.

"There you are," Ruby said, coming out onto the deck behind him.

"How do I look?" she said, showing him her new long-sleeved T-shirt and capri pants.

"Are these sneakers okay for a boat?" she said, showing off her pink Converse low tops. "I never went deep-sea fishing at night. Or actually during the day either, to be honest."

"You look marvelous, Lieutenant," Gannon said. "Especially the sneakers."

"How's your son? You called him, right?"

"He's doing fine," Gannon said. "The Brewers turned him down, but he got another tryout with the Mets in Port St. Lucie. Fingers crossed."

"That's awesome," Ruby said, holding up her crossed fingers on both hands. "The Messerly information drop just happened, by the way."

"He's back on his feet?" Gannon said.

"Uh-huh. It happened half an hour ago. The internet is going insane. It's all unredacted. Thousands and thousands of pages. Emails. Videos. Swiss bank account numbers. These intel people must be beside themselves."

"Intel people?" Gannon said. "Global mafia, you mean. Enough of those fools. Time to head to the dock. You ready?"

"As ready as I'll ever be," Ruby said.

"Good," Gannon said, walking over to the steel bucket by the door he'd already filled with ice and beer. "Grab the other end of this, would you?"

"Come on, guys. Time to catch us some fish," Gannon said excitedly as they came out on the lower deck by the pool.

"Actually, Mick, we're calling a mutiny," Stick said. "After a few more cervezas, me and little Jorge here are heading down to a club nearby. He's going to introduce me to some *las chicas bonitas* he knows."

"*Las* what?" Gannon cried. "The blues are biting, Stick. The blues! And Little Jorge. How could you? You're going to let me and Ruby here go out on that fine vessel we rented without a first mate?"

They heard the honk of their taxi sound as Little Jorge sat there giggling.

"It's okay, Mike," Ruby said. "I think we'll be okay by ourselves."

"Just you and me?" Gannon said, squinting at her.

Ruby looked up at the stars that were just now starting to show themselves in the darkening sky.

"Just you and me," Ruby finally said with a nod. "I think we'll be just fine."

★ ★ ★ ★ ★

ACKNOWLEDGEMENTS

The author would like to thank the following for their professionalism, advice and belief in this book:

Josh Getzler and everyone at the Hannigan Getzler Agency

And especially Peter Joseph and his excellent team at Hanover Square Press

ABOUT THE AUTHOR

Michael Ledwidge is the author of *The Narrowback*, *Bad Connection*, and most recently the coauthor, with James Patterson, of *The Quickie*, *Step on a Crack*, and *Worst Case*. He has coauthored several *New York Times* bestsellers.

THRILLINGLY GOOD BOOKS
FROM CRIMINALLY
GOOD WRITERS

CRIME FILES BRINGS YOU THE LATEST RELEASES FROM
TOP CRIME AND THRILLER AUTHORS.

SIGN UP ONLINE FOR OUR MONTHLY NEWSLETTER AND BE THE FIRST
TO KNOW ABOUT OUR COMPETITIONS, NEW BOOKS AND MORE.

VISIT OUR WEBSITE: WWW.CRIMEFILES.CO.UK
LIKE US ON FACEBOOK: FACEBOOK.COM/CRIMEFILES
FOLLOW US ON TWITTER: @CRIMEFILESBOOKS